Austen University Mysteries
BOOK 2

The PORTRAITS OF PEMBERLEY

ELizabeth GiLLiLaNd

the portraits of pemberley

book two in the austen university mysteries

Elizabeth Gilliland

praise for elizabeth gilliland

"Gilliland puts her expertise on Jane Austen, the subject of her doctoral dissertation, to amusing use in this promising series launch set at Louisiana's Austen University, where many of the staff and students have names that will be familiar to Austen readers....Gilliland has fun with the conventions of the closed-circle mystery....The idea of a modern versions of Austen's heroines joining forces to solve a murder is a clever one and is likely substantial enough to sustain several sequels."

Publisher's Weeky Review

"I LOVE this book! It's so fun to see favorite Austen characters with a modern twist. Very well written and such a fun book! I can't wait for the next book to come out."

Reader Review

praise for elizabeth gilliland

"Best of all is the humor which doesn't hit a single sour note, even with the seriousness of the topics under discussion. I found myself thoroughly charmed by the truly awful amateur sleuth at the center of the plot and more than ready to see what mystery she bungles next." -

Cassondra Windwalker, author of *Idle Hands*
and *Love Like a Cephalopod*

"If you're an Austen fan, you'll appreciate the author's obvious Austen-cred. She seems to know her stuff and how to weave it into a cozy, Janeite murder mystery. The plot kept me guessing and the Austen Easter eggs kept me nodding along the way."

Reader Review

To my sister, Sarah,
For enabling my Austen addiction

character list

Delta House:
Elizabeth (Lizzy) Bennet *(Pride and Prejudice)*
Elinor (Nora) Dashwood *(Sense and Sensibility)*
Marianne Dashwood *(Sense and Sensibility)*
Lucy Steele *(Sense and Sensibility)*
Mrs. Jennings *(Sense and Sensibility)*

Theta House:
Fo-Hian Darcy *(Pride and Prejudice)*
Jay Rushworth *(Mansfield Park)*
Charles (Charlie) Bingley *(Mansfield Park)*
*George Knightley *(Emma)* - graduated

Kappa House:
*Emma Woodhouse *(Emma)* - graduated
Karoline Bingley *(Pride and Prejudice)*
Catherine (Caty) Morland *(Northanger Abbey)*
Anne Elias *(Persuasion)*

Sigma Rho:
George Wickham *(Pride and Prejudice)*
Henry Tilney *(Northanger Abbey)*

Brandon Colon (*Sense and Sensibility*)
Wa'il Parsa (*Mansfield Park*)

Faculty/Staff:
President de Bourgh (*Pride and Prejudice*)
Mr. Collins (*Pride and Prejudice*)
Professor Palmer (*Sense and Sensibility*)
Ms. Bates (*Emma*)
Professor Elias (*Persuasion*)
Professor Grey (*Sense and Sensibility*)

Other:
Detective Lucas (*Pride and Prejudice*)
Detective Wentworth (*Persuasion*)
Fania Parsa (*Mansfield Park*) - Freshman, no house pledged yet
John Willoughby (*Sense and Sensibility*) - Graduate student

volume one

"There is, I believe, in every disposition a tendency to some particular evil."

Jane Austen, *Pride and Prejudice*

one

november - 10 days
after the event

GEORGE WICKHAM WAS FOUND (by a freshman of no real importance) on the campus square, tied up, spread-eagle, hungover, and it must be noted, completely naked.

While there were many at Austen University who felt the punishment fit the crime, there were also those who failed to see the poetic justice–among them, naturally, Wickham himself, along with the Austen University administration, including President de Bourgh.

And, as it was rapidly becoming clear to Elizabeth Bennet as she sat in the waiting room outside her office door, whatever President de Bourgh thought, so too thought her office assistant, Mr. Collins.

"You've made us quite upset, Miss Bennet," Collins informed her, glaring across his desk. "*Quite* upset."

Along with having his lips permanently attached to President de Bourgh's ass, Mr. Collins was, unfortunately, Lizzy's first cousin once removed. Up until recently, this relation had not seemed quite so unlucky, since it was at Mr. Collins's encouragement that Lizzy had applied to Austen University and gotten a full-tuition scholarship for academic achievement. Coming from a family with five daughters, Lizzy knew this was no small financial feat, and thus managed to hold her tongue at her distant cousin's strange habit of insisting on being called "Mr. Collins," even by his relatives.

Observing this sycophantic behavior in her cousin, however, Lizzy felt a twinge of worry about her genetic makeup. She'd already had her concerns from her mother's side, but now she had to worry about what unpleasant dormant lurkers might be hiding on her father's side, too.

"I'm sorry to hear that, Mr. Collins," Lizzy told him evenly, and could not help herself from adding, "*quite* sorry."

Collins's face furrowed with the effort of determining if he was being apologized to, or mocked. Fortunately before any permanent wrinkles could be fixed in place, the intercom buzzed, and President de Bourgh's imperious voice snipped over the speaker. "Is she here?"

"I'll bring her straight in." With that, Collins opened the office door and glared Lizzy into entering.

With her Southern flair for the dramatics, President de Bourgh had kept the back of her office chair turned toward the door, waiting for Mr. Collins to come to stand behind the desk with an outraged glower, before slowly turning to face Lizzy.

Caren de Bourgh was precisely the sort of woman who looked as though she would never die, which is to say, she had the appearance of a hardy tangerine left out in the sun for just a bit too long. Her hair was dyed a deep black which nobody had believed to be her natural hair color for at least the last twenty years, and it was styled in a gravity-defying bouffant that betrayed her age more than any grays could. She had a penchant for wearing bright-colored shirts and distinctive pieces of jewelry, the bigger the better, that was perhaps matched only by her love of pralines, of which she always had a tin on-hand.

"Elizabeth Bennet," she drawled in her distinctly Charleston accent, "take a seat."

Lizzy did so, careful to keep her back straight and to only cross her legs at the ankles. These old Southern women had eyes like hawks, and took any sign of comfort or familiarity as an indication of bad moral character.

"I suppose you know why you're here?"

"I'm assuming it's because of my article."

"If you can even call it that." Mr. Collins' own fairly mild accent always became much more pronounced in his boss's presence.

President de Bourgh retrieved the offending article from the *Juve-*

nilia–the weekly university publication–and placed it squarely in the middle of her desk. "Would you care to explain to me what this is?"

Lizzy observed where President de Bourgh's finger had landed. "I believe that's a penis, President de Bourgh."

A *pixelated* penis, but still it took a full minute for the furor to die down, with President de Bourgh alternating between loudly condemning Lizzy's forward, Yankee ways, and Mr. Collins following his boss in an awkward echo as he hurried to repeat everything de Bourgh said and match her ire for ire.

Lizzy waited for the commotion to die down before supplying, "I suppose you were referring to the article itself? It would have been strange if the school paper didn't cover the incident." Wickham's public display had been huge news across campus, after all–and hard to miss, with so many people posting pictures before security was able to cut him loose.

"We made it very clear to your faculty chair that nothing about the incident was meant to be broadcast through school media. Professor Palmer led me to understand that you were instructed not to write the article, but printed it anyway."

Lizzy raised an eyebrow. "I was advised not to, but 'instructed'? That sounds an awful lot like censorship."

"Your point being?"

Propriety be damned. Lizzy crossed her legs, taking pleasure in the little hitch of distaste on President de Bourgh's upper lip. "Look, the article is out there. Can't undo it. No use crying over spilt milk–or loose nuts, as the case may be."

She'd hoped the phrasing might incur another outcry of moral outrage, but instead President de Bourgh glared at her. Not so much a glare of dislike, although the emotion in question was certainly present in that steely blue gaze, but one of calculation. "You're awfully self-assured for someone so young. Pray tell, how does someone of your age get to be quite so confident?"

"Pray tell," Collins echoed with a sneer, until President de Bourgh waved a hand in his direction and he all but clapped his hand over his mouth, mortified at having spoken out of turn.

This felt like a trap. Lizzy tread carefully. "I don't know. I mean, I always eat my Wheaties..."

Alas, de Bourgh did not crack even the smallest of smiles. "Tell us, Miss-Know-It-All-Bennet, what should the administration do, rather than—as you put it—cry over spilt milk?"

"Well, I guess I'd put my effort toward trying to find out whoever tied Wickham up in the first place."

Somehow, and Lizzy did not quite know how, she had stepped onto a hidden landmine. President de Bourgh smiled. "Marvelous plan, don't you think, Mr. Collins?"

Even Mr. Collins seemed a bit taken aback by her abrupt shift in mood, and had to double-check President de Bourgh's expression before parroting, "Marvelous!"

"Great. I'm glad that's settled." Lizzy rose to her feet, hoping a hasty exit might save her from whatever unpleasantness was bound to follow.

President de Bourgh's voice reached her before she managed to make it out the door. "You'll let us know, won't you? As soon as you figure it out."

"As soon as *I* figure it out?" Lizzy was beginning to understand Mr. Collins's propensity for echoing.

President de Bourgh's smile was a full-on, cat-that-ate-the-canary grin now. "Very generous of you to volunteer to discover who tied George Wickham up in the campus square. Of course, as this is a time-sensitive issue, we'll need an answer by a week from today. Or we'll have to assume that you—as a person with vested interest in seeing Mr. Wickham publically humiliated—are the culprit. And what do you think the punishment for such a crime should be, Mr. Collins?"

Mr. Collins looked thrilled, and maybe even a little aroused, at the sudden power that had been placed into his hands. "Suspension?"

"For an infraction this significant, Mr. Collins? I'd hate to think you'd gone soft."

He was practically quivering now with the ecstasy of it. "Expulsion."

"Yes, Mr. Collins, I believe that would be the most fitting solution."

Lizzy kept her face perfectly composed, not wanting to give either the satisfaction of seeing her panic. And most certainly, it would be satisfaction that these two sadists would feel at the thought of seeing her squirm. "Then I suppose I'll see you in a week."

And it wasn't until she was safely in the windowless stairwell that Lizzy let herself collapse against the wall, sliding down to sit on one of the steps. "Well, shit."

chapter **two**

IT IS a truth universally acknowledged that a woman at risk of being expelled for a crime she didn't commit must be in want of some chocolate.

Granted, it didn't take much to make Elizabeth Bennet crave chocolate. Chocolate was the elixir of choice when celebrations were in order, and the drug of choice when life was at its most trying. She had long ago come to terms with the fact that she would never have the so-called ideal body, and that she would always be just a little bit "plush" (as her diplomatic older sister, Jane, had once phrased it in an attempt to be kind). In every other aspect of health, Lizzy could practice moderation. She ate mostly fruits, vegetables, whole grains, and lean meats; she loved to take long, vigorous walks; she could take or leave drinking, and drugs were a hard pass for her, except for marijuana (which was basically the state flower of her home state, Colorado, as well as a personal favorite of her father's). But chocolate? Chocolate, she believed, was the only thing not meant to be enjoyed in moderation. Whoever said that "nothing tasted as good as being thin felt" (an adage her mother tried not-so-subtly to ingrain in her daughters' young minds) had obviously never had a fresh-baked chocolate-chip cookie. Chocolate-dipped strawberries. The perfect cup of hot cocoa.

It was this last item that Lizzy purchased for solace from the Crescent as she confided the events of the morning to her roommate, Nora

Dashwood. The Crescent, Lizzy believed, had the best cup of hot chocolate in town, if not the country, if not the entire world. Most coffee shops made their cocoa an afterthought, putting together a treacly substance that was more sugar than chocolate, but the Crescent had just the right balance of sweet and rich, a true sensory pleasure—and not something for the faint of tongue. Even Lizzy didn't normally partake of something so decadent on a weekday morning, but it was a needed antidote to that meeting with de Bourgh.

Nora watched her with thinly masked concern as she drained the dark chocolate concoction. "Do you think she could have been bluffing? Maybe she won't really expel you."

Lizzy sighed glumly as she scraped what remained of the chocolate dregs at the bottom of her mug. "De Bourgh doesn't bluff," she returned bleakly. Anyone that used to having the world at her beck and call didn't make idle threats about getting her way, after all. "It's fine, though. My mom says you don't need a college education to get married and pregnant, so all I have to do is find someone to knock me up and make an honest woman out of me."

"Well. You haven't been expelled yet, so don't poke any premature holes in the condoms."

One of the nice things about Nora, and the reason that Lizzy had immediately gravitated toward her back in their pledging days at Pi Kappa Sigma, was her unflappability in the face of any crisis. On paper, that might not seem like the most exciting or alluring quality in a person, but having grown up in the Bennet household with an array of high-strung personalities, Lizzy appreciated a person who could take things in stride. It had also made immediate sense to her, after meeting Nora's younger sister Marianne, why there was very little that could ruffle Nora's feathers.

The cup sufficiently drained, Lizzy sighed and set it back on the table. "I'm afraid it's only a matter of time. De Bourgh's been wanting a scapegoat from the Austen Murder Club for a while. Bad luck that it had to be me, I guess."

Before Nora could answer, her gaze caught on something over Lizzy's shoulder, and she stiffened. Frowning, Lizzy turned to see that Fo-Hian Darcy and Charlie Bingley had just entered the coffee shop.

Lizzy felt herself tense, too, overcome with a swift and paralyzing sense of confused embarrassment at the sight of Darcy. She hadn't seen him since...well, since the night that Wickham had been tied up and left naked in the campus square. Not that it was unusual for Darcy and Lizzy to go long periods without being in contact; they were barely acquaintances. In fact, it would have been strange for him to reach out to her–only she'd called him that night, and texted, more than once, and there had never been any response. That in and of itself was a response, she supposed–but there had been something strange and charged between them that night at the gala, hadn't there?

All of this moved so quickly through Lizzy's mind that she didn't have time to make herself look away before Darcy noticed her staring. For a moment they were mutually staring at each other, Darcy's face inscrutable. At last, he leaned over to say something to Bingley, who did a double-take at the sight of Nora. *His* feelings, at least, were clear; he was embarrassed, but too well-bred to pretend he hadn't noticed her. After a brief moment's deliberation, the two boys began to make their way over to the table.

Finally, Lizzy was able to wrench her gaze away from Darcy, exchanging a quick, wordless glance with Nora. She would have offered some sign of solidarity between them if Nora's eyes hadn't communicated so clearly that she didn't want any kind of fuss. Nothing to indicate that her heart had been smashed to smithereens by Charlie the previous semester. It was completely in keeping with Nora's personality–logos first and foremost, barely any pathos–but even so, Lizzy had to be impressed by her friend's fortitude. No one looking at her now would have ever guessed there'd been anything between her and Charlie, last year or *ever*.

"Hello, Nora. Elizabeth." Darcy stopped just short of their table, not so much oblivious to the stares he drew as he crossed the room as accustomed to them. At well over six feet and with an aesthetically appealing combination of tall, dark, and handsome, Darcy had the easy authority of someone who'd had every door in life open to him, always.

Bingley was softer, sweeter, with his boyish good looks and dimples, though he also topped just over six feet and was just as athletic as Darcy. Even the little bit of stubble he'd apparently grown in Paris couldn't make him look like less of a baby-face. His hair was shorter than Lizzy had last seen it, buzzed into a fade that ended just above his ears.

As he met Lizzy's gaze, he grinned, seeming genuinely happy to see her. "Hey, Lizzy. How you been?"

Lizzy faltered for a moment, uncertain what the protocol was for seeing the guy who'd almost dated one's best friend but abruptly left midway through the previous semester without saying goodbye. Should she be standoffish, in solidarity with Nora? But then, Nora didn't seem to want to let on at all that Bingley's departure had fazed her, so it would be strange for Lizzy to be cold when Nora herself seemed so collected. She would just be undermining Nora then, wouldn't she?

And anyway, it was impossible to be indifferent to that puppy-dog expression, those dimples. Lizzy rose to her feet, giving him a quick embrace. "Hi, Charlie. It's good to have you back. Are you *back* back?"

Bingley's gaze darted to Nora before he caught himself, looking instead to Darcy. "To be determined." Steeling himself visibly, he faced Nora. "Hi, Nora."

Nora stood, too. She made no move to hug Bingley, but her smile was friendly. "Hi, Charlie. It's nice to see you."

"Nice to see you, too."

A long pause followed that interaction, as no one seemed entirely sure how to proceed. They were rescued–or at the very least, distracted–by Karoline's loud, distinct voice.

"Charlie! Darcy! There you are." Lizzy looked up at the sound of Karoline's heels clacking across the floor. Behind her, Lucy Steele was dressed in obvious imitation of Karoline's flashy style, and was apparently now following her like a lapdog–which was a kind of surprising turn of events, but in hindsight, shouldn't have been. "Please tell me you have my oat milk latte–I'm in desperate need of caffeine."

Karoline drew up short at the sight of Lizzy and Nora, doing an admirable job of pretending to notice them for the first time. If life as a soul-sucking harpy didn't work out for her, she might be able to fall back on a career in the theatre. "Oh, Elinor. Elizabeth. I didn't realize today was coupon day at the Crescent."

Lucy smirked, exchanging a conspiratorial look with Karoline–which was a bit rich, all things considered. Lizzy only just managed to suppress an eyeroll. She hadn't thought Lucy could manage to get any more annoying, but sometimes people could exceed expectations. "Well, some things are actually much worse when you get two for the price of one," she returned, smiling sweetly at the two newcomers in their matching lavender dresses.

Karoline spared Lizzy a brief glare before casting her gaze, nervously, to her brother in such close proximity to Nora. Lizzy saw the exact moment that Karoline realized all of her evil machinations to keep them apart might come to naught if they actually had the opportunity to talk to each other again. "Charlie, you should probably be getting back to the Theta house. Knightley said he was going to drop by today to say hello."

"He said he *might* drop by." Bingley returned, sounding embarrassed for Karoline's obvious intervention. Then, glancing around the group gathered at the table–and probably calculating how awkward Karoline could make things for Nora–he seemed to reconsider. "But there were some other Thetas I wanted to catch up with…"

"Are you walking?" Lucy spoke up, seemingly oblivious to the tension around the table. "I was going to head back to the Delta house and it's on the way."

"Um. Sure, yeah." Bingley cast a quick glance at Nora before waving to the group without quite meeting anyone's eyes. "Bye."

Silence, awkward and painful, followed in their wake. Karoline was smug, Nora stoic, and Lizzy simmering.

Darcy was the one to break the silence. He shifted, looking almost–uncomfortable? His features had always seemed incapable of making such an expression. It didn't sit well on him. "I heard you met with President de Bourgh." Darcy never referred to the woman in question as his aunt. It was almost cute, that he had deluded himself that everyone hadn't already pieced their relationship together. Or maybe it was just gauche in his social circle to throw that kind of information around.

"I did," Lizzy confirmed.

Another shift from Darcy, a slight bob of his throat. "What happened?"

Lizzy drew in a breath, torn between fully outing President de Bourgh's scheming and putting Darcy in an awkward position. Which, in itself, put Lizzy in an awkward position, because it had never once crossed her mind in her past interactions to worry about how Darcy, of all people, might be feeling, and the world suddenly felt off-kilter in a way that left her feeling unsteady on her feet. "Not much," she hedged.

To her surprise, Nora spoke up. "She'll be expelled if she can't figure out who 'assaulted' Wickham within a week."

Lizzy blinked at her friend, incredulous, but Nora looked completely unapologetic as she met her gaze. And maybe she was right. Maybe Darcy *should* know. Peripherally, Lizzy was also aware of Karoline trying desperately to fight back her gleeful smile–God, she must just be loving this–but her eyes fixed on Darcy, needing to see his reaction.

He blinked at her, as if he was uncertain he'd heard Nora right. "She actually said that? That you would be expelled?"

"Those were her exact words." Now Lizzy did look at Karoline, raising an eyebrow. "You got something you wanna say, Karoline?"

Karoline remained silent, pressing her lips together, though her eyes danced gleefully.

When Lizzy looked back to Darcy, his face was expressionless. "I see," he said, then looked down at his watch. "I have a meeting." And with that, he turned and left the cafe.

Lizzy wasn't the only one flabbergasted by the response. The mirth fled from Karoline's face, replaced with dismay. "But...I thought we were getting coffee?" She followed after him, heels clattering in her wake.

That was...weird. Lizzy knew that things had become complicated between her and Darcy, but she'd expected him to at least pretend to care that she might get expelled. But maybe that would involve admitting that his aunt had done something wrong, and he just couldn't bring himself to do it.

Lizzy did her best to shake the encounter off, looking over to Nora, who was watching her with a strange expression on her face. "What?" Lizzy asked.

A beat, and then Nora shook her head–slowly, as if she were piecing things together. "Nothing," she said, then raised her mug to take a long sip of coffee–her eyes darting back to Lizzy's face again in a long, silent appraisal.

chapter
three

THOUGH LIZZY THOUGHT the threat of expulsion should be a reasonable justification for an 'excused absence,' Nora reminded her that she was already being watched closely in Professor Eliás's class and shouldn't "poke the bear."

"If I get expelled it won't matter if Professor Eliás fails me," Lizzy reminded her.

"And if you don't get expelled and you fail, you'll have to take the course with Eliás again."

The thought of this was so unpleasant that Lizzy at last gathered up her things. "Doesn't it ever get tiresome, being so logical and *right* all the time?"

Nora considered this a moment. "No," she said at last.

The class itself was relatively uneventful, save be Professor Eliás's thinly disguised gloating every time he made eye contact with Lizzy during the lecture (clearly, he and de Bourgh had been in communication), and the notable absence of Wickham. Apparently being tied up naked in a public space was an excusable absence, no matter how well-deserved the punishment might be.

In truth, Lizzy was grateful to not have to come face-to-face with Wickham again—a sentiment she felt generally, but especially after their last encounter. If he had to take the rest of the semester off, she certainly wouldn't make any complaint in her end-of-term evaluation. (The university would, however, be hearing about her displeasure about the temperature in Kellynch Hall, which seemed to have only two settings: Arctic Tundra or Death Valley. Nothing in between.)

Afterward, Lizzy hurriedly gathered her things and left with the general throng of students to avoid any direct encounters with Professor Eliás. She was so preoccupied with hurrying down the hall that, in true rom-com fashion, she didn't pay attention to where she was going and collided with someone coming around the corner.

Unlike a rom com, Lizzy's entire body hurt from the impact. Groaning in pain, she looked up to see who she'd run into, and felt the breath knocked out of her for an entirely different reason as she realized she'd bumped into Wickham.

–only, no, Lizzy realized in the next instant, feeling her heartbeat start to slow back to normal, it wasn't Wickham. It was Willoughby, which was only marginally better, but it was a margin she would take. Face-on, Willoughby and Wickham didn't look too much alike–their facial features were distinct enough–but they had the same size frame, the same artfully tousled dark curls, the same confident swagger.

That last trait, at least, Lizzy had the pleasure of seeing deflate in front of her eyes as Willoughby recognized her. "Lizzy. Hi." He seemed to not know how to behave around her, after everything that had happened. "How is–?"

Lizzy had recovered enough by now to realize she had neither obligation nor desire to speak to him. "Let's not," she said, eagerly side-stepping him to hurry out of Kellynch Hall.

 δλε

Now that Lizzy had forced herself to sit through both a meeting with President de Bourgh and a lecture with Professor Eliás, she thought she deserved a well-earned reward of pajamas by 6:00 p.m., Netflix, and some kind of food that came in a box and required no cleanup. She knew there was a timeline on finding whoever had attacked Wickham, but that could wait until tomorrow. Tonight, Lizzy deserved some TLC.

Alas, upon entering the Delta house, Lizzy immediately realized an evening of uninterrupted rest and relaxation was not in the cards for her. Various cardboard boxes littered the living room, and several bright pink suitcases of various sizes lined the entryway.

Taking all of this in, Lizzy exchanged a wordless look with Nora, who simply shook her head in silent, resigned irritation.

A moment later, Lucy Steele clattered down the hallway, still dressed like the department-store version of Karoline's couture. Under her arm, she carried a stack of plates.

Lizzy darted another quick glance at Nora, afraid to get her hopes up. "Where are you going, Lucy?"

"I'm moving out. I know it's been such a stressful time for you two—what, with Marianne, and all. So I thought I'd get out of your hair. Plus, Karoline thinks I'll be a much better fit in the Kappa house."

Lizzy resisted the urge to do a spontaneous Irish jig. Finally, some good news, in a day—a week, a month, a *year*—that very much needed it. "Oh no," she said with as much feeling as she could muster, "such a shame. But if you have to go..." She wondered if it was tactless to ask just *when* Lucy would be vacating the premises. With any luck she'd be gone by that night, and Lizzy and Nora could reclaim the television. (Apparently Lucy got migraines from watching anything on her computer, so she *had* to use the television, even though no one else liked any of her shows, and using her computer for anything else didn't seem to pose any problem.)

It seemed Lizzy's half-hearted attempts to look disappointed were too effective, because Lucy stopped mid-stride and gave her a pitying look. "Don't worry, you can still follow me on TikTok. I'm sure you'll enjoy seeing all the fun things I get to do with the Kappas—it'll be like you get to do them, too."

Lizzy refrained from reminding her that she'd actually received a bid from the Kappas her freshman year, unlike Lucy, who seemed to be content to be passed from sorority to sorority like an HPV infection. "Can't wait," she agreed.

Her eyes narrowed on the plates under Lucy's arm, which most definitely did not belong to her. "Um–" she started, but Nora met her gaze and shook her head emphatically. Even without words, Lizzy got the message loud and clear. They shouldn't risk the chance of stalling Lucy's departure–or, God forbid, changing her mind–by picking fights over unimportant things like plates. Who needed plates, anyway? They could use paper products from now on. It would be terrible for the environment, but it would rid the Delta house of Lucy Steele, so...tie?

Lucy put the plates into one of the boxes and tucked it closed. "Well, I think that's it for now. I can always come back if I leave anything behind."

"No," Nora said quickly, then pressed her lips together as she caught herself. "I mean, we'd be happy to bring it to *you*. I'm sure you'll be much busier than we are with all of your Kappa activities."

Lizzy had to bite the inside of her mouth to keep from laughing.

Seeming to accept this narrative, Lucy checked her phone for the time. "Karoline should be here any minute. She's coming over here, personally, to pick me up. I guess she really sees a lot of potential in me."

Potential to be an even bigger ass-kisser than her, which was really saying something. Lizzy kept this thought to herself, too, nodding in bland-faced agreement. "Exciting."

"I'm sure I'll be spending lots of time with Karoline from now on. And everyone in her crew. Emma, Knightley, Rushworth. Darcy and Charlie, and everyone. I'll be part of the inner circle in no time."

Lizzy thought that was a little ambitious, even for Lucy, to think that she was going to become best buds with the richest, most notoriously exclusive group at Austen University. But again, she did not want to engage, or argue, or do anything that might drag out Lucy staying in the Delta house any longer than necessary. "Where *is* Karoline?" she asked, checking her phone for the time. "Are you sure you don't want me to call you an Uber...?'

The question was answered by a loud knock on the door. Lucy beamed. "That must be her!" She flounced down the entryway, leaving Lizzy to freely exchange a giddy glance with Nora at their good fortune. To her surprise, Nora looked distracted, maybe even a little troubled.

But Lizzy did not have too much time to ponder this, as a cacophony of high heels thundered into the living room. (What was the plural of heels? Did they have a cool name, like a pride of lions, or a murder of crows?) Before Lizzy could pretend to be civil at the sight of Karoline–again, for the sake of expediting Lucy's departure–she was accosted by the wannabe Kardashian in question.

"You had something to do with this, Bennet. I know you did!" Karoline thundered. Even though she was roughly the width of a broomstick, with her spike heels, she was alarmingly tall, and there was more rage in her eyes than that time an unwitting pledge had given her full-fat cow's milk in her coffee.

Despite herself, Lizzy fell back a step, raising her hands in surrender. "You wanted her–no take backs!" she protested.

"I'm talking about Darcy, of course." Even amidst her outrage, Karoline paused to take in the room, eyes narrowing with distaste. "My God, is *all* of your furniture from IKEA?"

Lizzy's heart gave a little stutter at the mention of Darcy's name. "What are you talking about?"

Karoline motioned to the TV stand. "This is obviously particle board."

"Darcy, Karoline. What are you talking about with *Darcy*?"

As Karoline remembered the reason for her initial rage, her eyes narrowed on Lizzy once again. "Darcy turned himself in to de Bourgh. Claimed that *he* was the one who attacked Wickham."

For a moment, Lizzy could only stare at her, too truly stunned to process what it was she'd just heard. "He did *what*?" she managed finally.

Karoline folded her arms, and Lucy mimicked her stance behind her, lines in the sand clearly drawn. Well, she certainly hadn't taken long to jump ship. Lizzy could probably forget about any vicarious TikTok adventures now.

"You're really gonna pretend you don't know anything about this?" Thing One (aka, Karoline) demanded. "That you weren't sneaking around, pulling the strings behind the scenes?"

Lizzy really, really wanted to know what had happened, especially if it had to do with Darcy, but she couldn't help but roll her eyes at this Machiavellian description of her. "Take it down a few notches, Karoline.

I'm hardly Lady Macbeth. I have too much homework and laundry for that."

"She does go an alarmingly long time in between washing," Lucy confirmed.

Lizzy wasn't entirely sure what that comment was meant to insinuate, and anyway she was too preoccupied trying to figure out why Darcy would have confessed to attacking Wickham. The most obvious answer was that he had, in fact, been the person to attack Wickham. But even if that were true, why own up to it, with Lizzy so conveniently placed to take the fall?

An idea presented itself to Lizzy, but it felt a little too much like wishful thinking, so she pushed it aside.

Karoline narrowed her eyes at her again. "If you think I'm going to let Darcy get expelled, you have another thing coming, Bennet. I will not survive in this godforsaken place without another person of taste. Do you hear me? Fix this!"

With that, she turned and stormed out of the room, with Lucy awkwardly following in her wake. "Um, Karoline. What about my bags?"

"Postmate them!" Karoline snapped back, and with that, the two *Shining* twins left the Delta house, slamming the door behind them.

four
october - 7 weeks before the event

THIS WAS HORRIBLE. Terrible. The worst thing imaginable. Okay, so that was hyperbolic, because Lizzy could imagine quite a bit that would be worse than this, including war and plagues and really unflattering photos posted to social media, but this current moment was nonetheless perplexingly awful.

She had gotten a D on her midterm exam for Cognitive Neuroscience.

Not to be one of *those* people, but Lizzy didn't get Ds on exams—especially not those she had actually studied for, since Professor Eliás was a notoriously hard grader, priding himself on failing at least a third of his class every semester. Granted, for most of her life she'd been hometaught and it wasn't really all that hard to maintain an A average when her sisters Lydia and Kitty were in the same grading pool, but even throughout her first two years at Austen University she'd been a solid A and B student; she'd one time gotten a C on a biology quiz, but a D on an exam? *Never.*

For a good thirty seconds, Lizzy merely stared at the grade in question, as if through sheer will she could morph it into something a little more digestible. But alas, there the offending grade remained, even long after Lizzy's row in the lecture hall cleared.

Up at the front of the room, Professor Eliás was looking very busy and important as he typed something on his laptop. He was not the most approachable professor by reputation, with a solid 1.2 (out of 5) on Rate my Professor; and in practice, Lizzy had once seen him flat-out ignore a student who tried to ask him a question after the lecture finished, until the abashed undergrad had finally given up and left the room. There didn't seem to be much of a point in attempting to approach him and ask why she'd received the grade she did, even though her academic advisor—Miss Bates—was always telling her to *talk to her instructors, they were there to help their students achieve their best.* Somehow Lizzy doubted that Professor Eliás gave a single shit about her achieving her best.

Still... a D. The worst Professor Eliás could do was ignore her, she supposed. But maybe she might catch him in an unusually good mood, and he'd agree that of course he'd meant to write a B instead of a D because she had an uncanny grasp of cognitive neuroscience, especially for someone who was only minoring in psychology. So uncanny, in fact, that she didn't have to bother with coming in the rest of the semester, she could just coast from now on and know that an A was guaranteed. (Hey, as long as she was dreaming...)

Bracing herself, Lizzy made her way down the auditorium stairs, aiming toward the podium where Professor Eliás was still busily typing away at his laptop, looking very professor-ly and important.

"I wouldn't do that if I were you."

Lizzy halted, caught off guard by the voice coming from her right. Turning, the first thing she saw were a pair of converse sneakers propped up on the back of an auditorium seat—which she knew, without even looking up to his face, belonged to Sexy-Pants TA.

This was not his actual name, of course. His actual name was George-something, but 'George' didn't really capture the sexy essence of the Cognitive Neuroscience TA. He was one of those guys with slightly mussed hair and a smirky smile and an air that everything he did was effortlessly cool. But he also seemed to be something of a science nerd, and she'd witnessed him being nice to all the girls in class, not just the hot ones, which was a courtesy that seemed like it should be a given, but definitely wasn't.

As of yet, Lizzy had never spoken to Sexy-Pants TA because a) there had never been a reason and b) she didn't want to shatter the illusion of who he *seemed* to be from an observant but non-creepy distance. However, it seemed imprudent to ignore a warning like that. "And why is that?"

"Professor Eliás likes to check his H-index after class," Sexy-Pants TA informed her. "It's, like, his happy place, or something, and he really doesn't like to be interrupted." He sat up, leaning toward her. "If you have a question, I can help you out."

Lizzy weighed her options. She didn't especially feel like getting chewed out by her professor during his Zen Internet time, but she also didn't relish the thought of her first actual conversation with Sexy-Pants TA being about her appalling grade. Still, if there was any chance that her grade had been a mistake, there was no use jeopardizing that over a cute boy.

With a sigh, Lizzy produced her exam. "So, it's possible I just really misunderstood the lectures, or the exam instructions, and I'm not trying to be one of those entitled brats who thinks their education should just be handed to them on a silver platter—but where's my A?" She added a wry smile to this, lest there be any confusion about the irony in her tone.

Sexy-Pants TA laughed a little, taking the exam from her and flipping through a few pages. After a minute, he looked back to the title page, doing a double-take at the sight of her name. "Oh. Uh. Elizabeth Bennet."

"Lizzy," she corrected him, frowning at his tone. It sounded like the name was familiar to him for some reason, which it definitely shouldn't have been. She'd flown under the radar the whole first half of the semester, and she'd only ever stalked his Instagram under a burner account (kidding—mostly). "Why do you sound like you've just stumbled across a known serial killer?"

Sexy-Pants TA laughed again, running an awkward hand through his hair. "Well... the thing is..." He leaned in closer to her, giving her a sudden and alluring whiff of his aftershave. "I can't say this officially. *Unofficially*, I graded all the other midterms. But Professor Eliás specifically asked to grade yours."

Frowning, Lizzy processed this. She didn't know what was stranger—that a TA would be put in charge of grading one of the biggest point-value assignments for the class on his own, or that she should be singled out by Professor Eliás, who had never before even so much as acknowledged her existence. "But—why?" A sudden thought struck her. "Does he always choose a random exam to grade?"

Sexy-Pants TA snort-laughed at that. "Um, no. Professor Eliás does as little grading as possible, which is to say, none."

Mind still whirring, Lizzy tried to piece it together. Had she somehow caught the professor's attention, incurred his wrath in some way? She had never fallen asleep in class, or posted anything about the course on social media, or contradicted any of Eliás's ideas during a lecture. There was no reason that he should have noticed her above anyone else in the crowded hall.

Sexy-Pants TA crooked her even closer with his index finger, glancing over first to make sure Professor Eliás was still absorbed in his laptop before continuing in a hushed voice, "Between you and me, if I were to take a guess? Is it possible you've done anything to piss off President de Bourgh?"

Unbe-frickin'-lievable. "Oh," Lizzy seethed through clenched teeth, "it's possible."

The previous spring semester, Lizzy had been invited to a dinner party that turned out to be a setup to uncover the murder of a girl on campus. Unbelievably enough, the ruse had worked, and would-be detective Caty Morland had managed to figure out who killed her roommate, Isabella.

On the surface, it might sound like the administration of Austen University should be thankful to the girl who'd uncovered the murderer and his accomplice, both of whom had ties to the school (Frank Churchill was a student at the university, and Mrs. Norris was the house mother of one of the biggest sororities on campus, the Pi Kappa Sigmas). On the surface, the administration gave every appearance of being glad the crime had been resolved. However, Lizzy and the others who had been there that evening—dubbed the Austen Murder Club by one of the other attendees, Henry Tilney—soon found themselves under added scrutiny. It seemed many in the university administration didn't mind having a murderer on campus so much if his father was a tenured professor and his family were major donors, and an accomplice to the crime working with a group of young girls if she had connections to a famous evangelical preacher. No one ever said anything outright, of course, but Lizzy hadn't been the only one to notice she was suddenly being watched more closely, upbraided for even the most minor of offenses. Others from the Austen Murder Club, like Caty and Marianne Dashwood, had reported similar experiences.

Notably that short list included those at the dinner party, like Lizzy, who were at Austen University on scholarship, who didn't come from connected or wealthy families, and whose name didn't carry much weight in the small Southern town of Highbury. Whatever camaraderie that had connected the Austen Murder Club members after Frank's arrest and Norris's firing had begun evaporating once the richer, more elite members of the group began insisting that Caty, Marianne, and Lizzy were simply being paranoid.

There were those there that night who remained more supportive– like Tilney, who was Caty's ride-or-die besty and always had her back, and Jane Fairfax who no longer went to AU but was rightfully jaded about bougie Southerners and their twisted ways–and others who were more neutral, like Rushworth, who usually cared more about the food than taking a side on important issues, which was kind of frustrating but at least understandable in terms of his priorities. John Thorpe hadn't spoken to anyone since that night, for which everyone was grateful and wouldn't be complaining any time soon.

Then there were the others. The elite. Lizzy could grant some lenience for Emma Woodhouse and George Knightley, who were seeing the world through love-tinted glasses and just wanted everyone to get along, even if that meant ignoring the glaring issues right in front of their eyes. But the others, Lizzy had a harder time excusing. Namely, Fo-Hian Darcy and Karoline Lady-Bastard Bingley. It had been a tentative truce, at best, between Lizzy and the two rich snobs who had made her time at AU a mosquito bite in the ass, but she'd thought that maybe, just maybe, they'd all finally met each other as equals and fellow human beings.

But as soon as there had been any hint of privilege being exercised unfairly, the richest people in the group had (of course) combined forces and turned their backs on the poor peasants among them. If they'd all shown a united front to the administration, de Bourgh would have had to back down. She couldn't possibly bully students from two of the wealthiest families in the South, especially since Darcy was her nephew by marriage. Any grievances she might feel for the upset to the university's reputation (and bank account) would have had to begrudgingly be swept under the rug.

Unfortunately, Darcy thought they "lacked sufficient evidence that anyone was being targeted by the administration," and Karoline had been looking for the first opportunity to distance herself from the "basic bitches" she could find. The Austen Murder Club was no longer a group formed in solidarity over a shared traumatic experience. The lines had been drawn, in money-green, and there was no turning back.

So far the extra attention from the administration had been nothing but a slight annoyance. But now it appeared it might actually interfere with her grades, her GPA, her scholarship... Well, if President de Bourgh wanted to play hardball, then Lizzy was more than game. All she'd have to do is figure out what hardball was because sports really weren't her thing, but once she accomplished that? Watch out, de Bourgh. Homerun, or touchdown, or whatever. It wasn't going to be pretty.

Sexy-Pants TA let out a sympathetic whistle. "I thought that might be the case. Eliás is up for a Faculty Recognition Award and is doing some serious ass-kissing at the moment. Hence, the unnecessarily harsh grade. I would take it up with my academic advisor if I were you. See if they can put on a little pressure to get the assignment re-graded."

Lizzy considered the suggestion. Miss Bates wasn't the most intimidating person at the university, but she had one superpower, which was that she could out-talk anybody, any time. That might not sound like such an impressive feat, but Lizzy had once heard her carry on a completely one-sided conversation about chicken salad for twenty minutes. If she could get Professor Eliás on the phone, he might agree to re-grade the exam, just to shut her up.

"Thanks. I think I'll do that." Lizzy smiled at Sexy-Pants TA, who smiled back at her. After a companionable beat, his eyes flickered down to her lips for just the briefest of moments before moving back to her gaze. Something silent passed between them—a suggestion.

It all happened so quickly that Lizzy couldn't entirely be sure it had happened at all, except that Sexy-Pants TA seemed to be waiting for something from her. After a moment, realizing he wasn't going to get it, he leaned back in his chair again. "Cool. Godspeed."

It wasn't a lack of interest, it was a lack of understanding. Lizzy had never been very quick on the uptake in figuring out when boys were signifying their interest—was so notoriously bad at it, in fact, that sometimes she had to wonder if she wasn't just willfully misunderstanding them. Maybe a secret part of her just wanted to be a cat lady. But a not-so-secret part of her also wanted to make out with cute guys and get all the fun butterflies.

Too late, though. The moment was gone, and Sexy-Pants TA had pulled out his phone—the universal signal that any previously opened doors had officially been closed.

Oh well. She'd always had a fondness for cats.

δλε

Lizzy continued to think about her missed connection later that night as she and her roommates watched Netflix together. Normally Lizzy really enjoyed the competitive crafting reality show that they could only watch together (this was among the most sacred of roommate vows), but tonight she found her mind wandering back to that moment where Sexy-Pants TA had looked down at her lips, then given her that questioning look. She'd replayed it so many times that she had to wonder if she hadn't heightened the entire thing out of proportion. Maybe she just had spinach in her teeth, or something. Or maybe it had just been a really, really long time since she got the fun butterflies. Or any kind of action, really, unless one counted accidentally brushing hands with a stranger while passing them on a sidewalk. (She did not.)

What could be done about it, though? Lizzy couldn't exactly return to class on Monday, confront Sexy-Pants TA, and tell him she'd like a do-over and that yes, she'd like to kiss him now, if that option was still on the table.

Right?

As the credits rolled, Lizzy did the unthinkable and pressed pause. Both Marianne and Nora looked to her with expressions somewhere along the scale from surprise to concern. "Bathroom break?" Nora asked pragmatically.

Lizzy ignored that. "So, hypothetically speaking, how gross would it be for a TA to date a student in their section?"

This was an intentional question, with a very specific purpose. Though Lizzy considered herself to be a feminist, and virtually all of her friends would categorize themselves as the same, she had never met anyone quite so impassioned about Women and Gender Studies issues as Marianne Dashwood. Marianne had a particular interest in imbalances of power; as much as abuses of power could be anyone's thing, abuses of power were Marianne's *thing*. So if Lizzy could somehow finagle a pass from Marianne on dating Sexy-Pants TA, then that would be a sign from the feminist gods (goddesses?) that Lizzy should take another shot. Granted, this was a safe gamble to take, since she was almost positive that Marianne would decry the entire practice, thus absolving Lizzy of any guilt or FOMO she currently felt.

Marianne straightened, looking very aware of her own importance as she considered the issue carefully. "Well, any time there's an imbalance of power in romantic relationships"–(if ever Lizzy made a drinking game out of things Marianne said, 'imbalance of power' would definitely be on there, as would 'patriarchy')–"the parties involved should proceed carefully to make sure that no one is being taken advantage of. A TA holds the power of your grade in their hands, and as we all know, students from underprivileged backgrounds could have their entire futures jeopardized by one failing grade, a sliding GPA, scholarships and financial aid jeopardized..."

Just as she'd suspected. Lizzy couldn't help but feel a little relieved that Marianne was adverse to the idea. Putting herself out there could be exciting but it was also daunting and wasn't it better to just have pizza and pajamas while watching a group of expert crafters figure out how to repurpose pine cones?

Unexpectedly, Marianne shook her voluminous hair a little before continuing, "That being said, a TA is different from, say, a professor. A TA is a fellow student, and in many ways on the same level emotionally, intellectually, and socially. So the power dynamics aren't quite so imbalanced since both are likely to be pawns of the same patriarchal system."

Marianne said this entire speech without taking a breath, and by the time she was finished, a dark crimson flush had climbed its way up her neck and spread to the tops of her cheeks.

Noticing this, Nora sat up and frowned, looking between the two of them. "What's going on? Do both of you have the hots for a TA?"

Marianne's blush, seemingly impossibly, deepened. "Mine's a GTA— a graduate teaching assistant." The words came out of her in a rush, as if she could no longer contain herself. "So he's in a slightly different social bracket but not really since he's still *technically* a student so it isn't that egregious an imbalance of power, if you really think about it. He teaches my poetry seminar and he's brilliant and sensitive and has eyes the color of the sea. His name is Willoughby."

Her eyes turned expectantly to Lizzy, whose own confession felt a little flat following on the heels of that. "Um, well, he's a TA for my Cognitive Neuroscience class. Seems cool. No idea what color his eyes are, don't know his name. But he did that thing where he looked down at my lips meaningfully, so—basically we made out, mentally."

Nora sighed, leaning forward to gather napkins and discarded pizza crusts into the now-empty pizza box. "Dating someone who holds the power over your education, to be decided on a whim, seems like a colossally bad idea to me, for the record." She rose to her feet, heading toward the kitchen. "I don't know why people bother dating in college at all. Don't we all have enough on our plates...?"

As she left the room, Marianne and Lizzy exchanged a significant glance. Nora had always been the most pragmatic of the three, but this trait had been heightened the previous semester. Her first year at AU, Nora had hit it off with Charlie Bingley, a cute, sweet Theta she'd met through Charlie's older sister, Karoline. At the time, Nora and Lizzy had both been pledging as Pi Kappa Sigmas, and Karoline had been

Lizzy's "Big," meant to orientate her into the ways of the sorority. However, Karoline and Lizzy had been like oil and water from the start—no, scratch that; like kerosene and a live flame. Karoline had been nicer to Nora at first, until she realized that Charlie and Nora liked each other. Even though Charlie and Nora never went on an official date, and even though both swore up and down they were just friends, Karoline made it her life's mission to either get Lizzy and Nora kicked out of the Kappas, or pressure them to leave themselves.

The antagonizing had eventually driven them out of the Kappas, but as a nice bonus, it had resulted in Lizzy and Nora becoming inseparable friends for life. The two had decided to start the Deltas on their own, as a sort of alternative sorority for those who didn't fit into the traditional Greek mold. (Side note: it was really difficult to get by at a small Southern school like Austen University with a long, rich Greek history without being pressured into joining one of the houses. Not belonging to a fraternity or sorority was sort of like being faction-less: Possible, but not pleasant.) So far there were only three members, including themselves and Nora's younger sister Marianne, but Lizzy held out hope that this next pledging season they'd actually get some pledges, provided that no more undergraduates were murdered. (Fingers crossed!)

Another added bonus—at least at first—was that Charlie hadn't seemed scared off by all the drama. He continued to drop by the house for visits, and was a regular for Friday night pizza nights. Despite the mounting frustration for Marianne and Lizzy that Charlie *still* hadn't asked Nora out on an official date, he kind of acted like her boyfriend in every sense of the word outside of actually being her boyfriend—texting regularly, installing anti-spyware on her computer, having regular study dates at the library, remembering her coffee order. Plus, there was the way he always looked when he first spotted her in a crowd, like she was the human personification of Christmas.

The two of them were both impossibly shy and sweet and stupid for two such smart people, and Lizzy had been in no doubt of them eventually finding their way to each other, where they so clearly belonged.

And then, out of nowhere, Charlie took a sabbatical from the university, finishing out his spring semester in Paris. That had been in

March. It was now October, and so far as Lizzy knew, Nora hadn't heard a single peep from him, even though he was rumored to be state-side again.

Bastard. It was still hard to think of Charlie being just another player. And technically he wasn't really since there had been no *playing* (at least, not that Lizzy knew of). But he had emotionally screwed Nora over, and hadn't even had the decency to explain why.

Ever since then, Nora had been understandably wary of campus relationships. As a result, Lizzy and Marianne often found themselves doing a careful tightrope act around her, where they didn't want to exclude her from things but they also didn't want to bring up anything that might be needlessly painful.

Right now, they communicated silently with one another via eyebrow, gaging if they should drop the conversation altogether or see if Nora needed to talk about her feelings. She never actually wanted to, but it felt like something that should be offered nonetheless. Then Marianne started doing something really dramatic with her left eyebrow, and Lizzy realized she might have been misinterpreting their previous silent conversation because she genuinely had no idea what was going on, and before anything had gotten back on track, Nora re-entered the room, folding her arms.

"You don't have to get all weird and quiet. I'm not having an emotional meltdown. Merely expressing that jeopardizing your future over a guy is shortsighted–advice I would have given regardless of any alleged heartbreak."

This seemed true enough. Lizzy couldn't ever imagine a scenario in which Nora encouraged anyone to pursue their feelings recklessly. Marianne seemed to be driven by her passion (whether it be for music, poetry, or feminist issues), but apparently she'd gotten all the dosage of that particular trait and Nora had gotten none. The only thing Lizzy had ever seen her get remotely excited about was a Cyber Monday deal for a new laptop battery.

It was, in truth, entirely possible that Nora really wasn't suffering over Charlie's sudden and unexpected departure. Maybe she really could just compartmentalize her feelings, and whatever she'd felt for Charlie had been tucked away into a neat, organized little box in her mind that very much resembled Nora's neat, organized little room (with her color-coded cubbies and labels).

But, on the off chance that Nora really was trying to underplay her struggle, Lizzy decided to change the subject. As one of five daughters in a semi-dysfunctional family, Lizzy had long-since developed the ability to defuse uncomfortable situations. If there had been an Olympics of deflection, Lizzy was confident she would make it to the winner's podium. "Well, I got a D on my exam, so I wouldn't be jeopardizing my grade so much as trying to use sexual favors to build it back up." Lizzy smiled sweetly at Marianne. "What about that kind of relationship with a TA? Would that constitute an abuse of power?"

Marianne huffed, not amused. "I know you're joking, Lizzy, but there's a long history of women being pressured into non-consensual acts to progress their careers, and I really don't think it's funny to..."

This continued for quite some time, during which Lizzy slid her gaze to Nora's and shared a brief, glancing smile.

Before Marianne could get herself wound up for a second round, they were interrupted by a loud, distinct rat-a-tat knock on the front door, accompanied by a, "Yoohoo!" The three girls fell silent, exchanging ominous glances. Mrs. Jennings.

Instinctively, Lizzy looked to the curtains, cursing inwardly when she saw they were open. There was no use pretending no one was home. The lights were on, and the telltale glow of the television screen lit up the bay window. Damn, damn, and triple damn.

The woman in question was their Panhellenic sponsor, Mrs. Dolly Jennings. She was Nora's and Marianne's second cousin, as well as the Deltas' sponsor and house mother; one of the richest women in Highbury, Mrs. Jennings was a major donor to the university and had championed their small sorority. She was probably the only reason they'd been able to open a chapter, and was probably the only reason it hadn't been shut down after the debacle of Isabella's death, Caty Morland's subsequent dinner party, and all the fuss it had caused at the university. Mrs. Jennings was an extraordinarily generous, friendly woman.

She was also impossible to get rid of once she managed to get into the house.

Mrs. Jennings was a talker. She could talk about any subject, regardless of whether anyone else was actually listening or participating in the conversation, and the thing she most liked to talk about was gossip, of which there was never a short supply in the small college town. Lizzy knew more dirt about neighbors she'd never actually met than she ever cared to, and she had no doubt that Mrs. Jennings talked about the three of them just as freely to whoever else she could manage to get within earshot. A brief visit from Mrs. Jennings was never brief. One time she stopped by to "drop off a cheesecake" mid-afternoon and stayed so long talking that at last all three girls had just gone to bed and left her alone in the kitchen, laughing boisterously at her own joke.

Nora looked at her watch, sighing. "I was going to wake up early to study…"

"Yoohoo!" Mrs. Jennings called again. "Just a quick pop-by, girls! I come bearing gifts!"

What else could they do but let her in? At least with Mrs. Jennings the promise of gifts was not an idle one. Sometimes she came bearing food, other times iPads. Okay, that had been one time, but still.

"Brace yourselves," Lizzy whispered, shooting back one last mournful look to her roommates before plastering on a smile as she threw open the door. "Mrs. Jennings! We weren't expecting you."

The woman in question bustled past Lizzy, carrying a tray full of cupcakes (yay!) and settling herself down at the dining room table (boo). "Lord, I'm sweating like a sinner in church. What right does it have to be so warm in October?" Uninvited, she propped her croc-covered feet up on the chair next to her, fanning herself heavily with a used paper plate she'd picked up from the table. "Lucy, honey, come on in here and shut the door, before you let out all the AC."

Before Lizzy had time to even fully wonder who 'Lucy' was, a familiar-looking girl entered the room. She had long, dyed blonde hair and wore thick eyelash extensions as well as a full face of makeup, and her outfit looked like it could almost pass for designer. Lizzy couldn't quite place her, but knew she had definitely seen her somewhere. Maybe they'd had a lecture together, or Lucy had been a pledge the same year as her?

Answering the unasked question, Mrs. Jennings gestured to Lucy– proudly, as if she had had something to do with making her. "Girls, I want you to meet Lucy Steele. Lucy is a distant cousin of mine. Actually, she's a distant cousin of my son-in-law's, so no blood relation to the two of you, Nora and Marianne, but practically family nonetheless."

Mrs. Jennings's recently acquired son-in-law, Jeb Middleton, had made a brief appearance last summer at a get-together that Mrs. Jennings hosted at her waterfront mansion and insisted that the girls all attend. Jeb was an extreme hunter, having made his fortune off marketing a very particular kind of hunting experience that Lizzy didn't fully understand (Jeb was missing a few teeth and had a thick Mississippi accent) but somehow involved helicopters and bazookas. Apparently, it was very lucrative. Between that and his alligator vest (sans shirt underneath), Jeb had given Mrs. Jennings a run for her money in the most-eccentric-member-of-the-family department, which was saying something.

Lucy didn't look like she came from the same *colorful* background, so she was probably about as distant to Jeb as Marianne and Nora were to Mrs. Jennings. As if sensing their curiosity, she gave a bashful little smile–though her cat-like eyes peered up at them from under her thick false lashes, appraising.

"You've probably seen her around town," Mrs. Jennings continued. "She was part of the Omegas, and she works at that cute little coffee shop, the Croissant."

"The Crescent," Lucy corrected her, still smiling that bashful little smile.

It clicked immediately for Lizzy–*that* was where she had seen her. Lucy was a waitress at the cafe, though she didn't recall her having the hair extensions then, and she had never looked quite so made up. Maybe the wait staff had a strict dress code they had to follow. "That's right. I've seen you there before." Lizzy offered her friendliest smile, knowing firsthand how uncomfortable it was to have Mrs. Jennings parade her around like her latest bag. "It must be fun working there. Do they let you have free pastries?"

Lucy's smile turned prim. "I try to avoid carbs as much as possible." She gave Lizzy a quick, assessing little look, as if to say *You clearly don't.*

O-kay. Lizzy put on her blandest smile, the one she'd grown accustomed to wearing around sorority bitches. No more sticking her neck out to try to make her feel comfortable anymore.

"Well, girls, we're simply in a flummox because Lucy's had a terrible falling out with the Omegas, and of course, I thought if anyone could understand, it would be my Delta girls."

Marianne had never made any secret of detesting Mrs. Jennings, but it just wasn't in her personality to abstain from the whiff of drama. "What happened?" she asked reluctantly, folding her arms over her chest.

Lucy took in a bracing breath. "I don't want to say anything negative against my Omega sisters. I'm sure there could have been some sort of misunderstanding." She didn't sound sure of this, at all. "But I couldn't ignore my growing suspicion that some of the girls might be..." she lowered her voice to a dramatic whisper, "*racist.*"

Lizzy exchanged a surprised glance with Nora, who asked, "What do you mean?"

Lucy looked up eagerly at the sound of Nora's question, meeting her gaze almost–hungrily?–before dropping it demurely to the ground again. "I really shouldn't say. I don't want to get anyone in trouble. But I also knew I couldn't be part of it anymore."

"Of course you couldn't." Marianne was properly fired up now. If there was anything that got her more inflamed than a good abuse of power, it was a racial injustice. "Any association with a system that oppresses makes us complicit to that oppression."

Mrs. Jennings didn't seem to entirely understand what that meant, but she gathered that the girls were receptive to Lucy's plight. "That's for damn tootin'. Obviously Lucy's had to step away from the Omegas for the time being, which means she's homeless and sisterless. Now, I'd love to take her in, but we're redoing the west wing, and anyway I thought it would be better for young Lucy to be around some girls her own age...?"

Another glance exchanged between Lizzy and Nora. Not much could really be said in protest, since Mrs. Jennings was not only their benefactor, but their landlady. At least Lucy's social justice plight would get Marianne on her side, which would be less of a headache for everyone involved.

Lizzy only had to wonder why Lucy would agree to go along with such a plan. She did not look like someone who'd want to willingly spend her time with the 'loser' Deltas, and she also struck Lizzy as someone who could have easily persuaded Mrs. Jennings to let her stay in her mansion and think it was her idea, too.

But for whatever reason, Lucy Steele had agreed to bunk up with them. Lizzy put on her most pleasant smile. "Welcome, roomie." Not quite willing to let go of the carbs dig previously, she added sweetly, "Tomorrow's pancake day, so I hope you brought your own syrup!"

chapter
five

IT HAS BEEN SAID that the newspaper industry is dying, and nowhere did this seem truer than during the bi-weekly meeting for Austen University's school newspaper, *Juvenilia*. What once might have been a competitive extracurricular was sparsely populated these days, with Lizzy and only a few small handful of others staffing what had once been a thriving publication. It had taken endless campaigning from Lizzy to finally persuade Professor Palmer to take the faculty chair position, and only then with the promise that he would only have to attend once a month and that he would only have to act mostly as a figurehead. Professor Palmer certainly hadn't risen above and beyond that promise, spending most of the meetings shamelessly scrolling through Twitter or playing games on his phone.

It certainly wasn't the glamorous introduction to journalism that Lizzy had hoped for. Last semester at least had been somewhat more promising. As terrible as Isabella's death had been, for the first time, Lizzy had felt like she was reporting real news. Respected publications were referencing her articles, and the student body actually seemed interested in what *Juvenilia* had to say.

It had been a short-lived thrill, unfortunately. The fraternities and sororities were all on their best behaviors this semester, thanks to rumors about cancelation that had circulated after all the dirt surrounding Isabella's murder investigation had been kicked up. So far this school year, Lizzy had written about a food poisoning outbreak caused by a popular food truck off campus, a shortage of Scantron forms and what it would mean for the future of testing, and a puff piece about why the school mascot (Petey the Peacock) deserved a makeover. Not exactly Pulitzer-winning material. Lizzy knew all writers had to pay their dues, but she had hoped this portion of her writing career would pass more like a colorful montage in a movie, not so much a slow-motion shot in a docuseries.

If Lizzy had known what was about to come, she might have embraced the monotony. As it was, she foolishly interpreted Professor Palmer's lack of phone in his hand as a promising development. Maybe something really juicy had happened, and Palmer was–for once–excited to engage in creating a quality paper.

(Foolish summer child.)

"Welcome. Glad everyone could make it." Palmer nodded in acknowledgement at Alicia Johnson, who wrote the gossip column, and James Benwick, who did cultural reviews; Lizzy was almost positive Palmer didn't actually know their names, and only slightly confident that he might know hers. "Nice fall weather we're having today."

Lizzy's first inkling of foreboding came along with those words. Professor Palmer being present in the moment was one thing; Professor Palmer making awkward small talk was... something else. It did not bode well.

"Before we jump into new business, I'd like to introduce a new member of our staff." Professor Palmer checked his watch. "He should be here any minute–oh, there he is."

If this had been a horror movie, the stringed instruments would have been in a frenzy. Lizzy felt an instinctive roller-coaster whoosh of dread as she turned toward the door, staring in blank disbelief as Darcy entered the room. His eyes slid to hers before cutting away; he took a seat far down the conference table, as if to dissuade anyone from assuming they might know one another.

"Fo-Hian Darcy," Professor Palmer was saying. "We're very lucky to have him. He's generously offered to contribute some photography to the paper for a special photo story we'll be including in the online edition."

He paused, clearly waiting for Darcy to say something, but Darcy just nodded silently, looking at each person in turn around the table–including, again only briefly, Lizzy–before staring straight ahead at nothing.

Lizzy stifled an irritated snort. Arrogant prick. He clearly expected Professor Palmer to do all the work of introducing him to the group, as if his reputation as a great photographer preceded him. She was willing to bet he'd gotten a camera for his birthday and fancied himself an expert after a few amateur shots, so Auntie de Bourgh had pulled a few strings so he could show off his budding talent. Barf.

Professor Palmer looked a little panicked at the realization that he was going to have to put in even more effort at today's meeting than he'd already exerted thus far; poor man must be absolutely exhausted. "Um, well. I've seen some of his work and it's very impressive. We're lucky to have him. Welcome, Fo-Hian."

"I go by Darcy, actually." Darcy actually sounded a little miffed that Professor Palmer wouldn't intuitively know this. It was one of the weirder things that Lizzy had encountered at AU–how many of the guys went by their last names. She didn't know if that was a Southern thing, or a carry-over from boarding schools, but it was yet another thing she found both annoying and perplexing. She couldn't wait to get back to the Southwest, where the states were newer and none of the family names were old enough to carry any real weight and people just used their first names like normal people.

Professor Palmer apparently felt something of the same, since the first sign of irritation cracked through this bizarrely polite facade he was putting on. "Welcome, *Darcy*."

This time, Lizzy did laugh a little, trying to keep it under her breath. Darcy looked over, glaring with his familiar stern, slightly perplexed look that seemed to say, *Why aren't you more impressed with me?* To which Lizzy responded with her usual *Bless your soul* smile, which was one of the only things about the South she actually liked: A way of essentially saying "Screw you" to somebody's face that was somehow socially acceptable.

"Welcome, Darcy," she echoed, unable to help herself. "I for one can't wait to see what you contribute to the quality of the school paper.

I'm sure we won't be able to understand how we ever managed to function without your help."

Darcy had had too many interactions with her now to misunderstand her words for sincerity. He simply blinked and looked away again. Professor Palmer gave Lizzy an exasperated, amused smile, because at his heart, he was a basic bitch who loved a good clapback, even though he'd obviously been instructed by de Bourgh to pat Darcy's head and tell him he was doing an amazing job.

"As one of our senior staff members, I'm sure you won't mind showing Darcy the ropes," Palmer said to Lizzy now, his smile deepening as her own faded. "In fact, maybe the two of you can work on his first story together."

Ohhhh, he really was a basic bitch.

"The story is a local women's shelter. The administration wants to generate some interest in getting students involved in local charity work as the holidays approach."

Of course they did, because the university needed all the good PR it could get after Isabella's murder. Lizzy wince-smiled, because what else could she do? Throw a huge tantrum over writing a story about helping displaced women and children? (She couldn't do that—right?)

As the other story assignments were made, Lizzy braced herself for the inevitable conversation with Darcy. She supposed it probably wasn't possible to get through working together without actually talking to one another (unless he agreed to some kind of arrangement with a plexiglass wall between them and a mediator who relayed their conversations to one another, which seemed both complicated and unlikely).

As the meeting concluded and everyone began to disperse, Lizzy reluctantly made her way over to Darcy—because of course, *of course*, he would not deign to be the one to make the effort to come over and talk to her. Sometimes it was exhausting being the better person.

She didn't wait for him to look up and acknowledge her, nor did she bother with any small talk. "So, women's shelters. Should we compile a list of a few, split them up, and figure out which would make the most sense for the article?"

"Actually, there's one that's already been determined by the administration." Darcy cleared his throat. "It's one sponsored by my family."

Of *course*. Any of the remaining pieces that hadn't yet been clear suddenly fell into place. If Lizzy were a betting woman, she would wager a sizable amount that Darcy was going to be starting his law school applications soon and de Bourgh was planning on forwarding this article to all her contacts in the Ivy League.

At least Darcy had the good grace to look vaguely embarrassed. He cleared his throat again. "I can send you the details."

Suppressing an eyeroll, Lizzy gave him her information, already dreading the day she'd see his name pop up on her notifications.

That accomplished, Lizzy found the first opportunity to excuse herself, deciding to check her *Juvenilia* email while it was on her mind. To her surprise, she actually had an unread message that wasn't a promotional advert from Hulu asking her to come back (she'd used up all the free trials on all her accounts, unfortunately). She almost assumed that it must be some kind of spam, though, since its sender was marked as 'Unknown'–but the subject line caught her eye before she moved it to the trash.

Subject: You didn't hear this from me

Okay, so that begged to be read, even if it was a link to a virus, right? Credit where credit was due, that was some A+ effort to steal her credit card information. (Ha! Good luck with that fruitless endeavor, scammers. She was fairly certain even the most heartless fraudster would *donate* her money when they saw the contents of her bank account.)

Opening the message, Lizzy quickly skimmed its contents, which were brief but to the point: **Ever heard of the Portraits of Pemberley? It's where the most depraved Sigma Rho bros post 'trophy' shots of their sexual conquests. Non-consensual photos. Pretty disgusting stuff.**
Signed, a concerned citizen

δλε

A quick Google search yielded no results for the Portraits of Pemberley, even combined with the key words 'Sigma Rho' and 'Austen University'–which probably shouldn't have come as any surprise, since if the site was real and the Sigmas running it had even a few brain cells, it would be either encrypted or on the dark web. Lizzy's next attempt to uncover more information was to send a reply email, but her message came back with an error message saying the email address no longer existed.

Well, shit. By far the most interesting piece of news that Lizzy had seen all semester, and it seemed to be a complete dead end. It was possible that whoever had sent it to her had just been trolling her, trying to stir up trouble where there wasn't any. But, why? She knew there was no use looking for sense in the behaviors of online instigators, but even so, it felt like a lot of effort if someone was just trying to rile her up, when they could do so much more easily–by, say, sending her a message saying low-rise jeans were coming back into fashion or that *Sex Education* was overrated.

The issue continued to plague Lizzy later that evening as she, Marianne, and Nora enjoyed a round of cocktails and off-key singing at the Crown Inn. It should be mentioned that Lucy was in attendance, too, but 'enjoy' didn't seem to be the right word to apply to someone who only ordered a water (because of the calories) and had spent the entire evening thus far engrossed in her phone.

Lizzy stirred her straw through her drink, at last sighing and pushing it back. "I have a dilemma."

"Another one?" Nora asked wryly, giving Lizzy a pointed look over her own gin and tonic. "Or is this a continuation of the dating-your-TA conversation? Because I think I've made my feelings on the subject clear."

Lizzy arched an eyebrow back at her. "I am a woman fully capable of instigating multiple dilemmas, thank you very much. This one has to do with my future career, and as an added bonus will pass the Bechdel test."

Marianne perked up at the sound of that. "I love a good Bechdel-friendly conversation."

"We know." Lizzy continued before Marianne had too much time to dwell on that. "I received an anonymous tip for a story that sounds potentially career-making, if I can verify that it's true. Unfortunately, none of the research I've done so far even remotely suggests that it might be. Do I continue to operate on good faith that this isn't a hoax–and sideline the other, less interesting assignment I've been given? All the while knowing of course, I'm only doing it because not only would it be an incredible story, but it would also undermine the Greek system, that I personally find to be archaic and corrupt?"

Lucy looked up from her phone long enough to blink at Lizzy a few times, before sighing and looking around the room, as if to say–*Is this really the best I can do?*

Nora narrowed her eyes at Lizzy. "What's the story?"

Lizzy explained the gist of the email as best she could, watching Marianne grow increasingly irate with each passing word. By the end, she was clenching her teeth, grasping the edge of the table until she was white-knuckled; and even Lucy looked vaguely interested in the subject matter.

"The non-consensual exploitation of a woman's body is one of the most reprehensible things in the entire world," Marianne seethed. "You have to take them down, Lizzy. Go for the jugular. Show no mercy."

Nora gave her sister a placating shoulder pat. "Breathe, Marianne. There's nothing that actually proves it's true–right, Lizzy?" This in the tone of someone speaking to another adult in front of a child, and asking them to confirm there was no such thing as the bogeyman to put the child's mind at ease.

"No," Lizzy conceded. "But I don't think it's beyond the realm of possibility that it *could* be true. I mean, we all know how entitled these fraternity bros can be. It wouldn't be that big of a stretch of the imagination to believe that some of them see women this way–as trophies to be passed around and collected like baseball cards."

"Some of them, maybe." Nora didn't sound convinced, and Lizzy didn't think it was entirely on Marianne's behalf. "But I can't see everyone agreeing to cover it up if this were some commonly known secret in the Sigma house."

"The Sigmas are the fraternity with ties to the military," Marianne reminded Nora. "And we all know the armed forces are just a weaponized branch of the patriarchy."

Lizzy frowned at this, in the uncomfortable position of having to play devil's advocate with herself. "That's a little extreme, Marianne. There are a lot of different people who choose to enlist in the military, for a variety of reasons, and it's an honorable thing to serve your country. I, for one, don't think I could do it."

"Of course you couldn't—because you're a free thinker." Marianne's nostrils flared, a signal of thinly veiled irritation. "I'm just saying, I could never date someone with the mindset of being a willing pawn to the government."

Nora and Lizzy exchanged a glance, a wordless agreement to move the conversation into less heated territory. "Do we know anyone in Sigma Rho? Maybe I could ask them if they've heard anything about it."

"No one comes to mind." Nora shook her head. "I just have a hard time believing high-ranking members of a fraternity would risk their reputations this way. I mean, think of Darcy, for instance—like him or not, you have to admit that he's honorable."

Now it was Marianne's turn to exchange a glance with Lizzy. One of the things that had come out the night of the fateful dinner party—aside from the truth about Isabella Thorpe's murder—was that Darcy and Karoline had schemed to separate Charlie and Nora from one another, encouraging him to finish his semester in Paris. Though they had never given a straight reason as to why Nora was deemed such an unacceptable match, Lizzy could easily guess it had to do with the difference in their families' incomes. Lizzy and Marianne had agreed not to tell Nora the truth about what they'd learned that night, mostly because Lizzy didn't know how it could possibly bring her any comfort—to know that not only had Charlie decided to leave her without so much as a goodbye, but also that his family and friends had disliked her so much that they'd teamed up to make sure it happened. If Nora knew the truth, Lizzy doubted she'd be singing Darcy's praises.

"I'll choose the 'or not' option, thanks." Lizzy took another long sip of her drink. "And I'd prefer it if you didn't bring up that name tonight—we're trying to have a good time."

Lucy once again perked up from her phone screen. "You mean Fo-Hian Darcy, the president of the Thetas?" She looked, despite herself, impressed. "Do y'all know him?"

"Unfortunately," Lizzy grumbled, just in time to turn and see Darcy standing behind her, one hand poised as if prepared to tap her on the shoulder. As their eyes locked, his hand hovered in place for another moment before falling back awkwardly to his side.

"Elizabeth." Darcy swallowed, reaching into his pocket. "You left your pen at the meeting today. I thought you might need it back."

Lizzy blinked at the sight of one of her pens, which she knew was hers by the telltale sign of absentminded chewing on the cap. It was just an inexpensive pen that came in a package of ten, certainly not anything that she would have fretted over losing; she lost about five pens a week, hence why she bought them on the cheap. Why would he bother returning it to her?

At once, it clicked into place for Lizzy. Darcy must think she was so poor that something like this lost pen might actually break the bank. And, okay, yes, she wasn't loaded, and yes she had only come to the Crown Inn tonight because it was ladies' night and she could get free drinks between 10 and midnight, and maybe she'd clipped a coupon or two in her day, but she wasn't so poor that she couldn't afford another packet of pens from the Dollar Store.

What a condescending twerp. Lizzy gave him her most glacial smile as she took the pen in question from his grasp. "Gee, thanks, Darcy. You've just saved Christmas for my family."

She'd barely had time to register his frown as Karoline Bingley approached, running a possessive hand down his arm. "Here you are, Darcy. I lost you in the crowd."

Lizzy did her best to suppress an eyeroll–not because the appearance of her nemesis was unexpected, but because it was all too predictable. Wherever Darcy went, Karoline was never far behind, tottering around him in her ridiculous heels and designer outfits, seemingly oblivious that it was a futile effort. No one was good enough for Darcy, at least not according to Darcy–and this was not just a thought born of bitterness because one time at a party Lizzy had overheard him saying she "wasn't his type" (with a cold, detached onceover of her body that implied he would never be quite that desperate. Well, the feeling was mutual, thank you very much). She imagined the only girl good enough for Darcy, in his mind, would be someone with the body of a model, the brain of a neuroscientist, and the pedigree of a Kennedy (but without so many annoying Yankee ideas).

Karoline's dream boy would, of course, be Darcy, or anyone who she thought might make him jealous.

There was no reason for the two of them to remain at the table, but Darcy shifted, seeming uncomfortable about just abruptly leaving. This was a very Southern thing, Lizzy had come to learn during her short time at AU. No matter how much you might hate somebody, if they were in your circle of acquaintance, you were seemingly obligated to make awkward small talk with them whenever you ran into each other. At least, that was the only reason she could attribute to Darcy so frequently seeking her out in public.

"Well," he said after a moment, and Lizzy could almost see the wheels turning in his brain as he tried to think of something, anything, to get him out of the conversation.

Surprisingly, it was Lucy who saved them all by speaking up. For the first time all night, she was completely engaged in what was going on at the table. "Aren't you Karoline Bingley?" At Karoline's blank stare, she fearlessly persisted, "I watch your makeup tutorials on TikTok. You're so talented."

Karoline's icy bitchiness melted at the first sign of praise, and she practically beamed at Lucy. "I'm just working with the gifts that God's given me."

Lucy smiled eagerly. "Has anyone ever told you that you look just like a young Rihanna? I could totally see you becoming a billionaire in the fashion and beauty space, just like her."

Karoline preened at the praise. "Who, me? Wow, I'd never even made the connection before, but I guess I *am* kind of like a young Rihanna..."

Blech. Lizzy resisted another eyeroll–she really was exerting Herculean levels of restraint tonight, despite having already had one and a half free cocktails. But better to remain silent and encourage Karoline and Darcy to move on quickly, than engage and cause them to linger any longer than necessary–a bridge they had already crossed, in Lizzy's humble opinion.

"You deserve every follow," Lucy gushed. "I've always wondered–do you have a younger brother named Charlie? I think I was in a class with him freshman year, and I thought you two had a strong resemblance."

Karoline's artificially green eyes sharpened as she cast a not-too-subtle gaze in Nora's direction. "Yes, I do have a brother named Charlie. He actually just got back from a semester in Paris. Well, not *just* back. He's been home for a few weeks now, so I'm sure he's had plenty of time to catch up with anyone who means anything to him."

Lizzy stiffened at the obvious insult to Nora, even as she saw Marianne reach under the table to take her sister's hand. Unless Nora was keeping some pretty intense secrets, she'd had no idea until just this moment that Charlie was back in Highbury, and he certainly hadn't reached out to her to let her know. It was an old wound, but Lizzy knew it would still be painful, despite Nora's stoic expression.

So much for keeping silent and trying to take the high road. If Karoline wanted to drag them down into the mud, then Lizzy wanted to get in a few good shots, too, especially if it would divert attention away from Nora and the pain that Karoline was obviously enjoying being the cause of.

"Karoline, where did you get that dress?"

Karoline spared her a quick, scathing glance. "Nowhere you could afford, Bennet."

"Oh, too bad." Lizzy feigned disappointment. "It's just, I think we're roughly the same size, and I know for girls like us, it's hard to find clothing that really flatters a fuller figure."

For the record, Lizzy was completely comfortable with her size, which was normal and healthy. However, she also knew that Karoline was the type to count every calorie and who prided herself on wearing a size 0-2, and who probably couldn't fathom anything more horrible than being Lizzy's–again, totally normal, healthy–size.

Sure enough, Lizzy saw the moment that Karoline gave up the ghost, the venom draining from her eyes and being replaced with sheer panic. "What? We're not the same size, Bennet. Not even close."

"Oh. Sure." Lizzy made her voice falsely bright, as if coddling a small child. "No, you're right. My mistake. I just thought–no, never mind."

"What? What is it?"

Lizzy grimaced. "It must just be the material. Or the lighting." She lowered her voice, leaning in toward Karoline. "Or did you maybe have carbs for lunch today?"

Karoline was gone before Lizzy had even finished the sentence, and this time Lizzy didn't bother to hide her grin. It faded a little as she met Darcy's gaze, but she held it, raising her eyebrow a little. "Thanks for the pen." And with that, she turned her back to him, a clear dismissal.

Waiting until she was sure he was gone, Lizzy leaned in toward Nora, brow furrowed with concern. "Are you–?"

Nora shot a quick glance at Lucy, who was listening with interest. Even with Marianne and Lizzy, arguably the two people closest to her in the world, Nora had never admitted how much Charlie leaving had hurt her, so Lizzy could only imagine that she wouldn't want to have this discussion in front of Lucy, who was virtually a stranger. Biting her lip in frustration, Lizzy sat back in her chair, feeling useless. She wanted to be there for Nora, but she didn't make it easy. It was almost as if Nora hoped by denying her feelings, they would truly just go away.

"Tilney," Nora said abruptly.

It was so out of the blue that Lizzy could only stare at her. "Huh?"

Nora persisted, "The guy who came to your Stinky Cheese and Bad Poetry night in September. Wasn't he in Sigma Rho?"

Now that she mentioned it, Lizzy could vaguely recall some surprise upon hearing that the charming, colorful Tilney was part of the military fraternity. And if there was anyone inside Sigma Rho who might give them a scoop on a secret sex scandal, it would be him.

"Why, yes," Lizzy grinned back at her. "He most certainly is."

chapter
six

WHERE THERE WAS ALREADY a likeness of intellect, interests, and disposition, there was nothing that could bond a group of people like having been responsible for uncovering a murder together. Lizzy felt a sense of kinship with most of the other attendees of the fateful Isabella Thorpe dinner party, tenuous as those bonds might be with some–like, say, Karoline and Darcy, along with Rushworth, and others she might like well enough, like Emma and Knightley, but with whom she wouldn't choose to regularly socialize.

However it was with real and unbridled glee that Lizzy welcomed Henry Tilney and Caty Morland into the Delta house, and not just because of the boxed wine and Oreos they brought by way of tribute. Even if they hadn't solved a murder together, Lizzy was confident she would have liked Tilney and Caty just as much as she did now, since both were so weird and clever (by far her favorite combination in a person). Even if she didn't see them often, every time they met felt like no time at all had passed between them. Having the shared history they did was just an added layer that gave some interesting texture to the friendship.

"No fair," Tilney groused good-naturedly as he followed Lizzy into the living room, eyeing her loungewear with unbridled envy. "I wouldn't have worn real pants if I'd known I didn't have to."

Lizzy wagged a finger at him. "Let it be known that the Delta house is always and officially the sweatpant house. Your jeans are no good here."

"Duly noted."

Caty dropped beside Tilney on the couch, cooing in audible delight at the offering of hot pizza on the coffee table. "But it isn't even pizza night!"

Friday, as everyone knew, was pizza night in the Delta house, but tonight Lizzy had made an exception, since she intended to ply Tilney for information. "Nothing but the best for my guests." She reconsidered, amending herself, "Nothing but the best five-dollar ready-made deal for my guests."

"Free pizza?" Tilney took a seat on the couch, studying Lizzy warily. "Oh, God. Who's dying? Is it you? Is it me?"

Lizzy had to laugh. "Nobody's dying. Well, lots of people are dying, but not currently in this living room, as far as I know. I just have a little tiny favor to ask you, so I thought an offering of pizza might make you more manipulatable."

Tilney let out a relieved breath. "Oh, thank God. I'm not the friend you want to have in your corner if you're having a long, protracted illness. But I am extremely bribable."

"And that's why we all love you." Lizzy waited until everyone had their pizza and their wine before settling into her own well-worn spot on the sofa and explaining the anonymous tip about the Portraits of Pemberley and its so-called ties to the Sigma Rho house. "I don't suppose you've heard any rumors?" she finished.

Tilney and Caty exchanged glances that were both horrified and titillated. "No, but I will definitely ask around," Tilney promised. "Unfortunately I can't say it's entirely out of the realm of possibility that some of the other guys might get up to this kind of shit, but if it's happening, it isn't commonly known."

"And if it is happening, someone will definitely slip up," Caty offered. "There's no way those Sigma guys are smart enough to run an operation like that without making some major mistakes—with the exception of yours, truly." She nudged Tilney affectionately with her elbow.

Tilney grinned. "I love being the exception. Almost makes being a Sigma worth it."

Lizzy didn't know the full story, but she had gleaned from .comments made here and there by Tilney that becoming a Sigma Rho hadn't been his first choice. Knowing that Tilney's father was a retired Air Force Colonel and ran the campus ROTC, Lizzy imagined there was probably significant pressure for Tilney to follow in his footsteps. Smart, creative, cool Tilney didn't fit the mold of the usual regimented, athletic types who gravitated to the Sigmas, but he seemed to have made the best with what he had, and most of his fraternity brothers had been surprisingly open-minded when he'd come out over the summer as bisexual. The South could be really set in its ways, but sometimes Lizzy had hope when she interacted with the younger generation.

Then she thought of people like Karoline Bingley and Darcy, and shuddered. *Sometimes.*

"I could do a little prodding if you like," Caty spoke up, interrupting that train of thought. "I know you have your methods so I don't want to overstep, but I could poke around, see if I find anything."

From almost anyone else at AU, this might have been a strange offer of help, but Lizzy had witnessed firsthand the way that Caty tirelessly hunted down Isabella's murderer. She'd had a few missteps, but her instincts were good overall, and she'd managed to spook the murderer into confessing to the crime. Lizzy personally thought it was the lethal combination of Caty's quick mind and incredibly innocent face. She looked like she couldn't harm a fly, which lulled people into a false sense of security, but she also possessed an incredibly morbid fascination for murder. Maybe lightning would strike twice, and Caty could somehow trick someone into confessing this crime, too–if it were actually happening.

"That would be great–" Lizzy started, but before she could get too much further, the front door opened and Marianne walked in, as if in a daze. Three times she reached behind her, trying to find the door handle, before finally managing to grasp it and push the door shut. Still she stood in the entryway for several seconds, merely staring into space, a small, vapid smile pulling at the edges of her mouth.

The three in the living room exchanged amused glances. "Hey, Marianne," Lizzy called finally, "you okay?"

Marianne blinked, coming out of a happy daze. She stopped just short of the couch, unable to contain her grin. "Oh, hi. I forgot you were coming tonight. How is everyone?"

Another exchange of glances. Even for Marianne, this was odd behavior. She seemed almost–serene? Which was not a term one would usually use to describe the intense, passionate red-head. "Well," Tilney said, tentatively, as if testing out a trap. Finding none, he continued, "I finally went out with that cute theatre guy. Yates."

This had been a topic of some intense discussion the last time Lizzy and Marianne had seen Tilney. The two had begun flirting intensely online but still hadn't met in person, as of September. Elated for her friend, Lizzy gave his leg an encouraging nudge. "And?"

"Pretty good, so far."

Caty rolled her eyes. "He's playing it so cool. They've been texting nonstop and seeing each other every other day."

Tilney–cool, unflappable Tilney–actually blushed at this. "Like I said, *pretty good*." He gave Caty an arch look. "And I'm not the only one holding back relationship news." He sing-songed, "Caty has a boyfriend."

"What?" Lizzy exclaimed, looking to Caty for confirmation.

It was Caty's turn to flush. "It's very new. His name is Robbie Martin."

"And he drives a motorcycle. And Knightley, of all people, introduced them. And Emma absolutely *hates* him." Tilney was all but cackling at these developments.

Lizzy didn't know what to fixate on first. Caty dating a guy with a motorcycle seemed a little out of character–again, that sweet, innocent little face. But motorcycles were no more dangerous than hunting down murderers, all things considered. The fact that Knightley had introduced them was surprising; he and Caty had once butted heads, seeing as Caty had been convinced he had murdered Isabella. But the fact that Emma hated the guy was less so. Emma was someone who liked to have control over her own little world, and Lizzy very much doubted that having her little protege, Caty, dating someone so far out of her social sphere was very comfortable for Highbury's own little empress.

She studied Caty's face closely. "And how does *Caty* feel about him?"

Caty looked embarrassed, but happy. "He's different. Surprisingly sweet. We're just taking it one day at a time. But I like him." Seemingly eager to turn the conversation away from herself, Caty diverted, "What about you two? Anything new?"

"I'm in love," Marianne blurted, as if she could hardly wait to get the words out.

The other three looked at her in open surprise, but Marianne was beaming too much to care. "I just came back from seeing him. Willoughby." She said his name on a wistful sigh, as if she were the heroine in a sentimental novel. "We met up for the first time tonight, but it's been building every time we looked at each other in class. Every time I could feel his eyes on me as I read my poetry, expressing the inner-most parts of my soul. Tonight he took me for a picnic on the Mississippi River, and we read our favorite poetry to each other, and we made love under the stars."

Tilney and Caty both looked like cartoon characters, their eyes almost simultaneously bulging to enormous proportions at this over-share. Lizzy was too familiar with Marianne's intensity to be shocked, although she was a little worried. If Marianne wanted to get hers on a picnic blanket by the Mississippi River, more power to her; but knowing how volatile her emotions could be, Lizzy worried that this might be the pathway to something catastrophic.

But Lizzy didn't want to overstep, and anyway, Nora would know how to handle this best. In the meantime, Lizzy did her best to look supportive but not like she wanted to know any further details (which she most certainly did not). "Wow. I didn't realize things had progressed with you two. You just told us about him for the first time, like, a few days ago."

Marianne gave Lizzy a small, wincing smile. "I know. I didn't want to say anything because... well, you haven't gone on a date in so long. Not that a woman needs a man to complete her, of course, but–we all get lonely, don't we?"

Um, *ouch*. "It hasn't been–" But Lizzy realized with a grimace that it *had* actually been quite a while since she'd gone on anything resembling a date. Adding salt to the open wound were the sympathetic looks that Tilney and Caty were both shooting her way. As if all four of them hadn't been grousing about their singledom just a month ago at poetry night. Smug bastards, all of them.

Marianne's phone chimed, and she fumbled for it, her face lighting up at the sight of the screen. "It's *him*. Listen to this– 'Dreaming, infinitely dazed and longing, tasting still the sweetly bitter dew of hope and fear and you.'"

Lizzy thought she would probably throw her phone across the room if someone texted her something like that, but Marianne seemed to find it meaningful, so she did her best to force a smile. "That's really great, Marianne. I'm happy for you."

Marianne scarcely seemed to have heard her; her fingers were already flying across the phone, typing out her response–one that was seemingly quite lengthy. Tilney watched her, alarmed. "Easy, Marianne. I know you like him, but you don't want to come on too strong, too fast."

Pausing only long enough to give Tilney a condescending smile and shake of her head, Marianne returned, "We're not like that. We don't need to play those games." And she hurried back to her bedroom, still typing furiously.

A stunned silence followed in her wake. After a moment, Tilney cleared his throat before asking, "So just how long has it been, Lizzy?"

It took her a moment to realize what he was asking, and once she did, Lizzy could not contain her surprised laugh, grabbing a nearby pillow to smack him in the face.

chapter
seven

LIZZY KEPT one eye on the entrance to the Merryton Library study hall as she worked on her Communications paper. She was meant to be meeting Tilney's graduate RA–Brandon Colón–in a few minutes and wanted to make sure she didn't miss him. From everything Tilney had told her about him, she expected him to be on time, if not a few minutes early. *COURTEOUS TO A FAULT* had been Tilney's actual description (via text), along with the not quite so flattering, *THE KIND OF GUY EVERYONE AGREES IS THE BEST BUT WOULD HATE TO BE STUCK NEXT TO AT A PARTY.*

Interesting. Lizzy knew that Tilney had a tendency toward going for the joke even if it was at the expense of others (a fault she couldn't very well blame him for, seeing as how she shared it), but it hardly sounded like Brandon was the sort of RA who would just look the other way while the undergraduates in his charge ran a pornography ring on the dark web. Still, Lizzy wanted to feel him out for herself. She and Tilney didn't always see eye to eye on everything, after all. For instance, he didn't understand the wonderful and terrible absurdity that was *The Bachelor* franchise, and was that really someone whose opinion could be trusted?

As soon as Brandon walked into the room though, Lizzy instinctively knew it was him. Older students just had a vibe about them; aside from looking physically older, they often dressed in ways that marked them as being other. Brandon himself was in a pair of jeans and a button-down shirt, an unremarkable outfit made remarkable only by the fact that he was in actual *clothes*, not basketball shorts, sweatpants, or t-shirts. Plus there was the air of bemusement the older students always had when surrounded by younger students, like they didn't quite know how they'd wound up in the same space as all these *kids*.

More specific to Brandon was the cane he walked with. This had less to do with his age and was more due to an injury he'd sustained in overseas combat. Still, considering the connotations of a cane and Brandon's obvious age discrepancy with the undergrads in the room, it seemed especially fitting.

"Brandon, over here!" Lizzy waved him over, quietly. It was one of the floors of the library where they were allowed to talk, which was why Lizzy had chosen it for a meeting–but she still didn't want to be an obnoxious asshole about it.

Brandon joined her at the table, giving a polite smile in greeting. "Tilney explained to me about the anonymous email. Do you mind if I see it?"

So they were going to skip straight past the small-talk portion of the interview. That was fine by Lizzy. Like most graduate students, she suspected his time was stretched to capacity, and she herself had her aforementioned communications paper to finish. "No problem." She pulled up the email, turning the screen toward him and watching his face as he read it.

When Brandon finished, he sat back with a frown. "Those are serious allegations, if they're true. However, they don't give you much to go by. Can you be sure this isn't some kind of prank?"

"That's what I'm trying to figure out." Lizzy gave him an easy smile, to show she wasn't the enemy, that she wasn't trying to accuse him of anything. "Have you heard any rumors, any rumblings, *anything* that might lead you to believe this is true?"

Brandon shook his head, definitively. "I wouldn't let it go on if I had."

Amazingly, Lizzy believed him. She'd come to the library today primed to be suspicious, but Brandon's entire demeanor screamed *trust-worthy*. Life of the party, this guy was not, but Lizzy understood now what Tilney had meant. Everything about Brandon–from the way he carried himself to his soft-spoken but firm tone to his direct gaze–gave the immediate impression of an upstanding, irreproachable individual.

As if to further prove her point, Brandon continued, "If any of the Sigmas are involved, I could make an educated guess as to who it would be. I'll talk to them, see if anyone knows anything."

Lizzy very much doubted that if Brandon uncovered anything through this route, she'd ever hear anything about it, but at least the problem would be taken care of. That was certainly more important than her story, but she'd nonetheless continue digging and see if she couldn't piece together a few things before Brandon managed it. That was the danger of getting the GRAs involved: potentially losing a good scoop.

Still, she smiled. "Thanks so much. I know you're probably busy and I don't want to take up too much of your time–"

Before she could finish the sentiment, Lizzy was interrupted as Marianne approached, looking beyond irritated. "Thank God you're here. I've been looking everywhere for you. I forgot my keys at home and Nora has her class until five, but I need to get back so I have time to change before my poetry reading tonight."

Far be it from Marianne to notice that Lizzy was in the middle of something. "Hi, Marianne," she said pointedly. "This is Brandon."

"Hi." Marianne slid her gaze to Brandon's in the most cursory of greetings before looking back to Lizzy imploringly. "Keys? Please?"

Lizzy might not be so annoyed if Marianne weren't always forgetting her keys at home. She seemed to think it was somehow an intrinsic part of her artistic, passionate persona (and not just deeply careless and self-centered) to never remember to take necessary items with her every time she left the house.

But before Lizzy could even begin to explain any of this, a commotion from across the room drew their attention. A pretty girl in a hijab was staring intently down at the keyboard of one of the library computers; behind her, a group of boys at a communal study table snickered as the boldest of their group threw out gibberish words that were probably meant to sound Arabic as he oafishly mimicked the prayer ritual.

Marianne was off like a shot, moving faster than when the last slice was up for grabs on pizza night. At 5'11, with massive spiraling bright-red curls that put her at nearly six feet, Marianne towered above the table of boys, her bright, almost inhumanly blue eyes aglow with right-eous fervor. She pointed a single index finger at them, wagging it in a way that should have been humorous, but which Lizzy knew from expe-rience (having once finished the last of the milk without buying another gallon) was absolutely terrifying.

"No!" she scolded, like a trainer bringing a dog to heel. "Bad racist. Bad xenophobe. Bad *human*. Shut your ignorant mouth, and learn something about the world around you before you even think about opening it again."

The combination of Marianne's intensity and her beauty was a potent one. The poor bigots didn't stand a chance. It was kind of like being yelled at by a supermodel in front of the entire library; there was no way for them to come out of this looking good.

The group of guys let out a few more half-hearted snickers, but it was clear the room had turned on them, and hard. As they gathered up their things to leave, everyone began applauding, not ceasing until the group of idiots had left the room.

Beaming with righteousness, Marianne turned toward the girl in the hijab, saying something in an intense, low voice. Watching all of this take place, Lizzy felt her stomach plummet. Oh, no. Marianne was at her absolute best in situations like the moment before, when she could exercise her passionate anger about the injustices of the world in a public spectacle and put ignorant assholes in their place.

It was in the aftermath, the one-on-one relationships, that Marianne often fell short, trying too hard and pushing too much in her attempts to be just and good that she often ended up bulldozing over the very people whose rights she was trying to defend.

Lizzy watched, helplessly, as the girl in the hijab reluctantly picked up her things and allowed Marianne to usher her over to the table where Brandon and Lizzy sat. "I'm about to leave, but this is my roommate, Lizzy, and her friend." Clearly she had already forgotten Brandon's name. "I'm sure they'll sit with you until you're ready to go. Lizzy, this is Fania Parsa."

Trying to convey with her smile that, regardless of what Marianne said, they would not be holding Fania against her will, Lizzy motioned to an empty chair. "You're welcome to join us, *if you want*."

"I'm about to leave for class in Delaford Hall," Fania said, so quietly that Lizzy had to lean forward to hear her.

"I'm headed that way, if you don't mind having a walking companion." Brandon rose to his feet, waiting for Fania's nod of confirmation, before looking back to the table. "It was nice meeting you, Lizzy. Marianne."

It was only the briefest of moments, but Lizzy saw the way Brandon took in Marianne, the admiration in his eyes and the slow bob of his swallow. Oh, no. Lizzy knew that look. He had been Dashwood-dazzled.

Marianne still barely gave him a glance as she turned back to Lizzy, waiting expectantly for the house keys. *Run, Brandon*, Lizzy thought to herself ruefully. *Save yourself. This one will eat you alive.*

eight
october - 6 weeks before the event

LIZZY CHECKED HER WATCH, noting that Professor Eliás had been talking for an impressive twenty-eight minutes without interruption. Most instructors would ask an occasional question, maybe have the class do a group activity, or turn time over to their TA to cover part of the lecture, but Eliás had a reputation around campus for being particularly long-winded. The longest he'd ever gone without any interruption whatsoever (even to take a drink of water) had been forty-three minutes, but Lizzy had faith in him that today could very well be the day that he broke his own record.

So she was doubly surprised when Eliás called her name–firstly, because he was interrupting his own rant, and secondly because he had never called on any student by name before. The class wasn't especially massive in size, but it was big enough that Lizzy felt conspicuously anonymous in the crowd, and Eliás had never previously shown any inclination for learning the students' names. Even Tom Parker, who always sat in the front row and raised his hand to answer any time Eliás asked a question, was referred to as "you" by the professor, and sometimes "young man."

In fact, Lizzy realized that even after Professor Eliás had said her name, he wasn't looking at her, but rather scanning the sea of faces. "Elizabeth Bennet? Is Elizabeth Bennet present today, or will she be receiving an unexcused absence?"

Being singled out this way couldn't be good–especially after being singled out for a personalized grade from Eliás on the exam. With a sinking feeling in the pit of her stomach, Lizzy reluctantly raised her hand. "Here."

At the front of the room, Sexy-Pants TA grimaced sympathetically. Oh, boy.

Professor Eliás gave Lizzy a smug, oily smile. "Would you like to explain the theories about the hippocampus and its role in depression, as outlined in last night's reading?"

Oh, thank God. She had actually done the reading on this. Lizzy wasn't one to take her education for granted–how could she, when her father so often reminded her of how much money they were saving by her getting a scholarship and how there was no way they would be able to afford sending five daughters to university, etc.?–and she wasn't one to skip class or eschew the assigned reading in favor of giving herself a Wikipedia education. However, the other thing that Eliás was notorious for, aside from being long-winded, was assigning hundreds of pages of reading for every class session that no undergraduate could possibly have time for. Lizzy often had to judiciously skim, and in truth when she was really busy with her other courses, she sometimes skipped altogether, knowing that Eliás would cover the material anyway in his monologue-style lectures.

But Lizzy actually remembered the hippocampus, and she scoured her memory for anything relevant she could say. "It's, um, believed that the hippocampus might be smaller in those who suffer from depression."

Eliás raised a disdainful eyebrow. "And?"

Oh. Lizzy hadn't expected a followup–but then, she realized that of course, she should have. If Eliás's purpose in singling her out was to report back to President de Bourgh that he'd made life miserable for one of the lowly members of the Austen Murder Club, then he wouldn't relent until he got her good and flustered, and ideally, made her cry.

Lizzy grit her teeth, determined not to let him get the upper hand. She had this inner stubbornness that always rose to the challenge any time someone attempted to intimidate her. "It's also theorized that stress can cause fewer neurons to be produced, which in turn leads to a smaller hippocampus."

Eliás yawned. "And?"

"Antidepressants try to increase neuron production in the hippocampus to counterbalance this process."

"And?"

With a sinking sensation, Lizzy realized there would be no winning this fight. No matter what she put out there, Eliás was determined not to be impressed and to make it seem like she was just skirting by in the class. Irritated, Lizzy sat back in her seat, arms folded over her chest. If she couldn't impress him, she could at least undermine him. "I'm thinking I might run to the student health center after class to see if I can get a prescription. It seems like I'll need it to get through the rest of the semester, if today is any indicator."

A few low snickers in the class. Professor Eliás did not look impressed, though he did look satisfied that he had at last found a reason to reprimand her. "In future, Miss Bennet, don't bother coming to class if you clearly haven't done the reading. You'll be receiving an unexcused absence for today, since you clearly showed up hoping to coast on my lectures alone. Although, according to your last test, you aren't even doing a good job of that."

As the class wore on, Lizzy stewed in angry silence, taking notes with such force that the pen ink bled through the paper. If there was anything she couldn't stomach, it was being treated unfairly. Lizzy didn't expect special treatment; she didn't expect to be handed anything in life, but she also refused to be targeted simply because she didn't have the family name or money to avoid becoming a scapegoat. If Eliás–or de Bourgh, for that matter–thought she would take this lying down, they were sadly mistaken.

It was in a fury that Lizzy stormed out of the class as soon as they had been released. The only reason she hadn't left earlier was because she didn't want to give Eliás any ammunition to claim she'd been behaving unreasonably or causing a disruption in class to justify his behavior. She didn't know quite how she was going to fix this, but she was going to put those rich bullies in their place.

"Elizabeth."

Lizzy whirled around, half-expecting that Eliás had followed her for round two, but instead drew up short as she realized it was Sexy-Pants TA.

He held up his hands in surrender. "Whoa. I come in peace." Closing the distance between them, he glanced over his shoulder to make sure Eliás wasn't behind him. "I just wanted to say that Professor Eliás was really out of line in there, and if you do end up going to your counselor for mediation, I'd be willing to act as a witness."

Oh. Well. That was very surprising, and chivalrous—an intriguing combination for someone with such a perfect ass. Lizzy shifted, anger properly deflated. "Thank you."

"No problem." Sexy-Pants TA put a commiserating hand on her shoulder, squeezing it briefly before sliding it down her arm and holding it there for a brief moment before releasing her.

Despite what Marianne thought, Lizzy was not so far out of practice that she didn't recognize this for the signal it was. Or at least, very much hoped it was. Summoning her inner courage, she gave him her most flirtatious smile. "I think I'd feel better prepared if we went over our stories together—say, over a drink?"

Sexy-Pants TA grinned back at her. "It's the only logical thing to do." Another arm squeeze. "Let me just get my things, Elizabeth, and I'll be right back."

She stopped him before he could make it to the door. "It's Lizzy, actually." She extended her hand with mock formality. "We should probably get that straight if we're going to be accomplices."

"Naturally." Matching her pomposity, he shook her hand. "Nice to meet you, *Lizzy* Bennet. I'm Wickham."

δλε

With two drinks under her belt, Lizzy quickly gleaned that Sexy-Pants TA—nee, George Wickham—was one of those rare and unexpectedly pleasant things: A person who turned out to be everything she had imagined of him. He was smart, clever, and irreverent, and though he came from Atlanta, was not at all impressed with the outdated and archaic Southern social systems.

"You mean you don't have at least *four* American flags outside your house? And you don't like Cane's sauce??" he demanded in mock outrage, clinking his drink down so hard on the table that it sloshed over the side. "I can't believe they haven't run you out of the state yet."

"Not for lack of trying," Lizzy smiled archly. "Just think what would happen if they found out I'm a registered Democrat."

His eyes widened with exaggerated fright, and he held a finger to his lips, lowering his tone to a harsh whisper. "Careful–legend has it if you say that word three times in the South, Tucker Carlson will appear in your bathroom mirror."

Lizzy laughed so hard at that one, she had to grip onto the countertop to keep from falling over, though this didn't distract her from noticing the way that Wickham gripped onto her–one hand on her shoulder, the other sliding over her knee. Lizzy took a sip of her drink to catch her breath, both literally and figuratively. It had been a very long time since she'd been so attracted to someone who wasn't a Marvel superhero. She had always enjoyed flirting, especially when she found an intellectual equal. At the risk of sounding arrogant, that pool had been running a little dry since coming to Austen University, at least in terms of people she was attracted to.

That wouldn't be the issue with Wickham, Lizzy realized as they locked eyes and an almost tangible electric spark passed between them. The bigger risk would be keeping a clear head when she was around him.

"So," Lizzy played with the end of her straw and pretended it was no big deal that Wickham still had his hand on her knee and was lightly caressing it. "At the risk of stereotyping here, how did you manage to grow up in the South and somehow escape the cult of Yes Ma'am-ing and Bless-Your-Soul-ing?"

Wickham grinned ruefully. "I wouldn't say I've escaped it altogether. More like, fine-tuned and twisted it into something I can use to my advantage."

"Intriguing. Tell me more."

"Well, I learned from the best." Wickham sipped from his drink, something dark passing through his expression. "My mother was the housekeeper for one of the rich old Georgia families, and I grew up right alongside them. Saw firsthand all the opportunities they were given and the way they played the game. And I picked up a few tricks along the way."

He kept his tone light, but Lizzy imagined there was a lot more to the story. Just as she was summoning up a delicate way to ask about it, Wickham's eyes locked on something over her shoulder, and his entire posture changed, his face and neck flushing.

Frowning, Lizzy looked back, doing a double take as she recognized Darcy a few feet away, looking like he'd seen a ghost—and one that filled him with disdain. The two of them were embroiled in such a tense glare-off that it took Darcy a moment to even notice her. When he did, he blinked in what could only be described as astonishment, looking back and forth between them before at last, clenching his jaw, he turned and strode away without a word of acknowledgement to either one of them.

Lizzy looked after him in what felt like equal astonishment, not fully understanding what she had just witnessed. She'd known for a while now that Darcy wasn't her biggest fan, that he thought her vulgar and beneath his notice, but she'd never seen such a look of contempt before. Whether that was directed toward her or Wickham or both of them, she couldn't be sure, but it was strangely disorienting. She didn't give two shits what Darcy thought about her, but she was intrigued to know what possible backstory between the two boys could have produced such a bizarre encounter.

She studied Wickham's profile. "I don't suppose the 'rich old family in Georgia' was the Darcy family?" She thought Darcy was from a small town, but it seemed likely that was closer to Atlanta than she'd previously realized.

Wickham blinked back at her, studying her closely for a moment, with a look that Lizzy couldn't quite decipher. "You know Darcy?"

"Unfortunately."

Another long moment of scrutiny, and then Wickham relaxed into his previous rueful smile, shaking his head as he drained his drink. "It's a long story."

Lizzy continued to watch him carefully. "Believe me, I'm no fan of Darcy's, if that's what you're worried about. And I like long stories."

Wickham's lips twitched upward. "They're better told in quiet places, don't you think?"

Another signal that would have been hard to miss. Lizzy felt her heart skip a beat, then hammer in her chest. "I like quiet places, too. As long as there's wine."

"Oh, there's plenty of that." Wickham's grin gleamed in the flashing lights of the bar as he took her hand and helped her hop down off her stool, guiding her toward the exit with one hand pressed to the small of her back.

chapter
nine

AS FORTUNE WOULD HAVE IT, Wickham was not exaggerating about the amount of wine. Though his small studio didn't have much by way of furniture or decoration, and she was willing to bet that his cupboards held little more than a few mismatched plates and cups and his refrigerator probably less than that, the boy had wine aplenty. They were well into their first box when Wickham began telling his story.

"To make a long story short, Mr. Darcy and my father grew up together. When my dad died overseas—"

Lizzy frowned, touching his arm. "I'm sorry to hear that."

Wickham reached up, interlacing their fingers. "Thank you. But it happened before I was born. Anyway, before he shipped out, I guess Mr. Darcy promised my dad that if anything happened to him, he'd look after my mother and me. My father was too proud to take any handouts, but he asked Mr. Darcy to help make sure I didn't have to follow in his path and join the military with no other options to take care of myself.

"Fast forward a few years. My mother is the Darcys' housekeeper, and we live in a little apartment over the garage. Fo-Hian and I grow up basically like brothers, playing together and whatever kids do until he gets shipped off to boarding school. I still naively think nothing will change between us and we'll still be close. I keep doing stuff with the family, looking after Guanyin like she's my little sister, whatever.

"But when Darcy gets back from school, he's changed. Big time. Has all these ideas about social class, keeping everyone in their place. Including me. Whatever." He waved his free hand to show he didn't care, but Lizzy suspected that wasn't true, based on the bitterness in his tone. "I keep my distance from him, but Mr. Darcy still thinks of me as almost like another son. He keeps inviting me to things, barbecues, baseball games, all this father-son type stuff, and I can tell it's driving Darcy crazy. But what can he say? His dad's the one with the bank account.

"Several times, when Darcy was there, his dad tells me how he knows I can achieve whatever I put my mind to and he's going to put me through undergrad and then law school. I didn't ask for it. He *offered* it, but it was common knowledge. Everyone knew–Darcy knew, Guanyin knew, everybody."

Lizzy had a terrible feeling she knew where this story was going, but she remained silent, biting her lip as she listened.

"So then Mr. Darcy dies, when Darcy's seventeen and I've been going to Georgia State for a year. I don't hear from Darcy right away, but I figure, he has a lot on his plate. Finally when tuition is due and I'm getting notices from the school, whatever, I reach out." Wickham gave a bitter laugh. "Long story short, Darcy says it's no longer a good investment to put money toward my future. So I do what I have to do–I enlist, the thing my dead dad didn't want for me, but what other choice do I have? I do my active duty time, and now I'm on reserves, going to AU on a government grant, and working as a TA and a bartender to pay the bills." Another laugh as he swept his free hand across the room. "Very glamorous, no? I'm sure Darcy would be jealous if he could see me now."

Lizzy could only stare at him. She'd known Darcy was an elitist snob, but this was far beyond what she'd thought him capable of. This was almost beyond what she'd believed anyone outside of the villain in a Hallmark movie capable of. She found herself actually sputtering with indignation. "But... there has to be something you can do, some kind of legal recourse–"

Wickham shrugged. "It was never in writing. It's his word against mine. Well, and Guanyin's, but... She's totally in his pocket, will do whatever he says." He grimaced, draining his glass. "Poor thing is worse off than me, in some ways. She might have the family name, but she can't do anything without Darcy looming over her shoulder like a watchdog. Almost makes you feel sorry for her–that he's making her into as much of a snob as he is. Especially since…"

Wickham trailed off, shaking his head as if he'd said something he didn't mean to; but Lizzy wouldn't let him get coy on her now. "Especially since what?"

"This is between us, right?" At Lizzy's nod of confirmation, Wickham reluctantly continued, "I probably shouldn't say anything since I'm still waiting on the results…but I'm pretty convinced that I'm Guanyin's half-brother."

Lizzy's jaw dropped open. Literally dropped open. There was no other logical response to a revelation like that.

Wickham ran a hand over his face. "Darcy's too, I guess, by default. I know it sounds crazy, but the more I think about it, the more I wonder why Mr. Darcy would single me out like that over the years. Unless…?"

"You're his illegitimate son." Lizzy could hardly wrap her head around it. It sounded like something out of a 19th-century novel. If it were true, then Darcy wasn't just being an ass to his childhood friend– he was being an ass to his own half-brother, and denying Wickham a relationship with his half-sister.

As Lizzy continued to process this, she became aware of Wickham's fingers, trailing through her hair, playing at the nape of her neck. When she blinked up at him, she found he had shifted closer. "So what's your story with Darcy? Did you two date, or something?"

Lizzy guffawed. "Um, no. That would require him to have to converse with a lower mortal, and me to have had a lobotomy."

"There was something between you two though, right?"

He was even closer now, close enough that she could feel the warmth of his breath against her lips. Lizzy licked said lips, trying and not quite managing a teasing tone. "A lady never kisses and tells."

"God, I hope you're not a lady."

"Ditto–" Lizzy started, but was cut off as he captured her lips in a kiss.

She would say this for Wickham: He really went for it. Lizzy had anticipated a little more buildup, a little more exploring, but the next thing she knew, his hands were up her shirt, fumbling with her bra. Lizzy twisted away, not quite ready for that. No shame to the Mariannes of the world who went for it on their first date on a picnic blanket under the stars, but she liked a little more anticipation. As much as she liked dessert, there was no reason to plow straight through dinner.

Wickham followed where she led, not quite taking the hint. "Hey," Lizzy started to say, but in his continued efforts to divest her of clothing, Wickham knocked over her cup of wine, perched on the top of the couch, and spilled it down the front of her shirt.

"Shit." Wickham was instantly all contrition, pulling back to examine the damage. "Oh, shit, I'm sorry."

Lizzy looked down at the garish red stain. "Bad day to wear white," she agreed, though in truth, she was relieved for the reprieve.

"Let me grab you a clean t-shirt. You can change in the bathroom—shower, if you want. Shit. I'm sorry."

He really did sound sorry, and now that they were no longer making out he seemed to have gone back to his charming, clever self. Still, Lizzy quietly locked the door after she was installed in the bathroom, just in case.

Removing her wet, sticky shirt, Lizzy examined the damage to her bra underneath. The shirt would probably need to be trashed, but the bra might be salvageable; Nora usually knew the best ways to get out stains, so maybe she could work a miracle. It probably would have been more comfortable to just remove the undergarment altogether, but Lizzy was not one of the fortunately small-endowed who could go braless, so she matted out what moisture she could with tissue and hoped what remained wouldn't leak through Wickham's borrowed t-shirt.

He was waiting outside for her, door to his apartment already open. "I went ahead and called you an Uber. It's waiting downstairs."

Lizzy had been prepping herself for excuses to leave, so this abrupt dismissal wasn't unwelcome, but it was unexpected. "Oh." She took her sweater that he was holding out to her, too taken aback to come up with anything cleverer. "Thanks."

Wickham kissed her cheek. "I'll see you in class, okay?"

And with that, she was effectively ushered out the door—which, she noticed, he locked as soon as she'd left.

δλε

Lizzy hadn't had a chance to debrief with Marianne and Nora—it was too late by the time she got home, Nora had left early for a morning class, and Marianne had apparently stayed the night at Willoughby's place. So as Lizzy waited to meet with her advisor, Miss Bates, she filled the two in on her night with Wickham in a group chat.

Sounds like you're better off without him, had been Nora's succinct advice.

Normally Lizzy would have expected Marianne to chime in with outrage about Wickham muddying the lines of consent by not being more attuned to Lizzy's reactions to his sexual overtures, or something along those lines. Instead, Marianne's earnest reply read: **We aren't always thinking clearly when passion overwhelms our senses. Self-doubt, fear of rejection, fear of vulnerability. We are all fools in love. If his feelings are true, he'll make them known to you.**

Lizzy doubted very much that Wickham was in danger of being overwhelmed by his love for her, and she honestly didn't even know if she was interested anymore. She'd enjoyed their conversation and bantering, but some of the allure of Sexy-Pants TA had definitely been tarnished. The fantasy was always much more pleasurable than the reality, especially when it came to dating.

"Elizabeth!" The door to Miss Bates's office opened, and the woman herself appeared—looking, as always, just a little bit frazzled, though always unfailingly welcoming and kind. "Please, come in. Come in. I'm sorry I'm running late..."

Lizzy knew Miss Bates well enough by now that she'd planned for an extra fifteen minutes, just to be on the safe side. Assuring her it was no problem, Lizzy took the proffered seat across from the desk and waited for Miss Bates to settle herself back in.

Most students didn't have such frequent interaction with their faculty advisors, but Miss Bates had only recently been promoted to full-time faculty (at the beginning of the semester, as a matter of fact), and as such, she took her role as a mentor seriously. Where Lizzy's previous advisor had been happy to meet with her once a year for about five minutes, Miss Bates insisted on monthly meetings. Lizzy didn't much mind. She enjoyed Miss Bates's benign absurdities, and there were always baked goods of some sort. Plus, it gave her a chance to hear about Jane Fairfax, Miss Bates's niece and Lizzy's friend who'd abruptly left Austen University at the end of spring semester when it was discovered her boyfriend was a murderer (bummer).

It was actually because Miss Bates was Jane's aunt that Lizzy suspected the woman had suddenly gotten the promotion to full-time faculty; if Miss Bates was tenure-track, her family was less likely to spread bad publicity about Jane's involvement with the university scandal, no? But of course, this had never been confirmed, and even if it were true, the promotion couldn't have gone to someone more hardworking or deserving.

Pushing a basket of homemade muffins across the desk, Miss Bates gave Lizzy a sympathetic frown. "I was so troubled to read your email about what you've been experiencing in Professor Eliás's class."

"It's been very trying," Lizzy agreed through her mouthful of double-chocolate muffin.

"Professor Eliás has a reputation for being...difficult. But I'm sure he isn't intentionally sabotaging your education. Nonetheless, I'm happy to intervene and make sure we clear up any miscommunications. Here's what we'll do..."

Lizzy listened as Miss Bates outlined her three-tiered plan to address any academic misconduct, content with her muffin and the knowledge that her education was no longer being hijacked by preferential treatment and classism.

Once all of this was established, Lizzy listened for another twelve minutes as Miss Bates detailed a recent email she'd received from Jane and went off on several tangents about music programs, then Ireland, then for some reason Bono, before she was able to extricate herself so she could make it to her next class.

As she was leaving the building, Lizzy was surprised to bump into someone who was coming in the door–and even more surprised to realize it was Karoline Bingley. Karoline yelped in outrage, looking down at her shoes in horror. "Watch out, Bennet. I know this doesn't mean anything to you, but these are Bottego Venetas."

"My God," Lizzy returned with mock horror. "How would I have ever lived with myself?"

"Someday you might actually own something of value, Bennet–I don't know, maybe a minivan or something–and then you'll understand my pain."

Lizzy had to begrudgingly laugh. That was actually a pretty good burn.

Seeming surprised at this reaction–as unfamiliar as she must be with anything resembling true human friendship–Karoline recoiled a little. Then, realizing that Lizzy was actually laughing *with* her, she gave her own begrudging smile in return.

Lizzy had to almost–almost–feel sorry for her. She so clearly didn't have any meaningful relationships. "Good one, Karoline. I guess I have no choice but to retreat in shame."

Still smiling, Karoline turned–then abruptly turned back. "Listen, Bennet. Let me do you a favor. I hear you were at the Merryton Bar with Wickham last night."

That truly was not what Lizzy had been expecting to hear. She blinked in surprise, then irritation. Why didn't any of these people have anything better to do, apparently, than talk about her? Weren't they supposed to be rich? "And?" she asked, folding her arms.

"Don't get salty with me, Bennet. This is a genuine warning, woman to woman. That guy is bad news."

It was the second time in a five-minute window that Karoline Bingley made her laugh. Oh, this was rich. Darcy royally screwed over Wickham and tried to deny him the opportunity to get his education, but *Wickham* was the one who was a problem.

The really funny thing was, Karoline probably actually believed it. Everything Darcy said was gospel to her. "Okay, Karoline. Thanks for the tip. I'll stay away from the Big Bad Wickham, just in case his working-class background is contagious."

Lizzy didn't even think she liked Wickham anymore, but she would still choose him any day of the week over someone like Darcy.

"I was just trying to help," Karoline called after her, sounding royally irritated to be brushed off. "Don't say I didn't warn you!"

chapter
ten

WHEN LIZZY SAW she had an email from one Fo-Hian Darcy, her first (irritated) impulse was that he might be trying to continue Karoline's assertions that Wickham was "bad news" and that she should stay away from him. Instead, to her surprise, Darcy had written her only a short, terse message:

ELIZABETH,
HERE IS THE ADDRESS FOR THE WOMEN'S SHELTER: 1813 DERBYSHIRE PLACE.
SUNDAYS WOULD BE BEST FOR ME.
BEST,
DARCY

Logically, Lizzy knew she couldn't be equally as irritated that Darcy hadn't brought up Wickham at all, as she had been by the thought of him bringing him up in the first place, but she was. How like Darcy it was to send someone else (Karoline) to do his dirty work, and then completely ignore the elephant in the room as if it would just go away with his insistence that they not look at it.

Furthering her irritation was Darcy's assumption that she accommodate her schedule to his. She wrote back a hasty, CAN'T DO SUNDAYS, and sent it off. Only belatedly did she realize that, while there was a certain moral satisfaction in undermining Darcy and his pomposity, she had just opened herself up to further conversation with the person she most despised in the world.

(Well, no, that was probably too hyperbolic–there were Neo-Nazis and whatnot whom she despised more. But Darcy definitely made the list.)

She had just set about pouring a bowl of granola (with a handful of chocolate chips added in, because her nerves required it) when the sight of a male passing through the kitchen caused Lizzy to do a double-take– and then a triple-take at the sight of Wickham.

But as wonderfully awkward as that might have been, Lizzy quickly realized the male in question was not Wickham, just someone who looked an awful lot like him. They had the same build, the same dark wavy hair, but this guy's eyes were blue while Wickham's were brown, along with other minute details that might have set them apart in a police lineup. Still, the similarity was uncanny.

Whoever this guy was, he looked a little sheepish at having been caught out first thing in the morning in the kitchen, especially as he was wearing a short, floral-trimmed robe that (no judgment) *might* have been his but more likely belonged to one of her roommates. "Marianne didn't think anyone would be awake yet," he said apologetically.

Ah, yes, that made sense. The not-Wickham was the renowned Willoughby: Poet, GTA, and picnic-blanket seducer. (As in, he seduced *on* picnic blankets, not that he seduced picnic blankets– most likely.) "You must be Willoughby. I've heard so much about you." Lizzy thought that was a diplomatic way of putting things.

With Lizzy's help, he procured the coffee he'd been sent to fetch and disappeared back to Marianne's room. In a low voice, Lizzy gave Nora a head's up when she came into the kitchen, and by the time the two love birds had come out of their rooms, Lizzy and Nora had managed to put together something resembling a festive breakfast.

Willoughby looked touched by the gesture, one arm slipping around Marianne's shoulders as comfortably as if they were long-time boyfriend and girlfriend and not as though he were meeting all the roommates for the first time. "This is too kind, ladies. I was actually just telling Marianne that I was planning on treating all of you to breakfast, but you beat me to it."

Lizzy was trying to be on her best behavior, but she couldn't help herself, truly. "Well then you'll just have to ravish Marianne again sometime soon."

What might have once earned her daggers from Marianne passed virtually unheeded as the girl in question gazed adoringly into Willoughby's eyes, and he did the same back to her. They seemed so genuinely oblivious to the rest of the room that by some unanimous agreement, Nora started tutting about moving the plates and utensils and Lizzy cleared her throat, just to remind them they were there.

"We're starving," Marianne said at last, taking a seat beside Willoughby and promptly placing her feet across his lap, as though she needed to be as close to him as humanly possible. And perhaps she did, since she'd already started to refer to them in the plural. They were starting that weird merging thing that happened with new couples where their identities completely melted into one.

Lizzy exchanged a quick glance with Nora over their coffee. "Good thing we made extra waffles, then. Please, help yourselves."

Marianne complied by preparing a stack of waffles, which she proceeded to cut up and feed to Willoughby, as Lizzy and Nora struggled to not look at them.

"So," Lizzy said loudly, as if through sheer volume she could drown out the sight of Willoughby sucking syrup from Marianne's fingertip, "I think it's supposed to rain sometime this week."

"How interesting." Nora, the coward, had not removed her eyes from her coffee cup since the PDA had begun.

For the first time since she had come to stay with them, Lizzy was actually relieved by the intrusion of Lucy Steele. Not one to be tactful or, really, thoughtful of others' feelings, Lucy entered the room and gave Willoughby a long, reproachful look. "In the Omegas, we had to get clearance from the other girls before we had overnight visitors," she said pointedly.

That, at least, was enough to burst Marianne's little love bubble, her eyes sharpening. "That sounds like an effective way to police each other's bodies."

Willoughby leaned forward, placing a placating kiss to her temple. "Consent is important, Mar, even in non-romantic relationships. I'll let the three of you sort things out, and maybe I can make it up to everyone with dinner sometime this week?" With a round of charming smiles and a few more parting words, he was gone, leaving Marianne glowering at an oblivious Lucy, who hummed to herself as she spooned out her non-fat yogurt and honeydew.

"Well," Nora said after a moment's pause, in that tactful way of hers, "the two of you seem to be getting really close."

As someone who had done her fair share of managing high-spirited younger sisters, Lizzy had to admire Nora's tactics in reigning in Marianne. A mere mention of Willoughby, and some of the fire drained from Marianne's eyes, replaced with a dreamy wistfulness. "He's incredible. I've never met anyone like him."

"He seems great," Lizzy agreed. "The two of you seem very...like-minded." How was that for diplomatic?

Beside her at the table, Lucy sniffed, clearly unimpressed. "You said he's a poet? That doesn't sound very lucrative."

Marianne set her jaw. "Writing poetry isn't about job security or playing it safe. It's about living a life of passion and feeling."

"I'm sure you'll both be 'feeling' hungry when you can't afford to buy groceries." Lucy laughed to herself at her own little joke.

Marianne's glare intensified. "Luckily I can make my own living and not depend on a man to provide for me, thank you very much. And anyway, I'd rather be self-fulfilled with a man I love than trapped in a mindless existence with a 401K."

Lucy didn't look very impressed by this argument, and Lizzy could see this was going nowhere. The two of them clearly would not be seeing eye-to-eye on the issue. She was just about to tactfully change the subject when Nora spoke up.

"I'm glad you like him, Marianne, but it's only been a week. You don't need to be planning your future with him already."

Marianne blinked at her sister, puzzled. "When two soulmates meet, time doesn't mean anything. In seven days I feel like I know more about Willoughby than some people could know about each other in seven years."

Lizzy looked to Nora, trying to gauge how she was taking this. Nora was always the voice of reason in the room, but it seemed that it was more than just practicality driving her. She looked genuinely troubled.

"All I'm saying is, it doesn't hurt to take a little time to get to know someone before you invest too much in them. If he's as wonderful as you think he is, you'll have all the time in the world to discover that. And if he isn't, then you will have done yourself a favor later by being cautious now."

Marianne looked affronted at first, until recognition dawned in her eyes, and she gave Nora a smile that was probably meant to look compassionate but had definite patronizing undertones in it. "Not everyone leaves, Nor."

Lucy shook her head. "I disagree, Marianne. Men are fickle. If you want to snag him, you'd better give him ample reason not to wander, if you catch my drift."

She continued eating, oblivious to the mutually horrified stares exchanged by Lizzy, Nora, and Marianne, as they silently and unanimously agreed then and there that Lucy Steele was probably not Delta material.

δλε

To save herself from having to hear more about Marianne's favorite facial expressions on Willoughby, Lizzy begged off a morning walk around the lakes with her roommates. Truthfully, she did have to check in on the situation with Professor Eliás. True to her word, Miss Bates had already set the mediation gears in motion, and Lizzy had been emailing back and forth with Eliás's daughter, Anne, who would be acting as her graduate student mediator.

Having known Anne only briefly, Lizzy nonetheless felt completely safe putting her education into Anne's competent, trustworthy hands. In her last email to Lizzy, she'd explained that she'd be sitting in on the lectures until the end of the semester, and that any future assignments would be forwarded to her. Lizzy was only waiting to hear what Anne

had decided about the past exam and Eliás's grade, though she anticipated it would be re-graded shortly.

It was a huge relief that going to Eliás's class would no longer have
to be such an ordeal—especially with the added weirdness of seeing
Wickham. It had been clear to her the next time she'd gone to class that
Wickham was done with her. He hadn't been rude or anything, but
she'd noticed him chatting with a tiny blonde after class in a way that
she felt was a little *pointed*. As if he wanted to make sure that she saw
him and understood that nothing further would be happening between
them.

Frankly, the feeling was mutual. What surprised Lizzy was how little
she cared. Just as she'd suspected, actually speaking to Sexy-Pants TA
had tarnished the fantasy. Their short interaction had proven that they
weren't quite on the same page when it came to dating, but she held him
no ill-will. Anyone who had managed to overcome the sabotaging that
Darcy had put him through was okay people in her book.

That didn't mean she wouldn't be suggesting a pint of Ben & Jerry's
with Nora in the near future. She might not be broken-hearted over
Wickham, but it was still an age-old ritual of womanhood that the end
of a relationship (whether real or imaginary) necessitated the eating of
ice cream with one's closest friend. And they would do it in secret,
because Lizzy didn't want to hear Lucy explain to them how many calories were in each pint, or God forbid, watch Marianne and Willoughby
lick it off each other's faces.

Before Lizzy could pull up her email to check on the status with
Anne, she saw to her surprise that she already had quite a few texts from
Caty Morland. What was surprising was not so much that Caty was
texting her in rapid-fire succession, but that she was doing so in the
"early" morning hours. (Caty seemed to live by a strict sleep-in-until-
noon life policy.) Curious, Lizzy opened up the thread:

**Did some digging on the Portraits of Pemberley.
I've found a few rumors about the site, but
nothing substantiated. So far.**

Truth be told, with everything going on with Professor Eliás and
then the non-starter with Wickham, Lizzy hadn't really been doing her
due diligence with the Portraits of Pemberley story. She'd even forgotten

for the most part that Caty had even said she'd look into it. Too bad it was sounding like it might all be a dead end. Nonetheless, Lizzy read on.

BUT, I DID FIND SOMETHING WITH THE NAME PEMBERLEY.

Ooh! Intriguing.

AND IT'S CONNECTED TO SOMEBODY FROM AUSTEN UNIVERSITY.

That was all Caty had sent so far, but Lizzy could see the bubbled ellipses, indicating there was more to come. Surely Caty could have included that information in the same text message–but then she wouldn't be the drama queen they all knew and loved.

FO-HIAN DARCY.

Any traces of a smile fled instantly from Lizzy's face, and she promptly ignored the protocols of being Gen Z and used her phone as a phone to call Caty right away. "Tell me everything," she demanded.

chapter
eleven

IT WASN'T easy being right all the time, but somebody had to do it. From the first day she'd met him, Darcy had rubbed Lizzy the wrong way, and not only because he'd insinuated that she was frumpy. Some, like Nora, had suggested that Lizzy was projecting onto Darcy, that she was stereotyping him into the mold of a preppy rich boy, but some part of Lizzy had known it went deeper than that. Deeper than the enraging entitlement and the thinly disguised superiority. And now, finally, here was the proof.

Caty's digging had revealed a few interesting tidbits of information. Apparently, William Darcy–aka Darcy's father–had been a very successful corporate lawyer. Successful enough that he'd privately funded a number of charitable enterprises, eventually starting up a non-profit organization. This organization wasn't given much press–apparently it was gauche in the world of the obscenely rich to take too much credit for one's philanthropic work–but it had been used to set up youth centers, arts programs, homeless shelters, and the like throughout the South.

And that non-profit organization? Was called Pemberley Estates.

Curious that a secret site funneled through Austen University should be called 'the Portraits of Pemberley' when one Fo-Hian Darcy attended that school and had deep family ties to the college, no? In fact, the very women's shelter that Lizzy and Darcy had been ordered to cover in the school paper had been funded by one Pemberley Estates.

Lizzy truly didn't know what was the most reprehensible part. That Darcy, who always acted so disdainfully toward others, was secretly running a site that posted naked, non-consensual photos of women. Or that he seemed to be trying to tarnish the reputation of his do-gooder father by correlating the name otherwise used to help people and build up the community, with dehumanizing and objectifying women.

Disgusting.

All thoughts of ice cream now fled, Lizzy paced her room, wondering how to best approach the situation. She and Darcy had finally landed on Monday as the day of choice to visit the women's shelter. However, knowing what she did now, there was no way Elizabeth could wait that long to confront Darcy. She snatched up her phone.

DARCY, THIS IS ELIZABETH BENNET. SOMETHING CAME UP MONDAY—CAN WE DO TOMORROW? I'M FREE ALL DAY.

She waited anxiously, hoping he wasn't one of those people who didn't keep his phone on him or waited several hours out of principle to respond to texts. (God, he seemed like one of those people.)

To her relief, the phone pinged almost immediately. Lizzy leapt for it, taking a brief moment to appreciate the irony that she was more excited about getting a text from Darcy, of all people, than she had been about any romantic interest since... maybe ever.

TOMORROW DOESN'T WORK.

Lizzy rolled her eyes. No explanation, no apology, no pretense at human emotions. **WHAT ABOUT SUNDAY?** she typed.

YOU VETOED THAT OPTION EARLIER, SO I MADE OTHER PLANS. LET'S REVISIT WHEN WE MEET THIS WEEK FOR THE PAPER.

Lizzy threw her phone across the room in frustration. The meeting wouldn't be until Wednesday, and by then Darcy could have worked his way through an entire dorm of girls. Still, she knew any protest would be futile. Darcy had decreed his decision, and in his world, he was used to his will being akin to law. And she needed him to be pliant, cooperative—at least until she lured him into a confession so she could write an expose that would derail his twisted website. Get him blacklisted from any self-respecting law schools. Maybe even see him prosecuted for his crimes?

She didn't kid herself that someone like Darcy would get more than a metaphorical slap on the wrist. But still, a criminal record, a damaged reputation? That would surely take him down a peg or two.

Lizzy would just have to figure out a way to ambush him as soon as possible—tomorrow, ideally—in a way that would seem plausible.

"Where would I go if I were a repressed scumbag who hates women and thinks I'm better than everyone else?" she asked herself aloud.

Alas, nothing came to mind, for which Lizzy couldn't help but be grateful. She was glad to confirm that she was nothing like Darcy, even if it was inconvenient for tracking him down.

And then, the most genius of genius ideas sprang into Lizzy's mind. "Karoline Bingley," she muttered to herself, and lunged across the bed for her phone.

δλε

It has already been well-established by this author that wherever Darcy went, Karoline Bingley was surely not far behind. While it was not in character for someone like Darcy to loudly broadcast his whereabouts on social media, it was most certainly on-brand for Karoline. Thus, Lizzy spent the rest of the night stalking Karoline's accounts, trying to find any clue of where Darcy might go on a Saturday morning.

This search provided Lizzy with a few key discoveries. The first, and most blatant, was that Karoline really needed to cool it with the Vignette filter. The second, and most surprising, was that Karoline did have some good tips on her makeup channel that Lizzy would need to try on one of the rare occasions that she deigned to put effort into her appearance. And the last, and most important, was that Darcy started every morning with a swim.

Like, EVERY morning. Lizzy loved a good, brisk walk herself, but swimming an hour every morning—at 8 a.m., no less, when any self-respecting undergrad was still sleeping–felt excessive. She imagined it somehow had to do with his repression and secret hatred of women.

Lizzy didn't much like the idea of waking up that early, herself, to confront him the next morning, but she'd unfortunately unearthed no other information about where Darcy might be the remainder of the day, and she'd hate to miss her only chance. So, begrudgingly, Lizzy set her alarm for 7:20 and went to sleep (or tried to, since her brain insisted on acting out all the scenarios she might encounter in her righteous confrontation with Darcy).

7:20 a.m. arrived with a falsely bright cell phone chime, shouts, curses, and epithets, and more than one pressing of the snooze button, before at last Lizzy managed to rouse herself from bed and head to the AU indoor pool.

Her original intention had been to confront Darcy before he had a chance to escape into the pool, but the snooze button had prevented this, along with Lizzy's desperate need for a cup of coffee. By the time she arrived, Darcy was already well into his laps, and to her surprise, there were others also swimming lengths in the adjacent lanes.

That put a bit of a damper on her original plan. Lizzy had, for some reason, assumed that Darcy would be alone in the pool, but having so many witnesses around as she tried to conduct her interrogation might prove more of a challenge. Give him the advantage.

No, she decided, it would be better to wait for him to finish rather than causing a scene. And if that meant she had to sit on the bleachers and drink more of her coffee, well, Lizzy would bite the bullet. Anything for her journalism.

Lizzy watched the swimmers as they silently cut through the water in their monotonous laps, wondering what the appeal was. She would take a long walk–out in the sunshine, with sights to see and audiobooks to listen to–over a cold, over-chlorinated pool any day. But then, considering Darcy, that was probably the appeal of lap swimming–not having to converse with people or see off-putting sights like children or puppies.

At last, Darcy stopped his swimming–at 9:00 exactly, like clockwork. It was difficult to tell between the different swimmers, with their goggles and caps, but she'd figured out which one was Darcy because she recognized his water bottle. Not that she'd paid undue attention to Darcy or what kind of water bottle he had, but she'd remembered seeing him drink from it at a party and remembered thinking how strange it was a) that he carried around a water bottle with him at a frat party and that b) he somehow managed to find a water bottle that looked *expensive,* when she hadn't even realized such a product could exist. Having successfully located him, Lizzy had been watching his lane like a hawk ever since to make sure he didn't somehow manage to slip out of her sight.

Now as Darcy removed his cap and goggles and took several long drinks from the aforementioned water bottle, Lizzy hurried to intercept him before he could disappear into the men's locker room. On a purely hypothetical, ethical level, Lizzy wanted to believe she was the type of journalist who would brave war zones, gang turf, and yes, even men's locker rooms to get a story if needed, but she also really, *really* didn't want to encounter that many speedos in close quarters.

As Lizzy watched from across the pool, Darcy hoisted himself onto the pool deck. He moved to a bench behind the diving block, reaching for a towel.

She was too far away, and he was too close to the locker room entrance. Without really intending to, Lizzy called out his name. "Darcy!"

Darcy turned, facing Lizzy full-on to expose his body in all its speedo-ed glory. She skidded to a halt, staring without wanting to. The guy was a snob, a jerk, and most likely a pervert, but credit where credit was due, he had the sort of body that didn't look ridiculous in a skimpy little piece of fabric.

For a moment, they simply stared at one another. Then, blinking, Darcy finished wrapping the towel around himself and cleared his throat. "Elizabeth. What are you doing here?"

Lizzy could feel her cheeks warming, and she hated this involuntary reaction, not only because it undermined her position in calling him to justice, but also because it suggested that she was somehow embarrassed or maybe even something worse, which she wasn't. She was just discombobulated, and the room was unseasonably warm, and she'd run across the length of an Olympic-sized pool to catch up to him. She raised her chin a fraction of a degree, should he be in any doubt that she was completely and totally in control. "I need to talk to you about the paper."

"Oh." Darcy still seemed confused, but at least this answer was semi-plausible. "Can I change first?"

"No." Lizzy motioned for him to follow her—which, after a brief moment of hesitation, he did.

She took him to a remote corner of the bleachers. It would be better, of course, to have a little more privacy, but Lizzy was afraid to let him out of her sight for even a moment in case he disappeared or lawyered up, so this would have to do.

After allowing him a brief moment to pull on a white t-shirt—which was somehow *more* distracting, all damp and clingy—Lizzy jumped right in. "What can you tell me about the Portraits of Pemberley?"

If she hadn't known better, Lizzy might have almost believed the slight furrow of the brow, the slow blink. "I'm sorry?"

Okay. She would play his little game. "Your father's non-profit is called Pemberley Estates, correct?"

The furrow deepened. "It is, but I don't know what you mean by 'portraits'." A sudden thought seemed to strike him, and he shifted. "It wasn't my idea to take the photographs at the women's shelter, if that's what you mean. President de Bourgh saw some of my pictures and thought it might be good PR for the university, but we can choose somewhere else if you think it's a conflict of interest."

Damn him, he was being purposefully obtuse. Well, Lizzy wouldn't let him off that easy. "We both know those aren't the pictures I'm talking about, Darcy." She shook her head, not bothering to hide her disgust. "I know we haven't always seen eye-to-eye, but I never actually thought you were a bad person. How would you feel if someone did this to you without your consent?"

Darcy rocked back, posture straightening almost as if in second nature. That must be his private-school training kicking in; when in doubt, sit up straight. "I genuinely have no idea what you're talking about. All the women at the shelter will have to sign waivers and agree to sit for pictures—I would never force anyone to do it. And if they're worried about their safety being compromised—"

Dragging the women from the shelter into the conversation as a sort of moral shield was too much for Lizzy. "The Portraits of Pemberley, Darcy. I know all about it. You and your little fraternity brothers posting pictures of your conquests. I came to you first to give you a chance to explain yourself–" Not precisely true, but it sounded good, "– but if you can't even do me the decency of being honest–"

Darcy reeled back as if she'd slapped him. Drama queen. "What are you talking about?"

"You've been tipped off, buddy." Not her cleverest turn of phrase, but Lizzy was too worked up to care. She pulled up the email about the site on her phone, showing it to him to prove she meant business. (Normally, she'd never reveal a source, of course, but the address was both anonymous and now defunct, so she figured it was safe.)

For a long time, Darcy just stared at the screen. Then he blinked at her. "Is this some kind of joke? I never understand your humor..."

"I guess not, since you seem to think posting non-consensual pictures of half-dressed women is a hoot." Lizzy shook her head in disgust. "Let's see how funny the police think it is, huh?"

That would have been a good segue to rise to her feet and storm away, but before Lizzy could manage, Darcy had taken to *his* feet and began to pace in front of her, running an uncharacteristically discomposed hand through his wet hair, over his face.

At last he turned to face her. "This is what you think of me?" He took a step toward her, then seemingly stopped himself from progressing. "I never have and never will be part of anything like what you're describing. I would never, *ever* devalue a woman like that."

The Marianne in Lizzy's head wanted to snark that women didn't need such overly chivalrous proclamations guarding their virtue, but the surprising emotion in Darcy's voice caught her off guard. This was *personal* to him in some way, and not just because of some nebulous sense of honor.

He took in a deep, shaky breath. "Why do you think I would be involved with something like this?" He blinked, voice faltering a little. "Did Wickham have something to do with this?"

The mention of that name snapped Lizzy out of whatever sympathy she might be feeling toward Darcy. "Wickham is completely unrelated to this. But since you decided to bring up that name, Wickham *did* tell me about what you did to him. What you took from him. So when I found out your family has ties to a business called Pemberley, it was surprising, sure. But maybe it shouldn't have been. You've already proven your true colors."

"What I did to–" Anger flashed through Darcy's eyes as he cut himself off abruptly, sucking in a deep breath. "Have you verified that the site even exists, or are you just going off hearsay?"

Lizzy bit her lip. "Well–I haven't found anything yet. But where there's smoke, there's usually fire."

He scoffed. "And so without ever having actually seen this website, you made a link to a non-profit organization run by my family–a public organization, that any number of people could be familiar with–and decided that was proof that not only does the site exist, but also that I'm behind it?" Lizzy opened her mouth, but Darcy barreled on. "And even though you've known me now for years, you decide to take the word of some guy you met at a bar, who you know nothing about–"

Lizzy gritted her teeth. "Okay, hold on. He's my TA, not just some random dude I picked up at ladies' night. But even if he weren't, I have to say—knowing you for longer hasn't done anything to persuade me that what he accused you of couldn't be true. If it wasn't bad enough that you're basically the poster child for privilege, remember that little incident where you broke up my best friend and yours?"

Darcy had the good grace, at least, to avert his gaze. "They weren't dating."

"But they were headed down that path–which you very well know, or you wouldn't have encouraged Charlie to take off mid-semester to Paris."

Darcy shook his head, any pretense of shame taking a backseat to his ingrained certainty that he must always be right. "There are things you don't understand."

Lizzy rose to her feet, suddenly hating the fact that he was standing over her, lording his presence. He was still significantly taller than her, which wasn't ideal, so she lifted her chin, as if to even the distance between them. "Please do enlighten me–on the record, of course. I'll make sure to include your side in the article, for the sake of fairness."

But Darcy didn't seem to have registered what she was saying. Her advancement on him, which was intended to daunt him out of his smugness, seemed to have been misinterpreted as something else altogether. At her sudden nearness, Darcy swallowed, then—as if he couldn't quite help himself—looked down at her lips.

The first thing that Lizzy felt was confusion—and then, a dawning sense of horror. That couldn't be right. She had always assumed that if he thought of her at all, Darcy must find her annoying. He had all but called her ugly, back when they first met. But there had been no denying that look, the long, slow swallow.

Everything she was feeling must have played out across her face (this, Lizzy knew, had always been one of her curses), because Darcy took a step back, looking flustered—and, dare she think it, embarrassed?

"I'm not..." But whatever it was that Darcy meant to say, he apparently found it too futile to utter. Instead, running his hand over his face, he turned and abruptly retreated into the locker room.

chapter
twelve

IT WOULD HAVE BEEN an exaggeration to say that Lizzy did not sleep that night, but not by much. As much as Lizzy believed herself to be completely morally in the right–and she most certainly did–the entire encounter with Darcy kept replaying over and over again in her mind. Mostly she thought of cleverer things she could have said to him, better clapbacks that would have shut him down more efficiently. She also, despite herself, kept replaying that moment over and over where he looked down at her lips.

Was it possible she could have been mistaken? Lizzy very much hoped so. The idea of Fo-Hian Darcy getting turned on by arguing with her was repulsive, but strangely, it was something Lizzy could live with. She did not know much about the psychology of over-privileged males, but she imagined that many (if not all) probably had some fetish about being told off. If that moment had been a weird, passing flash of attraction, it would be disgusting, but bearable.

But if it signified something more... if there was any possibility that Darcy liked her, had feelings for her...that was when it would become officially unbearable. She examined over and over the exchanges they'd had together–not just this last heated confrontation by the pool, but other encounters that she'd brushed over as simply Darcy being Darcy (re: awkward and arrogant and inscrutable). She thought of Darcy returning her cheap disposable pen to her. Darcy suddenly wanting to join the school newspaper. Darcy insisting on coming over to speak to her at every social function, even though he looked miserable and usually had nothing to say.

Insufferable. Lizzy knew, logically, that she couldn't control what Darcy thought or felt, but illogically, the thought of him pining for her, maybe even fantasizing about her...it was just one more instance of him showing off his privilege. Assuming that a woman he'd barely spoken to, that he'd never been anything more than passably polite to, and often quite rude to, must be receptive to his attraction to her just because that was what *he* wanted.

It was intolerable. It was infuriating.

More infuriating, still, was that for the second day in a row, Lizzy was out of bed before the sun had risen. On a weekend. For that reason, if for no other, Darcy deserved to suffer.

Lizzy put on a pot of coffee, determined to think about anything but Darcy as she waited for her caffeine. New day, new beginnings, and all that. Hearing a rustling at the kitchen door, Lizzy rose eagerly to her feet. That must be Marianne, coming back from Willoughby's place—and, as usual, sans keys. Normally Lizzy wouldn't especially want to hear Marianne gushing about her love for Willoughby and how it was the purest ecstasy that any human soul had ever known, but this morning she welcomed the distraction.

But when Lizzy swung open the door, she found not her statuesque ginger roommate, as expected, but rather Darcy, crouching by the step. He looked up at her in surprise that swiftly gave way to embarrassment.

By the time he rose to his feet, he'd managed to school his features. "I didn't know if anyone would be awake yet, but I brought this for you. If you would read it. Please." This last word sounded unfamiliar, almost like he was tripping over a foreign pronunciation; but then, he probably had very little experience using it.

Nonetheless, Lizzy was so taken aback by it that she took the item that Darcy thrust toward her: a sealed envelope. Before Lizzy could ask what it was, or say anything, really, Darcy turned and swiftly disappeared around the house.

Stunned, confused, and even more in need of coffee than she had already been, Lizzy shut the door, locking it for good measure. She didn't really expect Darcy to come back or try to barge his way into the house, but then she hadn't expected him to be at her back door on a Sunday morning, so it was probably best to err on the side of caution.

Lizzy poured her coffee, sending wary, sidelong glances at the envelope on the table. It had her name written in clear, un-flourished handwriting (of course he had good handwriting, she thought with an eye roll). It was also ominously thick, suggesting a lengthy letter.

A confession? The thought made Lizzy brighten temporarily. It would be much more convenient to publish her article about him with a signed confession, so as to avoid any libel issues. Although she had kind of been looking forward to her first libel suit...

Another thought, far more horrifying, struck her. What if it was a love letter?

Oh, God.

Lizzy allowed herself to finish two cups of coffee and a bowl of granola before she at last begrudgingly took the letter in hand. No time like the present, or some other such nonsense that was meant to be bolstering.

Elizabeth,

Yesterday you made some accusations at the pool that I was unprepared to address. This letter is an attempt to do now what I couldn't do then. You can, of course, destroy this letter or refuse to read it, but I hope out of a sense of fairness and a commitment to the truth, you'll read it in full. Not everything I have to say here is pleasant, but it is, to the best of my knowledge, true.

First I'll address your comments about Nora and Charlie. It's true that Karoline and I made an effort last semester to persuade Charlie to leave Highbury. The reason behind that was not entirely to do with Nora, but I won't pretend that she wasn't a factor. There are parts of the story that I'm not privy to disclose because they aren't my story to tell. What I can say is that, in the past, Charlie and other members of his family have fallen prey to people who take advantage of their good natures. I never believed that Nora fell into this category, but Karoline thought it would be in Charlie's best interest to leave Highbury, and I deferred to her judgment. Having watched Nora's interactions with Charlie closely, I believed that, although they shared a close friendship, her heart would not be too deeply damaged by his departure. Charlie, on the other hand, might be in danger of getting in too deep, too fast, as he is very prone to do. As her friend, I suppose you can be the better judge of the depths of her feelings, but no ill will was intended toward her specifically.

Some other charges you've made will involve me disclosing some information that I hope I can entrust in your hands. I think it goes without saying that I would prefer you not publish certain aspects of what I'm about to tell you.

The more serious of the two accusations is my alleged involvement with a website called the Portraits of Pemberley. If the site actually exists, which still has yet to be proven, I can say with the utmost sincerity that I had no involvement whatsoever in any part of it. If the site does exist, however, I believe I know who was behind it. Earlier you accused me of unfair bias when I suggested that Wickham might have something to do with this, but some of the details that I'm about to tell you will hopefully explain why I would make such a weighty accusation.

I've heard some versions of the story that Wickham has told about me over the years, so I can guess the basic gist of what you probably heard from him. Rather than trying to refute him point for point, I will simply tell my side of the story as I experienced it.

Wickham is the son of our former housekeeper, and his deceased father was a childhood friend of my father's. My father did make promises to Captain Wickham to look after his son and provide him with different opportunities so that he wouldn't be forced to join the military as his only option in life. Wickham often joined us for family vacations, holidays, birthday parties, and other celebrations, and I considered him to be a close family friend, as did my sister, Guanyin. Beyond the obligation to his childhood friend, my father genuinely liked Wickham and thought he had a promising future. Wickham got a half-tuition scholarship to a local university, and my father offered to pay the difference on the condition that Wickham keep up a 3.5 GPA. There was also an informal agreement that if Wickham graduated Summa Cum Laude, my Father would pay his first year of tuition for law school.

After my father's sudden and unexpected death, I was overwhelmed with a number of new obligations, as you can no doubt imagine. When Wickham approached me to ask for his tuition money for the semester, I gave him a blank check, trusting him to fill in the correct amount. Instead, I received notice from the bank a few days later that the check had been made out for a much larger sum. When I confronted Wickham about it, he confided to me that he no longer wanted to finish university and go to law school as he had discussed with my father, but wanted to instead try his hand at becoming a musician. The money would be used to help him promote his gigs and help him stay financially afloat while he tried to make his name in Nashville. I tried to discourage Wickham from taking this reckless course, but Wickham was set on this idea, and he reasoned that the money was equivalent to what my father had promised him to start his life. I finally agreed, with grave misgivings, but made clear to Wickham that there would be no further financial support after this point.

In less than a year, Wickham had blown through all of the money and came back multiple times insisting that he was owed more. At first, we were still able to meet as friends and Wickham was still welcome at family events, but as he became increasingly belligerent, I felt it was better for us to part ways for the time being. I wished him no ill will but I felt that money would continue to be an issue between us until Wickham could sort out some of his issues. For over a year, I didn't hear anything further from him.

However during this time, without my knowledge, Wickham continued to stay in contact with Guanyin. I'd tried to keep the strain on my relationship with Wickham under wraps for her sake, because she looked up to Wickham and I knew she'd always had a crush on him. After losing both of our parents in such a short amount of time and at such a young age, Guanyin was understandably emotionally vulnerable and I didn't want to add any extra stress to her life.

I soon learned, unfortunately, that in keeping my sister in the dark, I made her easy prey for Wickham. During that year of no contact, Wickham had been grooming my then-16-year-old sister. Over a series of several months, Wickham convinced Guanyin that they were in love and persuaded her to send him some compromising pictures that could be used to blackmail her and extort money from me.

This has understandably been a very difficult time for my sister and for our family. The immediate problem has been contained, but the emotional repercussions have been severe—compounded by the absurd claims that Wickham has recently been circulating about being my father's illegitimate son. Wickham obviously has no proof of this, but even if it were true, it makes his actions toward Guanyin even more troubling.

Perhaps it's more understandable now that, when I heard a site like the Portraits of Pemberley might exist, my thoughts turned to Wickham. It would be too much of a coincidence, I think, for it to be anyone but Wickham, considering the nature of the site, as well as the seeming attempt to disparage my family's name. I hope that these prove to be just rumors, but I would strongly suggest looking more closely at Wickham if you want to discover the truth.

I will, of course, help in any way that I can.

Best,
        Darcy

thirteen
november - 1 week until darcy is expelled

RATHER LIKE A SMALL ENGLISH VILLAGE, word traveled around a small campus town remarkably quickly. No one could be quite sure who had spilled the beans about Darcy confessing to attacking Wickham. Darcy himself seemed unlikely, since in true, stoic form, he had refused to say anything about the incident to even his closest friends (even Lucy Steele, who had been part of his innermost circle for three whole hours now!). President de Bourgh was out of the question–she, who guarded Darcy's reputation even more carefully than he did his own. And the only person who perhaps cared more about de Bourgh than de Bourgh herself was Mr. Collins, so he, too, seemed an unlikely culprit.

Most likely, some lowly student worker who happened to be in the office had spilled the beans. Having neither wealth nor social clout, as evidenced by being a student worker, the worker had likely been grouped into the same category as a stapler, a wastebasket, or a printer: Necessary for the function of the office, but not worthy of any particular notice unless unable to perform its proper utility. As such, said worker had been completely overlooked by Darcy, de Bourgh, and Collins, and had been free to escape the office without signing an NDA.

Regardless, word had gotten out, and what had started out as a promising evening for Lizzy (getting rid of Lucy! Yay!) had quickly devolved into chaos (confusion, anxiety, and yes, even guilt, about Darcy's confession–Boo).

Eager to be apprised of any new developments, Lizzy quickly texted Tilney and Caty. In addition to being fun, clever, and surprisingly good at beer pong, Tilney and Caty had established themselves as the experts of the dark underbelly of the university. Where there was scandal at AU, Caty and Tilney could be trusted to get to the bottom of it.

TILNEY: THE GENERAL SAYS DE BOURGH IS FURIOUS THE WORD HAS GOTTEN OUT.

Tilney referred to his father, retired US Air Force Colonel and head of the campus's ROTC program, as "The General," and he was (presumably) the fount of all the knowledge Tilney was able to obtain about the inner workings of the faculty and administration. It seemed even retired colonels liked a good gossip every now and then.

TILNEY: I GUESS UMBRIDGE WAS HOPING TO KEEP IT UNDER WRAPS SO SHE COULD PERSUADE DARCY TO RECANT.

Apparently it was only fun to expel students if they were poor and not from one's family. Lizzy supposed she should be relieved. She was off the hook now, after all, both from potentially getting kicked out of AU and having to conduct an investigation into Wickham's assault.

So why, then, did she feel such an inconvenient sense of dissatisfaction? foreboding? remorse? at the idea of Darcy leaving Austen University, for a crime she just couldn't bring herself to believe he had committed?

Caty, too, seemed to have a hard time wrapping her head around it. **DARCY ALWAYS SEEMS SO COMPOSED. HARD TO IMAGINE HIM JEOPARDIZING EVERYTHING LIKE THAT.**

THE RICHER THEY ARE, THE HARDER THEY SNAP, Tilney returned sagely.

Lizzy wasn't as well-versed in crime as her two weird, macabre friends, but even she had listened to enough true crime podcasts to know that it wasn't uncommon for a seemingly sane, together person to lose it if the right set of circumstances was set into play. In fact, of all of Lizzy's four sisters, the one she knew without a doubt was most capable of murder wasn't loud Lydia or prone-to-hysterics Kitty, but quiet, studious Mary. If any of the Bennets was capable of plotting the perfect crime, it would be Mary. That was why Lizzy never borrowed her sweaters without asking–not because of common courtesy, but self-preservation.

Lizzy also knew that Darcy had good reason to exact revenge on Wickham–and frankly, knocking him out and stringing him up naked in the campus square was letting Wickham off pretty lightly for what he'd done. Further, she was no expert on Darcy or his personality. They barely knew each other, all things considered. And yet...

She could not wrap her head around it. It didn't fit with the Darcy she knew, however little that might be.

Of course, Lizzy could have texted Darcy himself. They didn't communicate on a regular basis, but messages had been exchanged. Considering everything that had passed between them in the past several weeks, it wouldn't be so completely out of left field. Considering, especially, that if Darcy hadn't owned up to the crime, Lizzy would have been the one punished for it, didn't she deserve to get some answers?

Only every message that Lizzy tried to compose seemed woefully inadequate. Too gossipy, too aggressive, too familiar.

And if Darcy had wanted to be in contact with her, he would have reached out, wouldn't he? Maybe that was all the answer Lizzy needed.

δλε
November, 6 days before Darcy is expelled

Sleep that night for Elizabeth Bennet was woefully disrupted. Her dreams weren't so obviously about Darcy or Wickham or the Portraits of Pemberley, but the anxiety they produced had clear roots back to these people and events that had populated her subconscious all semester. Burning buildings, dark streets with ominous strangers, and the obligatory naked-in-the-classroom nightmares plagued her until she was unceremoniously roused from bed by a loud pounding on the front door.

It took Lizzy a moment to process the sound. The Delta house was not accustomed to many visitors, and certainly not those who chose to come in the still-dark early morning, repeatedly and insistently pounding on the door. This kind of thing might more commonly happen in some of the more popular sororities, with drunken Stanleys calling for their Stellas. But the Deltas had very little experience with these sort of shenanigans. A bleary Nora and Lizzy met up in the hallway, exchanging uncertain, mystified looks, unclear how to proceed.

"We don't have any drugs!" Nora called out finally.

"Try the Omegas," Lizzy added.

"Elizabeth Bennet, you open that door this instant!"

Lizzy placed the voice immediately, but had a harder time justifying its presence, given the place, time, and persistence. "Mr. Collins?"

The man in question stood in what appeared to be his natural state—quivering outrage—as he glowered down at her. He was already fully dressed, suit and all, even though it was only 5:13 in the morning. "President de Bourgh needs to speak with you."

"Now?"

"Now," Collins insisted, gesturing toward the Bentley in the driveway.

Exchanging another bemused glance with Nora, Lizzy obliged, following Collins toward the waiting car—not so much out of desire, or even curiosity, but because her caffeine-deprived brain didn't know what else to do.

Mr. Collins ushered her into the back of the car, where President de Bourgh was waiting, decked out in her usual pantsuit and gaudy jewelry like some kind of crossdressing Tony Soprano. Lizzy thought Collins might climb in after her, but instead he shut the door behind her. (To avoid any witnesses?!) The president of the university surely didn't go around murdering students—although, if she did, 5:14 in the morning would be the ideal time to do it, as no one on Greek Row would be awake to see it.

Lizzy glanced toward the front of the car to see if the driver could, at least, act as a witness, but saw there was none. Did Collins drive President de Bourgh around? That seemed beyond the job duties of an administrative assistant; yet it was both entirely plausible, and completely depressing, to think that this might actually be the joy of his life.

"Miss Bennet," said de Bourgh, reclaiming Lizzy's focus. "I'm sure you know why I'm here."

"I have absolutely no idea," Lizzy assured her.

For a long moment, de Bourgh glared at her–that same, strangely assessing but also aggressive stare–before she sat back with a sniff. "I'm assuming you've heard that my nephew confessed to assaulting Wickham."

There was no need to reply to that, as *everyone* had surely heard about it by now. President de Bourgh continued, "As we both know that Fo-Hian could not be capable of such an act, I can only assume that you had something to do with this confession."

Lizzy rolled her eyes. It was too early to try to hide her annoyance. "What's that old idiom about assuming, President de Bourgh? Something about making an ass out of yourself?"

President de Bourgh spoke on as if she hadn't heard her. "Should I further assume that you have some kind of sway over him? Blackmail, perhaps, for some other infraction?"

The leaps in logic were astonishing. Lizzy had published an article in the school paper about an event that happened on campus, which just so happened to be a crime, so she must be somehow responsible for it. Darcy had claimed responsibility for said crime, so Lizzy must be blackmailing him. It was difficult to know whether to be offended or flattered that de Bourgh would think her capable of such masterminded plotting and scheming.

"President de Bourgh, I mean this with all due respect, but I have no idea why you're so obsessed with me." This said with all of the dignity that could be mustered in avocado-print pajamas. "I don't know how to put this more clearly, but I had nothing to do with Wickham's assault, and I'm certainly not blackmailing Darcy."

What could she possibly blackmail him with, anyway? Pictures of his hair slightly unkempt after taking off a hat, or proof that he spent fraternity parties completing crossword puzzles on his phone instead of getting plastered like any self-respecting undergraduate?

Lizzy reached for the car door. "Feel free to forget my name and ignore me until I graduate. I'll happily reciprocate."

"Wait!"

It was the panic in de Bourgh's voice, not the instinctive, sharp authority, that caused Lizzy to reluctantly pause, waiting to see what might come next.

"Fo-Hian didn't do this," de Bourgh reiterated. "But he won't retract. He's as stubborn as any Darcy ever was. I've tried everything–ordered, begged, even asked Guanyin to plead with him. Nothing! Even though I've explained to him, in every way possible, that this will ruin his future. What ivy-league school will take him into law school if he gets expelled for a petty crime? And what is he supposed to do–go to a *state* school?" She shook her head at the indignity of it, blinking back tears.

The obvious privilege in the last part had lost Lizzy a bit, but she couldn't be insensible to the root of what de Bourgh was saying: Darcy hadn't committed this crime, but he was still going to suffer the consequences.

"You could always just *not* expel him," Lizzy reminded her. "You are the president of the university."

De Bourgh shook her head. "I can't be seen to show any nepotism." No, that was only acceptable so long as it wasn't obvious. "And even if I risked the ire of the board and let him off with a warning, Wickham will almost certainly press criminal charges. He'll do anything he can to sully the Darcy name."

Lizzy wondered just how much de Bourgh knew about that story, and further, just how much she should let on that she herself knew. Deciding that the answer was none, she remained silent, not entirely certain why President de Bourgh was unloading all of this onto her in the first place.

As if the older woman had read her mind, de Bourgh rounded on Lizzy, her sharp blue eyes piercing. "You and your friends, you solved the murder of that girl in spring term."

Lizzy could have reminded her that she'd played a pretty minor role in that whole thing–and further, reminded her that *that girl* had had a name, one that shouldn't have been so easy for the president of the university to forget–but both points felt a little exhausting at such an early hour. "Yeeaaah," she hedged, wary of where this was going.

"Solve this." It was unclear if this was a request, or a command. "Find out who really did it. Absolve Darcy."

The order hung in the air, loaded and heavy, as Lizzy considered it. She didn't particularly want to see Darcy get expelled for something he might not have done–might have even had a night of restless sleep because deep down she knew she couldn't let it happen. But damn, if it wouldn't feel good to be the one to say no to something de Bourgh really wanted.

"What's in it for me?" she asked, deciding that if she had to capitulate to what de Bourgh wanted, she could at least make it as painful a process as possible.

President de Bourgh looked obligingly irritated, though also a little too assured that she was going to be getting her way for Lizzy's liking. "I would be grateful, of course."

Lizzy rubbed her fingers together in the 'pay me' gesture. "Gratitude don't pay the bills, Caren."

That, at last, got the reaction she'd been wanting. President de Bourgh audibly ground her teeth together. "A little piece of advice, Miss Bennet. You catch more flies with honey than vinegar."

"I'll make sure to consider that the next time I want to catch flies," Lizzy returned, unfazed. "In the meantime, I want immunity. For me, and everyone else in the Austen Murder Club."

"I don't know what you mean."

Lizzy leveled her with a look. "Yes, you do. Stop punishing us for what happened with Isabella last year."

President de Bourgh held her gaze for a long moment, before curtly nodding. "What else?"

Lizzy blinked. She hadn't realized she could make more than one demand–but she was determined to get the most mileage out of this, now that she knew she could. The problem was, she couldn't think of anything else on the spot. Afraid to lose the upper hand, Lizzy blurted the first thing that came to her mind. "Coffee."

"Coffee?"

"I want a coffee machine for the Delta house. A nice one. With one of those steamer things to make the milk all fancy."

President de Bourgh did an admirable job of pretending this wasn't an absolutely ludicrous request. "Fine."

"Fine," Lizzy echoed. She hesitated a moment, not knowing how to proceed. "I'll let you know when I find something, I guess."

She reached again for the door, and again, President de Bourgh's voice caught her. "I meant what I said about honey and vinegar, Miss Bennet. You might want to take it to heart. You're clearly a clever girl. But you're brash, rude, even at times vulgar. Instead of courting people who could be in a position to help you—help that you very much need, I might add—you alienate them with silly jokes to show off how witty you think you are. You're trouble, and anyone with any grain of sense can smell that a mile off."

Lizzy considered the words as she exited the car, pausing just outside to give de Bourgh her best shit-eating grin. "You know, I think I'm going to take that as the highest compliment, coming from you."

And with that, she slammed the door behind her.

chapter
fourteen

THE AUSTEN MURDER CLUB was officially back in session. The membership might have shifted, the crime in question might be different, but all things considered, Lizzy was glad to be back, even under these circumstances. It was possible she was spending too much time with Caty and Tilney, getting such a kick out of solving mysteries, but at least she was in good company.

The company in question had been significantly altered since the night of the murder dinner party last spring. From the original group, in attendance were Tilney, Caty, and Lizzy. Marianne would be away indefinitely—possibly for the rest of the semester, but that had yet to be determined. Emma&Knightley (who now, apparently, came as a package deal) couldn't make it that afternoon, but Emma had sent a fruit basket, along with her assurances that she would see what Knightley could gage from Darcy (and what he would be willing to divulge). Rushworth hadn't answered his texts, Karoline and Darcy hadn't been invited, Jane Fairfax was still in Ireland, and Frank understandably wouldn't be attending. Also, by mutual agreement it seemed, John Thorpe and the other members of the group had happily not been in contact with one another since the spring.

Though the O.G. group member's numbers might be small, others had joined to fill out their ranks. Nora was present, along with Brandon

Colón (Sigma Rho GRA), Anne Elias (Pi Kappa Sigma GRA), and Fania Parsa (a freshman as yet unpledged).

"You're probably all wondering why I asked you here today," Lizzy began.

This collection of people was far too polite to jump at that segue, as a John Thorpe or a Rushworth certainly would have. After a brief pause, it was, surprisingly, Anne, who spoke up: "I honestly have no idea why I'm here."

Anne, as usual, wore no makeup, her long dark hair pulled back into a nondescript ponytail under a baseball cap. Her yoga pants, sneakers, sweatshirt, and heavy backpack all indicated that she had been pulled away from the library–the natural habitat of the PhD student.

"There's a very important reason you're here," Lizzy reassured her, knowing how much graduate students hated to be pulled away from their research. And there was, after all, an important reason she had invited Anne; it hadn't occurred to her until now to feel bad that it was because Anne drove a minivan, which might come in useful during the investigation.

Lizzy filled them all in quickly about President de Bourgh's initial ultimatum to her, Darcy's confession, then de Bourgh's early-morning plea that she solve the case.

"Are we all suspects now?" Tilney asked, sounding far too intrigued by the prospect. "My money's on Fania, but only because I've never actually heard her say anything. It's always the quiet ones..."

Tilney was clearly teasing, but Fania–a shy, quiet girl wearing a beige Shayla–simply stared down at the ground, clearly flustered by the attention. Knowing Tilney, he'd simply hoped to tease her a little out of her shell, but instead she had retreated back into it, turtle-style. They'd only just managed to get her to make eye contact with anyone in the group, and now this. Wordlessly, Caty reached over and pinched his arm, hard.

"No one here is a suspect," Lizzy hastened to say, not only for Fania's sake, but also because it was so obviously true. There were a lot of volatile, vibrant personalities at Austen University, but few of those were present here today at the new and improved Austen Murder Club. Lizzy had asked everyone here today because of their more practical qualities: their skills, their proximity to the crime, and yes, even their modes of transportation. She certainly didn't believe any of them capable of any kind of major crime, with the possible exception of Tilney after too many helpings of sangria.

"We're all here to help you," Brandon spoke up, as always the voice of reason. Lizzy imagined that even as a toddler, he'd been grave, thoughtful, and fond of the cardigans he seemed to favor. "No innocent person should have to be punished for something they didn't do."

Nora said nothing, but nodded at Lizzy with her quiet assent. Relieved to have everyone on board, Lizzy clapped her hands. "Okay, then. Let's start with motive. If Darcy didn't do it, why would he confess to the crime?"

"We're operating under the assumption that Darcy's innocent?" Caty had, from somewhere, produced a notebook and was already scribbling away.

Lizzy hesitated, wanting to tread carefully. No one here, not even Nora, knew the full extent of Lizzy's relationship with Darcy. She hardly understood it herself, truth be told. But she didn't want to come across as unduly biased. "De Bourgh seems convinced that he is. If he isn't, I'm sure the evidence will point that way. Either way, we can put any rumors to rest."

"He's protecting somebody."

Everyone looked up in surprise to confirm that it was, in fact, Fania who had spoken. Her gaze was trained on the coffee table, but she spoke evenly as she continued, "Or at least, he *thinks* he is."

Lizzy felt a little lurch of something in the pit of her stomach, but did her best to squash it down. "Okay, but who?"

Unfortunately, despite their combined skills, no one in the room knew Darcy well enough to wager a guess. Lizzy had a few ideas, but again, the information she was privy to was confidential. Even to save Darcy from expulsion, she didn't know if it was her place to reveal the things she'd been told in confidence.

"We should bring in someone who knows Darcy a bit better," Caty summed up what Lizzy herself had been thinking.

"Charlie Bingley?" Tilney offered. "Those two are thick as thieves, aren't they?"

Lizzy did her best not to look in Nora's direction. "That might not be the best idea." Along with the obvious awkwardness that might ensue for her best friend if Charlie were brought into the inner circle, Charlie was someone Darcy might very well be protecting, putting him as a definite suspect. She expressed the latter part of this sentiment to the group, leaving out the former.

"Knightley?" Anne suggested next. "He and Darcy were close, when Knightley was still the Theta's GRA. I imagine they still are."

Like Anne and Brandon, Knightley had been a graduate student resident advisor for the Thetas, until he'd resigned so he could date Emma. (There were rules, apparently, about GRAs dating undergrads, even those not in their respective houses.)

Lizzy shook her head. It was a good suggestion, but Knightley and Emma were in that cute but annoying first stage of love where they were completely obsessed with each other and barely remembered the rest of the world existed. Darcy could have very well knocked Wickham out cold in front of Knightley, and he would have been too absorbed texting Emma and smiling at how cute it was that Emma always used lowercase letters to notice. (This was a purely hypothetical scenario, of course; let it be known, for the record, that Emma's texting mechanics were above reproach.)

Caty sighed, meeting Lizzy's gaze grimly. "I think we all know there's really only one choice."

They *did* all know, or at the very least, Lizzy knew it. "Lucy Steele?" she joked, trying to buy herself even a few more moment's respite. But in her heart of hearts, Lizzy knew there was only one person obsessed enough with Darcy to track his every movement, know his every preference, and understand why he might lie about committing a crime.

Dialing the number, Lizzy braced herself, and was a little relieved when she was sent to voicemail. "Karoline, this is Elizabeth Bennet. I, uh, I need your help..."

volume two

"...your reasoning is very good, but it is founded on ignorance of human nature."

- Jane Austen, *Sense and Sensibility*

one
november - 5 days before darcy is expelled

IT WAS difficult to say who was more uncomfortable having Karoline Bingley in the Delta living room—everyone in the Austen Murder Club, or Karoline herself. The last meeting of the group hadn't exactly been a rollicking good time, but there had been a relative comfort and ease amongst those present. A security in the knowledge that no one present meant any ill will or was judging anyone else unduly.

That ease had flown out the window the moment that Karoline stepped into the room, with her imperious heels and impeccable outfit and her scornful, judgy eyebrows. (Lizzy didn't quite know how someone managed to have judgmental eyebrows, but Karoline Bingley *managed* it.)

The only slight comfort was that Karoline seemed to feel equally out of place in her present company. Smug, supercilious, and snobby, yes; but also so far out of her element that she still hadn't quite settled back all the way into her seat, even though she'd been there for fifteen minutes already. Granted, this might be due to the fact that she seemed to believe the (perfectly clean, respectable!) couch was somehow capable of damaging her dress, but still. It couldn't be a comfortable sitting position, and there was some rude satisfaction in that.

Still, someone should probably do something to break the awkward tension in the room. Lizzy resorted to her immediate go-to: food. "Scone?" she asked, holding out a plate toward her guest—for yes, somehow in this bizarro alternate reality, Karoline Bingley was an invited guest in her home.

Karoline looked at the proffered item disdainfully. "Gluten-free?"

"No," Lizzy returned just as disdainfully.

And they were once again at a stand-still.

"Thanks for agreeing to help us, Karoline," Caty rushed in diplomatically. She had picked up a thing or two from spending so much time with Emma, it seemed. "We really couldn't do this without you."

Karoline perked up a little at that, casting Lizzy a none-too-subtle smirk. "Of course. I always like to lend a hand when needed."

Lizzy wanted very much to blurt out that they only *needed* her because she was pathetically obsessed with Darcy. But she didn't. Because she was *Mature*.

Caty gave an encouraging smile. "We thought it might be helpful to list out the possible people that Darcy might be protecting."

Some of the smugness dissipated from Karoline's eyes. "Protecting?" she echoed uneasily.

"Well, that's the most reasonable assumption. Otherwise, why would he agree to take the blame for something that he didn't do?"

"Maybe he did do it," Tilney prodded, watching Karoline's expression carefully. "Seems like Darcy has plenty of reasons to hate Wickham."

Lizzy wasn't sure if Tilney truly believed this, or if he was simply trying to goad Karoline into overcoming whatever was holding her back. Regardless, it worked. "Of course he didn't do it," Karoline huffed. "Even though Wickham obviously deserves it."

Lizzy perked up at this, though she did her best to keep her interest off her face. Did Karoline know about what Wickham had done to Guanyin? Darcy's letter had made it seem like the whole affair was a well-kept secret, but Karoline was a close friend of the family.

As if mirroring her thoughts, Karoline went on, "Guanyin is the most obvious person. He takes the overprotective brother thing to a whole new level." This with a wistful sigh. "He's so sweet that way." (Barf.) "But I honestly can't imagine that Guanyin would have anything to do with it. She was just a kid when Wickham had the falling out with

Darcy's family, and anyway she's too sweet-natured. She wouldn't hurt a fly."

Hmm. It seemed as if Karoline might not know about what Wickham had done to Guanyin. Either that, or Karoline was a better liar than she pretended to be. Which didn't seem likely, considering that if Karoline was a good liar *sometimes* then she should be a good liar all the time, and Lizzy had definitely overheard some very obvious fibs in her brief time as Karoline's "Little" in the Kappas. ("Oh, Darcy, I had no idea you were a fan of history podcasts!" "Emma, you should definitely get the bangs–you have the perfect face shape for it!" Etc.)

Lizzy also didn't buy that Guanyin wouldn't be capable of hurting Wickham if she really put her mind to it. She'd never met the girl, but she shared a bloodline with Darcy, and that had to come with a certain level of calculation and ruthlessness.

"We'll go ahead and ask her where she was that night," Caty said, pleasant but firm. She seemed to be on the same wavelength as Lizzy about not wholly trusting Karoline's character assessment of Guanyin. "Just to dot our i's and cross our t's."

"Sure." Karoline's voice was pleasant enough, but her smile had gone a little sour around the edges, like she'd just sucked on a lemon. Or accidentally eaten a carb.

"Anyone else?" Tilney asked.

Karoline's face went a careful, calculated neutral. "No one comes to mind."

Lie! Aha, so maybe Karoline *wasn't* a secretly good liar. Lizzy exchanged a meaningful glance with Caty. A part of her wanted to pounce, but she sensed that doing so would devolve quickly into a battle of wills between herself and Karoline. Caty seemed to be having better luck at coaxing information from her–maybe because she was a fellow Kappa. Or maybe, Lizzy thought with guilty self-reflection, because unlike Lizzy, Caty had never hidden a remote-controlled fart machine under Karoline's mattress. (To be fair, there was important context behind that story.)

"What about your brother?" Caty prompted. "He and Darcy seem pretty close."

It was ridiculous. They all knew Charlie and Darcy were best friends. Karoline knew they all knew that Charlie and Darcy were best friends. Still, Karoline hedged, "Define close...?"

Lizzy couldn't help it; even though she'd just resolved to let Caty do her thing, she took the bait, hook, like, and sinker: "Close enough to take the fall so Charlie won't get expelled and ruin his chances at an ivy league business school?"

"Close enough to explore any sexual curiosity with a trusted confidant?" Tilney added. At the blank looks from the others, he sighed. "I just want to believe that it happened, even if only once." Caty patted his arm sympathetically.

Karoline ignored this entirely, glaring at Lizzy. "My brother did not beat up Wickham and leave him tied up naked in the campus square. He was an Eagle Scout."

As if those two things somehow canceled each other out...? Before Lizzy could point this out, Caty piped in, "So, good at knots?"

"He didn't do it. He barely knows Wickham. Different circles. They've had maybe two conversations total, in public settings, where it was mostly Darcy and Wickham glaring at each other and Charlie making awkward jokes because he can't handle confrontation."

That did track, actually. For someone whose sister was the literal embodiment of evil, Charlie seemed fairly unequipped to handle conflict.

But Lizzy had another idea—one that she couldn't voice aloud, because of the implied confidence in Darcy's letter. Maybe Karoline didn't know what Wickham had done to Guanyin, but what if Charlie did? As much as it pained Lizzy to consider it, there might be some truth to Karoline's strongly hinted suggestions about Charlie's and Guanyin's romantic connection. Charlie had obviously had feelings for Nora, and maybe still did, but that didn't mean he couldn't feel something for Guanyin, too. Maybe he'd found out what Wickham did to her and decided to avenge one of the (apparently many) girls he liked. And Darcy had, in turn, claimed responsibility to protect him.

It didn't seem like the most airtight motive, but stranger things had happened.

Not that Lizzy wanted Charlie to be guilty, or Guanyin either, for that matter. But if Darcy really was protecting someone, those two were the most likely candidates. Unless...

Unless Lizzy confronted another, more awkward alternative, one that she dared not voice aloud. Unless *she* was the one Darcy was protecting.

Thought he was protecting, anyway. She hadn't attacked Wickham, but she could see why Darcy might have drawn the conclusion that she had. After everything that had gone down with the Portraits of Pemberley, Lizzy certainly didn't begrudge whoever had gotten revenge on Wickham. There could be no one more deserving, in fact, of such an attack.

What was harder to believe was that Darcy might stake his reputation, his education, his *future*, on Lizzy Bennet. Even the thought of it felt supremely arrogant to Lizzy. Yes, there might have been a smattering of incidents where she'd wondered if Darcy might be attracted to her—the way he'd looked at her lips during that confrontation at the pool, and that night at the gala, his hand on her lower back, pulling her in closer—but she could have been imagining things. And even if she weren't, Lizzy wasn't the Romantic Grand Gesture Girl. She thought she was great—knew she was great, in fact, and had always had perhaps too high a sense of self worth (at least according to her mother). But she also knew herself well enough to know that she was not the girl who inspired boomboxes outside of windows, or love sonnets, or expulsion-worthy false confessions. (That girl was her older sister, Jane, and she was *perfect*, a real-life fairytale princess. Not the creator of Peanut Butter/Oreo sandwiches, patent pending.)

"It would probably be best to look into Charlie, just in case," Caty told Karoline, in such a reasonable tone that it would have been difficult to take offense.

And yet take offense, Karoline did. "Fine," she said, in a tone that made it clear it was *not*, "if you want to waste your time, feel free. I'm going to focus my attention on real possibilities."

Tilney looked amused, despite himself. "Such as?"

"The people who have the biggest reason to resent Wickham: the girls on the Portraits of Pemberley website."

Lizzy grudgingly had to admit that wasn't the worst idea. She wouldn't admit it out loud, of course, but she didn't make any snarky comment, which was basically conceding as much.

"That's not a bad idea," Caty said for her. "We don't want to limit our search prematurely."

Looking buoyed by the feedback, Karoline gave an imperious toss of her hair. "Plus, we should totally look into whoever was the whistler for the site in the first place."

"Whistleblower," Tilney corrected, though he, too, looked reluctantly impressed. Was Karoline kind of...good at this? "Not bad, Mattress Princess."

Mattress Princess? Was that some kind of obscure slut shaming? Lizzy waited for Karoline to rip Tilney a new one at the insult, but she only looked mildly perturbed, waving off the reference like she could physically bat it away with her hand. "Whistleblower, whatever. You never found out who they were, right? Even after the story came out? Seems a little fishy. Like maybe someone has something to hide."

Not the only one with something to hide, Lizzy thought as she did her best not to say anything pointed about Karoline's smug, self-satisfied little face. She thought she'd thrown Caty and Tilney off her brother's scent, but if so, she'd severely misjudged how tenacious those two could be.

"Great," Caty said brightly; and, as if confirming Lizzy's inner dialogue, continued, "Tilney and I will look into Charlie and Guanyin. That leaves the two of you–" this to Karoline and Lizzy, "–to figure out Darcy's alibi for that night, if there is one."

As Karoline and Lizzy exchanged a mutually horrified look at the thought of having to work together, Tilney cheerfully broke the silence: "Look on the bright side–maybe he won't have one, and the case will be solved."

It was a prospect that neither girl relished, and for reasons that might have surprised them in just how similar they were.

δλε

"What was all that about 'Mattress Princess'?" Lizzy asked Tilney after the meeting was officially over, but Caty and Tilney had lingered behind to eat the leftover snacks and bounce around ideas...but mostly just eat the leftover snacks. "Is that a fancy way of saying future porn star, and if so, why aren't you dead yet by Karoline's hands?"

Tilney choked a bit on his generous helping of Cheez Whiz on cracker. "God, no. Get your mind out of the adult film industry, Elizabeth."

"Lizzy's not from the South," Caty reminded him. "She doesn't know."

"Doesn't know what?" Lizzy echoed, looking uneasily back and forth between the two amateur sleuths, who were now wearing identical Cheshire grins.

Tilney fished out his phone, pulling up something on the screen. "It's like early Christmas..."

Lizzy leaned over to see the video he'd found on YouTube. It had hundreds of thousands of views, and looked to be some kind of commercial. A middle-aged black man who looked vaguely familiar wore a gaudy plastic crown and hammed it up for the camera. "Trouble sleeping? Come by and see the Mattress King, your one-stop-shop for a night of blissful dreams. With the Mattress King, you aren't just a customer, you're royalty, baby!" And with that, he jumped backward into a pile of mattresses.

It seemed like a pretty standard bad-quality commercial to Lizzy, but for some reason Tilney and Caty were both mouthing along the last tag-line, adding an extra punch to the word 'baby'. "What is this?" she asked, confused, handing the phone back to Tilney.

"It's hard to explain, but this thing was huge in the early 2010s, at least in the South," Caty informed her. "The Mattress King was every-where—billboards, TV commercials, ads in the movie theater, bus stop logos...It's hard to explain now why it was so funny, but I guess it kind of became this running joke, how bad it was? And the Mattress King just ran with it."

"You're leaving out the best part," Tilney joined in gleefully, pointing to the Mattress King's paused image on his phone screen. "The

Mattress King? Is Karoline's father. That's how the Bingleys made all their money."

Lizzy took the phone again, seeing a certain resemblance in the Mattress King's nose, the shape of his jaw. She'd always assumed Karoline's family got rich like all rich people got rich—inheritance, or stock trading, or hedge funds, or other rich-sounding words that she didn't really understand.

To know that snooty, entitled Karoline had gotten rich off her dad running a mattress store and going viral for having exceptionally bad-quality commercials? Lizzy grinned, hugging the phone to her chest. "I'm so happy."

"You're welcome," said Tilney. "Now give me back my phone so I can show you the one where he wears a blowup sumo wrestling outfit and knocks customers down onto the mattresses..."

chapter
two

"MAYBE WE SHOULD SPLIT UP," was the first thing Karoline suggested to Lizzy as they made their way up the drive to the Theta house at the appointed time. "I'll talk to Darcy, and you can... I don't know. Look through the dumpster or something."

Lizzy did not bother to hide her eye roll. "Or *I* could talk to Darcy and you could look through the dumpster." Not that she was especially keen to have a heart-to-heart with Darcy, but a slight like that could not go unchecked. Give Karoline Bingley an inch and she would take a Manhattan mile.

Karoline scrunched her nose at Lizzy. "Of the two of us, who's dressed for the dumpster, Bennet?"

"Yellow flag penalty," Lizzy snapped at her. They had agreed, before meeting tonight, to call a truce of sorts. No sarcasm. No condescension. No snide remarks. If one of them felt the other was violating these terms, "yellow flag penalty" was the code phrase to call them to accountability. (Lizzy knew next to nothing about team sports, but Karoline had assured her this was a thing; her ex, Elton, had been a lacrosse player, as she was excessively fond of reminding people.)

Playing nice with Karoline Bingley was not high on Lizzy's list of priorities, but she would put aside her pride for the sake of truth, and justice, and potentially clearing Darcy's good name. She could be mature enough to hold up her end of the bargain–but only if Karoline didn't start it first.

"Is it really a potshot if I'm just stating the obvious price discrepancy in our outfits?" At Lizzy's warning glare, Karoline sighed and muttered a sulky, "*Sorry.*"

"Much as it pains me to say it, it might be best for us to stick together." It really did pain Lizzy to say it–that wasn't just hyperbole. She was grinding her teeth hard enough to break the filling in her molar. But honestly, it wouldn't be the best idea to split up. She didn't trust Karoline to tell her the truth if she found out something incriminating about Darcy or Charlie; and she didn't trust herself to have the guts to confront Darcy on her own. The last time they'd spoken alone, well...

Things had gotten weird.

At last they reached the end of the interminably long drive. Karoline marched up to the front door with the ease of someone who had been at the Theta house, often, raising her hand to ring the doorbell. They'd decided the best plan was to show up without informing Darcy, so as not to give him a chance to come up with a cover story. Karoline had reassured Lizzy that Darcy would definitely be home at nine o'clock on a weekday night; eight to ten p.m. was study time, and he had lights out by 10:30. The fact that Karoline knew his schedule this well was concerning, but then again, it was also why they'd enlisted her help.

Even so, Lizzy stopped Karoline's hand before she could press the doorbell, feeling suddenly, unaccountably, nervous. Not wanting to show Karoline any weakness, she put on her most businesslike tone. "Maybe we should come up with a plan? Like what to do if Darcy isn't home."

"He'll be home." Karoline smug-smirked; but then, her face only really had one setting when it came to talking about Darcy, which was smug, so the adjective probably went without saying.

Before she could reach the doorbell, Lizzy stopped her again. "Okay, but maybe we should decide how to approach our interrogation."

An (unnecessary to mention, but notably 'smug') eyeroll from Karoline. "Calm down, Isles. It's not an interrogation. We're just asking a few questions."

Isles? That was a weirdly specific reference. (And if Karoline thought she was a Rizzoli, she was delusional.) "Fine, but what's the plan? Maybe you should be good cop, and I'll be bad cop?"

"Yeah right, Bennet." Karoline motioned to her outfit–a chic, all-black ensemble that looked simple but also, somehow, expensive. "I'm obviously bad cop."

It was Lizzy's turn to eyeroll. "But you're Darcy's friend. It would make sense that you take his side. Hence, good cop."

A tinge of whine crept its way into Karoline's voice. "But everyone knows the bad cop is the sexy one."

Lizzy huffed. "No one is the sexy one in this scenario. It's just a term for–never mind. Let's just knock and see what happens."

Before this could be accomplished, the door opened from the other side, revealing none other than Charlie Bingley. At first Lizzy assumed that he must have heard them arguing, but this idea was quickly dispelled by the surprise, then wariness, that crossed his always-transparent features. "Kar–what are you doing here? With...Lizzy Bennet." Forcing a smile, he nodded in acknowledgement, more out of ingrained politeness than real pleasure, it seemed. "Hi, Lizzy."

Suffice it to say, this was an unusual reception from Charlie, whom the Delta house had long ago dubbed 'the puppy' because of his exuberance and innate cheerfulness. The Charlie standing in front of Lizzy looked tired, as if he had been (metaphorically) beaten down by the world.

If Karoline noticed this, she didn't let on. "Here to see Darcy. Is he upstairs?"

"He's not here."

Dumbfounded, Karoline blinked at her brother for a full, uncomfortable, ten seconds (it was longer than it sounded). "What do you mean, he's not here? Where is he?"

Charlie sighed. "You tell me. I came by to talk to him, but..." He let the sentence trail off, shrugging, as if it would take too much effort to finish the thought.

Karoline whipped out her phone, typing furiously, as Lizzy watched Charlie with concern. "Are you okay?"

He didn't quite meet her gaze, trying for a smile. "Me? Yeah. I'm always okay. Just tired." He motioned toward the driveway. "I'm gonna..."

But again, he didn't bother to complete the thought. Lizzy frowned after him, watching as he disappeared down the dark driveway. Not looking up from her screen, Karoline let out a frustrated groan. "Ugh. Darcy isn't answering. Where could he be?"

It had only been about five seconds since Karoline had texted him, but Lizzy refrained from mentioning this, in case it might be a yellow flag penalty. (It felt very important to her to accrue less of these than Karoline during the hopefully short-lived duration of their partnership.) Instead, she motioned after Charlie. "Is something going on with him? He doesn't seem like his normal, happy self."

"He's fine," Karoline said too quickly, in a tone that clearly suggested she Did Not Want to Talk About It. "He's been that way since coming back from Paris. My parents are putting a lot of pressure on him to get serious about business school."

Lizzy supposed that could account for it. She had a hard time imagining bubbly, gentle Bingley in a cutthroat MBA program. But he hadn't seemed so glum when she'd run into him at the Crescent a few days before. Of course, Nora had been there then, so that might be the reason...

Then again, that had also been before Darcy had turned himself in for assaulting Wickham. Could that have something to do with Charlie's mood? Maybe it was only concern for his friend, or maybe something deeper–like, guilt?

"Something's wrong," Karoline announced, echoing Lizzy's own thoughts–only, Karoline's words seemed to be directed at the lack of response from Darcy. It had been ten seconds now–which, again, to be fair, was much longer than it seemed. "Darcy should be here. He is a creature of habit, Bennet–a creature of habit! This doesn't make sense. We're going in."

"What?" Lizzy barely had time to ask before Karoline was opening the door without invitation, barreling into the front entryway of the Theta house.

As the Rizzoli, Lizzy had no choice but to follow her inside. Because, for whatever reason, they were partners; and also it could not be said that Lizzy Bennet had cowered back in fear while Karoline Bingley charged ahead. Nonetheless, Lizzy cast a wary eye around the Theta front room. She had never had reason to enter the frat house before, and she was surprised at how quiet it was. Whenever she'd imagined the inside of any fraternity house, it was always like something from National Lampoon—a passed out guy in a toga, maybe, with a few scattered beer bongs and red plastic cups from whatever weeknight party they'd been hosting. The Theta foyer was quiet, however, and almost weirdly orderly, with a row of post boxes and two dedicated study carrels. Lizzy wondered, offhand, if this was a result of Darcy's presidency, or if this was the fraternity Darcy had chosen because it had study carrels. Or maybe it was more of a chicken and egg kind of scenario.

Karoline, it seemed, remained unimpressed by the quiet, library-like atmosphere. "Hello! Kappa President in the house." *Pay attention to me* was the unspoken subtext of this statement.

"Well, well, well," came a familiar voice from the top of the darkened stairwell. "Look who it is."

Karoline faltered, looking for once a little out of her element. Maybe even—embarrassed? Intrigued, Lizzy looked back to the staircase—

—to see Rushworth descending, grinning like a cat who'd gotten the cream.

δλε

"Karoline," Rushworth greeted the girl in question, maintaining some serious eye contact as Karoline did her best to pretend to be entranced by a painting on the wall. (It was a man playing polo on a horse, Karoline—nothing all that fascinating!) He spared a brief glance in Lizzy's direction. "And I want to say, Luz?"

"Lizzy," she corrected him with a frown. "We spoke, like, a week ago."

Rushworth either didn't remember or (more likely) did not care.

His eyes were honed on Karoline, like she was the last slice of pie on the table. Karoline, for her part, was still pretending to look at the painting; but, realizing that Rushworth was not relenting, she at last slid her eyes to him with what appeared to be the utmost reluctance. "Rushworth."

Never breaking eye contact, Rushworth took her hand and tried to bring it to his lips. Karoline pulled away before he could accomplish this, wiping her hand on her pants and darting a quick (embarrassed?) glance at Lizzy. "*Don't,*" she hissed at him.

The whole thing was maybe one of the most perplexing exchanges Lizzy had ever encountered. She had never seen Karoline even remotely embarrassed; this was the girl who all but begged for Darcy's attention on a daily basis, showing no sign whatsoever of shame, but now she could not make eye contact with anyone in the room.

As if wanting to reclaim her power, Karoline visibly steeled herself, meeting Rushworth's gaze with a glare. "We're looking for Darcy. Do you know where he is?" *If not, you'd better not waste our time*, was the unspoken warning clear in her tone.

"Sorry, beautiful. He's out."

Karoline all but stamped her foot in frustration. "We know he's *out*. But WHERE is he?"

Lizzy had been the focus of Karoline's ire on more than one occasion, but even she was taken aback by the vehemence in the other girl's tone.

Once again, Rushworth either did not notice or (more likely) did not care. Not much ruffled Rushworth–that was clear from even a few short conversations, which was basically what Lizzy had exchanged with him over the years. But whatever was going on here was more than that. He looked downright *amused* at Karoline's hostility, like it was cute that she was treating him like the valet. "Just *out*, honey britches. He didn't leave me a forwarding address or anything. Darcy and I aren't exactly commandants."

Lizzy frowned. "Confidants?" she guessed.

Rushworth blinked at her, like he was only now remembering she was in the room. "Hey, I saw you a couple weeks ago. The night that Wickham dude showed off his walnuts to the whole campus." He gave her a knowing look. "You were looking for Darcy then, too, as I recall."

Keenly aware of the daggers Karoline was glaring at her (it was possible Lizzy *might* have omitted this detail in the discussion of the case), Lizzy kept her focus on Rushworth. "That's right. And Darcy was missing that night, too. Can you remember anything about where he was going? What he was doing? Anything that might be notable?"

Rushworth shook his head. "Darcy is mad secretive, y'all. He wouldn't tell me *anything*–not even when I asked him where he got his shoes."

"His shoes?" Lizzy repeated.

"Yeah, I've been looking for a pair of all black. Like, not just mostly black with white soles, but *all* black. He had the exact type I've been looking for but when I asked, he was all, 'I don't know, Rushworth. A store.'" Rushworth shook his head at the injustice of it all. "Yeah, obviously, man. But *which* store?"

Lizzy had no idea what to say to any of that. "Darcy was wearing all black shoes?" she repeated. This detail, at least, might be somehow related to where he was going that night.

"Yeah, he was wearing all black, head to toe." Rushworth turned his gaze back to Karoline with a surprisingly soft smile. "Kind of like what you're wearing tonight, milady. But obviously not nearly as timelessly elegant as you are."

Lizzy felt something sink into the pit of her stomach. On the night that someone had attacked Wickham and tied him up, naked, in the campus square, Darcy had left his house late at night, dressed in all black. That did not bode well for the theory that he could be innocent.

Karoline seemed to have come to the same conclusion, based on that gut-punched look on her face. "You're sure it was that night and not another night?"

"Well, yeah. That night was the first time I noticed it, for sure."

Lizzy heard the oddness in the phrase and latched onto it. "What do you mean, the first time you noticed it? Darcy's left the house wearing all black more than once?"

"Every night since then. He may have done it before–I dunno. But that was the first night I saw it."

So Darcy was regularly leaving the Theta house at night wearing all black? It didn't sound great, especially on the night in question, but why would he *keep* doing it afterward? Was he going around tying up other undergrads on campus, but Wickham was the only one who's story had gone public? Maybe Darcy had learned his lesson, and was keeping his vigilante justice more low-key?

That all sounded a little absurd, to be frank. But then, the whole thing was kind of absurd. Wickham, exposed to the world. Darcy, about to be expelled from university. Lizzy and Karoline working together to solve a crime. Rushworth clearly hot for whatever Karoline was serving.

"Thanks, Rushworth. You've been a lot of help," Lizzy told him, and she was surprised to find she meant it.

They'd nearly made it to the door when Rushworth's voice caught them. "So, I'll leave the door unlocked, yeah, babe?"

It took Lizzy way too long to figure out what he was saying. She was too surprised to keep her gaze from sliding to Karoline, who looked both mortified and furious.

Rushworth tried to cover himself. "For when you come back later, to help me study." To Lizzy, he explained, "I study best late at night. 'Cuz of the endorphins?"

"Shut up, Jay!" Karoline stormed out of the house. If she'd been a cartoon character, there would have been a Karoline-shaped hole in the wall, that's how eager she was to escape.

Lizzy was doing her very best not to laugh. "A pleasure as always, Rushworth..."

Outside she found Karoline silently fuming on the porch. At Lizzy's approach, she held up her index finger, practically shoving it into her face. "Not a single word. I mean it, Bennet. Not so much as a syllable."

It might be worth a yellow flag penalty, all things considered. But seeing the look on Karoline's face, Lizzy realized they would never get anything accomplished in the investigation if she crossed this boundary now. It would be well and truly over.

Exercising all of her willpower, Lizzy took in a deep breath, and changed the subject. "So, where do we think Darcy's been going?"

Karoline shot her an (almost) grateful look, before segueing along with her. "I don't know. It does seem strange. Darcy's complexion doesn't *do* black. He's much better in jewel tones."

"Maybe you could ask him?" Lizzy suggested. Not about the jewel tones, but about where he was going; she hoped that much was obvious, but that shouldn't be assumed with Karoline. "Or maybe he might tell Charlie what he's been up to?"

"I have a better idea." Karoline nodded to herself in full agreement of her superior correctness. "We're going to follow him."

three
october - 4 weeks before the event

ELIZABETH BENNET WAS MISERABLE, and it was all Darcy's fault.

That letter. That letter! She'd read it at least a dozen times by now, and probably far more than that. The first time she had done so contemptuously, relishing the proof—as she initially took it—of Darcy's condescension, his arrogance, his thinly veiled contempt for women.

Until she got to the part about Guanyin. Reading about the young girl and what she'd experienced, it was hard to think of Wickham as anything but a monster. A manipulative, mercenary monster. And once Lizzy accepted this to be true, she'd been forced to renegotiate all the assumptions she'd made about Darcy. How quick she'd been to believe Wickham's story, to believe the worst of Darcy! How she'd relished in enhancing Darcy's so-called sins to something worse still! With some reflection, she realized that she'd been very quick to jump to the idea of Darcy being behind the Portraits of Pemberley, with no proof and only the smallest amount of suggestion. All because she disliked him, not because he'd ever done anything to indicate that he might be involved in anything so predatory and salacious.

So actually, if Lizzy was being honest with herself, she was miserable, and it was all her own fault. Until this moment, she had never truly *seen* herself, and she did not like what she saw.

The subsequent readings of the letter were at first to try to piece together all the information as best she could, see how it realigned both Darcy and Wickham in her mind. And the times after that were pure self-flagellation. She re-read, with particular shame, the parts about Darcy being orphaned at the age of seventeen and scrambling to keep together the family business and raise his emotionally scarred sister, only to have her maliciously targeted by someone he had once believed to be a friend.

Lizzy still couldn't excuse Darcy's behavior with Nora and Charlie, but she could understand it now. It must be very, very hard to trust people after going through something like that.

For three days, Lizzy didn't do anything beyond what was required of her–eat, sleep, go to class, even though she barely registered what her professors were saying. The rest of the time was spent holed up in her room, sometimes re-reading the letter, sometimes stalking various people involved in the letter on social media, and much of the rest of her time silently berating herself for just how badly she'd misread everything and everyone.

On the fourth day, Nora and Marianne coerced her to go on a picnic with them with the promise of fresh-baked chocolate-chip cookies. "A little fresh air and sunshine will help you feel better," said Nora as they prepared to leave.

"So would a shower," called Lucy from the couch. Alas, she had a seminar that afternoon and would not be joining them at the park. Shame.

Surrounded by nature, on a perfect, crisp October day, Lizzy did admittedly feel a little better. What were men to grass and trees, after all? She felt even better after telling Marianne and Nora about some (though not all) of the contents of the letter, after swearing them to secrecy–even from Willoughby, she said with a warning glare to Marianne.

Lizzy omitted telling them about Darcy's role in breaking up Nora and Charlie. Not to protect Darcy, but because she didn't know how raw that wound still was for Nora; she wasn't sure yet if it would hurt her less or more to know that Charlie really *had* liked her, though he'd

still been persuaded to leave her. Lizzy also alluded to Wickham manip-
ulating and pressuring Guanyin, but she didn't reveal the information
about the pictures. She knew how hard Darcy had worked to keep that
private, and she was sure Guanyin didn't want it to be common
knowledge.

When she finished, both Dashwood girls had been stunned into
silence, including Marianne. (That Marianne was involved in the category of "both Dashwood sisters" should have gone without saying, but
to actually rob Marianne of the capability of formulating a righteously
indignant speech was so notable that it deserved clarification.)

At last, Nora was the first to speak. "Wickham has to have broken at
least a few laws in the process of doing everything he did. Surely there
are due processes that could hold him accountable."

Leave it to Nora to fixate on the practicalities of the situation. Lizzy
thought immediately of Guanyin, and shook her head. "Darcy's grand-
father was a judge. I'm sure if anyone has the legal connections to make
Wickham suffer, it's his family. He must have a reason for not charging
him."

"Who cares what Darcy wants?" Marianne finally exploded. Nora
and Lizzy must have been matching pictures of surprise, because Marianne gave them both the same half-irritated, half-embarrassed glare. "I
mean, what Wickham has done to his reputation is terrible, but if
Wickham is really behind the Portraits of Pemberley then it no longer
just concerns Darcy's family. Think of all those poor women, powerless
pawns of the patriarchy." She attempted to add something further, but
she seemed to have become incoherent with rage, her face flushing a
bright red that nearly matched the color of her hair.

Marianne had a point, though it unfortunately felt like a futile one.
"So far the Portraits of Pemberley is only a rumor. There's no proof it
even exists, much less that Wickham has anything to do with it."

Nora looked at her sister's complexion in alarm, reaching out to run
a steadying hand over her back. "Breathe, Marianne. Breathe." As Marianne struggled to comply, Nora soothed her, "If it's true, we'll find a
way to put a stop to it. Won't we, Lizzy?"

"Of course we will," Lizzy agreed, mostly to keep Marianne's head from exploding, though in truth, she had no idea how they were meant to do that. Short of Wickham offering a full confession–unlikely–it seemed like they had nothing but dead ends. A suspect, but no proof that the crime had even been committed. No website, no photographs, no witnesses. Only one anonymous email, and one very angry Dashwood sister.

δλε

A text from Tilney was usually a very welcome break from the monotony of day-to-day life, but Lizzy knew immediately upon receiving this message that something important had shifted and fallen into place.

WE FOUND SOMETHING. CAN WE COME BY TONIGHT? BRINGING BRANDON.

The 'we' in question was, of course, Caty and Tilney, the indomitable duo. If it had just been the two of them, Lizzy might have been tempted to read the 'we found something' as an indication that she would be looking through a trove of shirtless gifs of Henry Cavill. The inclusion of Brandon, however, made that unlikely, although not impossible. (Who couldn't appreciate a good shirtless Henry Cavill gif, after all?)

Lizzy had intended to meet with them alone, but once Marianne got wind of it she insisted on being there. And, wherever Marianne was, so was Willoughby (matching her ire but also making sure to defer to her experience as a woman and not try to appropriate her rage as a cisgendered straight white male. They really were a perfect pair). Even Nora seemed interested enough to put off a night of studying at the library, and surprisingly, Lucy opted to sit in as well. But maybe that shouldn't have been so surprising, since she seemed to have developed a keen interest in Nora, always insisting they walk to class together, go to the grocery store together, and so forth. Most likely Lucy had gleaned that

Nora was the most socially acceptable of the Delta sisters and had latched onto her as the only lifesaver on this sinking ship of a house.

So all told, it was probably a bigger group than Brandon had anticipated. Still, he took it gamely, giving everyone in the room a cursory glance. His eyes landed on Marianne, sitting on Willoughby's lap even though there were more than enough chairs to go around, and held for just a beat too long. Then, looking to Lizzy with a curt nod, he began.

"After you mentioned the rumor about the Portraits of Pemberley, all I got from asking around Sigma Rho was a bunch of dead ends. I couldn't shake the feeling, though, that something wasn't quite adding up—and I wouldn't have been able to sleep at night knowing there might be a site out there like that, associated with Sigma Rho. So I enlisted the help of a cyber investigator. She should be here any minute..." He checked his phone. "Ah. There she is."

He stepped over the door, opening it and ushering inside Fania, the girl Marianne had "rescued" in the library the day Lizzy met Brandon the first time. She looked vaguely embarrassed as she entered the room, not quite fully meeting anyone's gaze. "Hello. Sorry I'm late."

Marianne perked up, a little too eager. "Fania! It's so good to see you again. Of course you're welcome here. Please, sit down. Do you need anything to drink or eat?"

Fania shrank away from Marianne's enthusiasm, looking not quite sure what to do with it. "Um... no?"

Lizzy decided to step in before Marianne over-exerted herself. "There's an empty chair by Nora. Luckily some of us have doubled up to ration our supply."

Nora smiled with the appropriate level of friendliness at Fania, who visibly relaxed as she took her seat, no longer at the center of the room—though she still, to her visible regret, was the center of attention. Tilney gave her an impressed nod. "You look young to be a cyber investigator."

Fania shifted at the term, glancing at Brandon. "I never said I was one. I'm just taking some cyber security classes."

Tilney shrugged. "But cyber investigator sounds much more impressive, no?"

He glanced over at Caty, who was staring at Fania with all but openmouthed shock, as if it were Beyonce sitting in the living room. Or knowing Caty and who she would be more likely to be starstruck by, maybe someone more aligned with true crime, like Amanda Knox. "Are you Fania Parsa? As in the foster daughter of Reverend Thomas Bertram?"

Recognizing the surname, Lizzy exchanged a brief, worried grimace with Tilney. Caty had been a bit obsessed with Marla Bertram, Reverend Thomas's daughter, who had once been a Kappa. According to former Pi Kappa Sigma president Emma, Marla had been kicked out for getting blackout drunk one too many times and nearly burning down the Kappa house in the process. However, Caty had become obsessed with her backstory after finding Marla's coded diary left behind in the Kappa house and had refused to believe that the story was quite so simple, especially after Mrs. Norris had been willing to commit blackmail to get it back.

After how deeply Caty had been investigating Marla Bertram, it must be surreal to be meeting her foster sister, Fania. Some of this must have registered on Caty's expression, because Fania's eyes skittered away nervously. "Um. Yes," was all she said in response.

For some reason everyone seemed intent upon giving Fania the attention she so clearly did not want, so Lizzy decided to tactfully change the subject. "Were you able to find the Portraits of Pemberley?"

Fania relaxed visibly, seemingly grateful to hide behind the technology of it all. "It took some digging, but I finally found it hidden on the dark web..."

As she went on to describe the site in detail, Lizzy felt physically ill. It would have been bad enough if these were just some pictures that guys were forwarding around on their phones, but this... this had required technological savvy. Lizzy didn't know much about this level of web design, but she imagined it would take several hours to construct the kind of hidden site that Fania was describing. Likely, too, that more than one person was contributing photos to it. The fact that there had been a paywall to access the photos suggested that there were still more people who knew about it and had been paying to—what, ogle unsuspecting women? There were millions of free pornographic images online, so the fact that people would actually pay to see these photos meant the enjoyment came from knowing the women were unaware of their involvement. It was about power as much as it was about sex, about demeaning women and objectifying them.

And of all the people who must have been involved with the site, no one had come forward. Well, no one except for whoever had sent the anonymous email to Lizzy.

Marianne was the first to speak up, looking pale as a ghost. "So that site is still just there–all those women still being looked at every day, and they have no idea?"

Fania shook her head quickly. "Someone must have gotten wind that we were looking, because the site has been taken down as of yesterday."

"Luckily Fania had the foresight to take screenshots," Brandon spoke up. At Marianne's sudden, sharp look, he flushed a little. "Luckily, in terms of being able to prosecute whoever put up the site, whenever we find them."

Marianne considered this for a moment, then accepted it, settling back against Willoughby, who rubbed her shoulders. Brandon blinked, staring ahead at the wall.

Reaching into her bag, Fania produced a thin manilla folder. "These were some of the most recent photographs."

Everyone in the room stared at that folder for a long moment, no one quite knowing how to proceed. "It doesn't feel right, to violate their privacy that way," Nora spoke up at last, voicing what everyone had been thinking.

"We should probably just turn it over to the police," Caty agreed, to Lizzy's surprise. Caty had never struck her as the 'turn it over to the police' kind of girl, as her behavior last semester had proven.

Seeming to read the thought on Lizzy's face, Caty grimaced. "Look, if those were dead bodies I'd be all over it, but sex crimes really aren't my thing."

Tilney smiled at her fondly. "You'd be 'all over' pictures of dead bodies? My weird, macabre little murder-gnome." He slung an affectionate arm around her shoulder.

Caty pressed on, "Besides, Detective Lucas is really good at her job. She's let me shadow her a few times and answered all my questions about the job. I basically want to be her when I grow up." She looked around the room. "She'll take this seriously, make sure it gets solved."

The idea absolved everyone of having to look at the pictures, and thus seemed to be widely accepted–until Lizzy took everyone, and herself, by surprise by speaking up. "I think I should look at them."

Tilney groaned. "Oh, God. I can't look after a murder-gnome and a pervert-gnome."

Lizzy spared him a glance before steeling herself. "No, listen–I don't *want* to look at them, but whoever wrote to me trusted me to break this story. I believe you when you say Detective Lucas will take care of this–" she looked to Caty before turning her focus back to the group at large, "–but as a journalist, I feel a duty to look these over before we hand them off so I can make sure the word gets out. If, for whatever reason, the police mishandle things."

The words hung in the air a moment before Fania silently handed her the folder. Swallowing, Lizzy gave one last glance around the room at all the apprehensive faces before opening the file.

It was somehow both better and worse than she'd anticipated. Better, because there was something clinical that took over her brain once she told herself to view this as evidence; and worse, because even having anticipated what she might see, she hadn't expected the pictures to be quite so invasive. These weren't staged shots, with models who were aware of being photographed posing for the camera. It was clear from the angles of the bodies that these women had had no idea their image was being captured. Women with their backs turned toward the camera as they took a drink of water, or scrolled through their phones. Women who were just stepping out of the shower, or just putting on their bra, and a dozen other variations on being in states of unawareness and undress.

The worst part, though, was that all of the photos had been cropped so that the women's heads were out of frame. Not, Lizzy suspected, to protect these women's privacy, but more likely to protect the privacy of whoever had taken the picture. If a woman couldn't prove she had been photographed, then she couldn't prove who had taken the picture. The other effect of symbolically decapitating the women was to dehumanize them even further. They weren't actual people. They were just bodies to stare at.

Lizzy paused, one photograph in particular capturing her attention. Frowning, she reached for it, staring at first in incomprehension, and then disbelief.

"What is it?" Nora asked quietly.

Lizzy blinked at her in shock. "This one is me."

chapter
four

IT WAS the bra that gave it away.

Lizzy had one 'good' bra–a clearance item from an upscale boutique that made her boobs look amazing. The other bras she owned were more everyday, get-the-job-done kind of support-wear, but the good bra only got trotted out on special occasions, when she needed an extra boost of confidence. Nonetheless, she'd had it for so long that one of the straps had begun to fray a little, so she'd reinforced it with some slightly off-color fabric in a small but distinct patch over the left shoulder.

Even if Lizzy hadn't recognized her decapitated torso, or her boobs, or the top of her jeans just visible over what looked like the cut-off edge of a bathroom counter, she would have known that bra anywhere.

Because the bra was used so infrequently, it was easy enough to pinpoint when she might have worn it in her recent history. Once to Ladies' Night at the Crown Inn at the beginning of the semester, once to her communications class where she'd done a mock television debate around the end of September.

And once to give her a confidence boost to talk to Sexy-Pants TA, nee George Wickham. She'd been wearing it the night they went out for drinks at the Merryton Bar, wearing it back to his place afterward, and wearing it still when he'd spilled wine all over her t-shirt and all but insisted she go to change in the bathroom. The background of the photo had been cropped and blurred out so any distinguishing features of the room would have been difficult to prove, but the very tip of the bathroom sink visible in the shot looked like the same one in Wickham's place. The picture appeared to be taken of her reflection in the mirror, though that wouldn't have been noticeable unless one looked closely; no camera was visible in the mirror, but then neither had there been one visible in the room. Lizzy thought back now on how Wickham had offered for her to take a shower, and shuddered, wondering how many girls that had worked on before her.

Tea was procured for her, a blanket for her shoulders, then a chocolate-chip cookie, and finally a vice-like but oddly comforting hug from Marianne. Nora joined, less forcefully, on the other side, and Lucy seemed to realize that she shouldn't be the only roommate not participating, so she gave Lizzy's shoulder an awkward pat from behind.

Once all this had settled, Tilney gave Lizzy a sympathetic smile, as Brandon paced the room just behind him, one hand covering his mouth. "Do you want to talk about it, or should we give you some space?"

"I'm okay. More angry than anything. I'll be listening to Alanis Morissette after this, if anyone wants to join me." Lizzy tried for a laugh, but it didn't sound natural. "I want to see some hell and justice paid, for sure."

Caty leaned forward now, visibly switching into detective mode. "Do you have any idea where this could have been taken?"

"Actually, yes, I do." Lizzy looked to Brandon. "Do you know someone named George Wickham, and does he have any ties to Sigma Rho?"

Brandon stopped his pacing, looking at her with a resigned expression that answered Lizzy's question before he had the chance. "Hijo de puta," he said on a sigh, taking everyone–maybe even himself–by surprise.

In a few minutes, the whole sordid history had been revealed in its entirety. Wickham had been a member of Sigma Rho until the previous spring, when he'd been kicked out for running an illegal gambling ring betting on university sports. It wasn't the first time that Wickham had gotten himself into trouble (Brandon refused to divulge details that hadn't been made public record and were therefore confidential, but

Lizzy took him at his word on the subject), but it was the first time Brandon had managed to gather enough proof to finally get him removed from the fraternity. The story might have made a bigger splash, if it hadn't been for the investigation of Isabella Thorpe's death happening almost simultaneously on campus. Also fortuitous for the chronically lucky Wickham was the intervention from the Darcy family, who had anonymously made a small but sizable donation to the Sigma Rhos to ensure the fraternity didn't press charges.

Caty noted that piece of information with a frown. "The Darcys intervened? Their family also owns Pemberley Estate, which is where the name for the Portraits of Pemberley site seems to have come from. We should look into Darcy—it's possible he might be financing the site in some way."

Lizzy squirmed internally, debating how much she should say. She knew Darcy wouldn't want her telling this group of people his sister's history with Wickham, but nor would he welcome being charged with a crime she knew firsthand he hadn't committed. "I actually already spoke to Darcy about it. It's complicated and some stuff is confidential, but I can say without doubt that Darcy doesn't have anything to do with the site."

The answer didn't seem to satisfy Caty. "But why would he have made that donation for Wickham to get him off the hook, only for Wickham to turn around and name the site after his family's company? That kind of seems like Wickham's biting the hand that feeds him."

Without anything else she could really say on the subject, Lizzy shrugged. Tilney nudged Caty, clearing his throat. "You know how you asked me to tell you if you ever got too weirdly intense about a case like you did last year? We're heading down that path."

Caty took in a deep breath, centering herself. "Okay, fine. I trust you, Lizzy." This said begrudgingly and, it must be said, not entirely convincingly. "But whatever you know, and however you know it, you should convince your source to let you take it to the police. I can put you in touch with Detective Lucas, and she can make sure that Wickham and whoever else is behind this gets charged."

Lizzy hesitated, then nodded. "All right. I'll talk to my source. And to Detective Lucas."

Meeting her gaze, Caty gave a small, encouraging nod.

The moment was interrupted as Lucy spoke up. "I'm not trying to be that person, or whatever–" Nothing that followed this statement could be good, "–but what can the police even really do? You can't prove who any of these girls are, or even *where* they are. And no offense–" Only worse things, still, could follow this statement, "–but how do we know all of this was non-consensual? And even if it was, what do you expect to happen when you take off your clothes with some random guy? You have to be smart enough to anticipate something like this might happen and deal with the consequences." She slid her gaze to Lizzy's, repeating again, "No offense."

Lizzy could have said a lot of things then, like how she hadn't taken her clothes off in front of some guy, she'd been tricked into a bathroom with a hidden camera, and there were probably other girls just like her on that site. Or more important still, how it shouldn't matter if she had intentionally taken off her clothes because that wasn't the same as agreeing to have her picture taken or posted on the Internet without her knowledge. Or that it was the 21st century and wasn't it finally time to stop shaming women about having sex instead of holding men accountable for these kinds of behaviors?

But Lucy was only saying what others would say, behind her back and in online forums. So Lizzy said to her what she might not get the chance to say to those nameless masses: "I would take offense, Lucy, if I gave even a single shit about what you think about me. But since I know that your opinion of me can't possibly be lower than your opinion of yourself, based on the truly shitty way you treat everyone around you, I'll extend my condolences to you for whatever happened in your life to make you this way."

And there was very little, it proved, that Lucy could say in response to that.

chapter
five

LIZZY WATCHED the clock anxiously in the few minutes leading up to the next meeting of the *Juvenilia,* anticipating with growing dread the moment that Darcy would arrive. With the conversation she would need to have with Professor Palmer today, Lizzy was already a bundle of nerves, and having this–the first meeting with Darcy since receiving his letter–hanging over her head wasn't helping.

Or maybe, in some strange way, it *was* helping. It was easier to focus on the potential unease with Darcy than it was to remember that half-naked picture of her posted on a site for dozens, if not hundreds, if not thousands of people to see.

Easier, but nonetheless still nerve-racking. Lizzy mentally practiced schooling her features, wanting to be a blank slate when Darcy walked in. She wanted to be able to treat him like any acquaintance, not a guy she'd accused of running a porn site and destroying peoples' lives only to discover that she'd misjudged him based on her personal biases against rich frat boys (and maybe a little because he'd implied she was unattractive, once). Plus that other thing she hadn't even allowed herself to think about, where there'd been that moment when he'd looked at her lips, which didn't seem all that important in the grand scheme of things, but somehow kept trying to wedge its way into her mind.

So, she wanted to go back in time, basically.

But then something quite unexpected happened. The clock struck three, and no Darcy. The boy was never late, unless he was trying to make an entrance–it was one of the things she'd always found annoying about him, although now she struggled to remember why chronic punctuality had been such a trigger. When the minute hand moved to 3:01, Lizzy knew with certainty that Darcy wouldn't be coming at all.

In all the scenarios she'd imagined about their first encounter after the letter, she'd never even let herself consider that he might drop the paper. This was supposed to be his showcase, after all, the padding on his law-school resume.

Unless, a little niggling part of her brain insisted, it had never been about his resume. But Lizzy wouldn't let herself think about that. She set her jaw and attempted to listen to Professor Palmer talk about the mundanities of running a school paper and tried very hard not to think too much about why she felt so very . . . disappointed.

After a few minutes of this, Professor Palmer looked up at her over the rim of his glasses. "You may have noticed that your photographer is MIA. The women's shelter photoshoot has been postponed indefinitely. Do try your best not to be too smug about it."

Lizzy knew he was joking, and it was the very sort of thing her father might have said to her, but for some reason it still made her want to cry. She forced a smile. "Smug? Me?"

Palmer made a "hmm-phing" sort of noise, moving the conversation along.

Afterward, Lizzy followed him back to his office, bracing herself against his groan of dismay. "What is it now, Bennet? I've been meeting with little shit undergrads all day–no offense–and doing all the pointless paperwork that the administration makes us do just so *they* can have something to do, and all I want is to listen to my podcast while I pretend to read my students' journal posts. Can't you just give me that?"

Lizzy lingered in the doorway, unmoved by his plight. "I need to talk to you about my new story. Since I won't be writing about the women's shelter."

He waved his hand at her, taking his seat behind his desk. "If you leave me alone, I'll give you carte blanche–as long as it's not that thing you keep pitching about university tuition being a Ponzi scheme. We all know it's true, but it is what it is."

"I have something else in mind, actually." Uninvited, Lizzy entered the office, shutting the door behind her.

When she turned back, Palmer was eying her warily at this unprecedented move. He knew she was no drama queen and wouldn't be shutting the door over nothing, but he was still reluctant to relinquish his free time. "This'd better be good," he said at last.

When she'd finished explaining everything about the Portraits of Pemberley, including her unexpected involvement with it, Palmer just stared at her for a few moments before sitting back in his chair, rubbing a bleak hand over his face. "Well, shit." He sighed, then reached into his desk drawer, pulling out a flask and offering it to her.

Lizzy frowned at him. This was unorthodox, even for Palmer. "I appreciate the gesture, but I'm pretty sure you shouldn't offer alcohol to a student, even under the circumstances."

"Eh, I'm tenured. What're they gonna do?" But Palmer put away the flask, his face sobering. "You okay? You want me to refer you to student counseling?"

"I want you to let me write about it."

Another sigh from Palmer. "Yeah, I figured that's where this was going." He shook his head, more to himself, it seemed, than her. "This is going to open up a real shitstorm. Might even get picked up by a national. Are you sure you want that attached to you–and I want you to really think about that. Don't do the young-person thing and give a knee-jerk response. I want you to think about the big picture. Your name, probably eventually your photo, out for the entire world to see. Every Google search with your name in it, every job interview, this thing is going to follow you around. Are you *sure* that's what you want?"

Lizzy struggled to find the right words. "The people who made that site, they wanted to shame us. Make us into *things* to look at and not *people* with opinions or voices or, God, even heads. I don't want to be the face of this, but I need us to have faces, you know?"

Palmer nodded, sighing again. "I'm truly sorry," he said, voice uncharacteristically solemn, "that this happened to you. And for what's to come. I hope I'm wrong, but you know, I'm usually not."

δλε
October - 3 weeks before the event

Since there is not much narrative interest in describing the process of writing an article, suffice it to say that in due time, Lizzy wrote her article and it was published in *Juvenilia*. Both of these feats were accomplished with the support of copious amounts of chocolate, almost as many tears, and one much-needed boxing session with Marianne's Feminist Fighters group.

As Palmer predicted, the story generated a good amount of buzz, eventually being picked up by several outside news sites. Even if the story had not been salacious enough in and of itself, its connection to Austen University and the previous media frenzy over the murder of Isabella Thorpe ensured that it was headline news. Lizzy had carefully checked the article with Caty's friend, Detective Lucas, to make sure it wouldn't impede the criminal investigation into the site, and to safeguard herself against any protests made by the university.

There was nothing the administration could legally do to have her article taken down, but they were nonetheless very displeased with the attention it was drawing to the school yet again, or so Palmer told her.

Other than this, the reception to the article had been overall pleasantly surprising thus far. There were the usual nasty online comments, a few conservative outlets questioning the role the women's brazen sexuality had played in the site, but Lizzy had also received emails from several people who had likewise had compromising pictures used against them. In her personal sphere, Lizzy had been overwhelmed by the outreach of support, both from the expected sources—such as Marianne, Nora, Caty, and Tilney—and those she hadn't anticipated, such as a lengthy email from Jane Fairfax, a fruit basket from Emma and Knightley, and perhaps most unexpectedly, a random but overall supportive Facebook shoutout from Rushworth.

Then there was Miss Bates, who was now requiring Lizzy to meet with her for weekly wellness check-ins. Lizzy could have begged off after the first meeting, but the baked goods were too delicious to pass up, and it was actually kind of nice to meditate and go through self-affirmations with Miss Bates.

As she left one such meeting, Lizzy had all of her inner calm immediately shattered as she came face-to-face with Karoline. The girl in question gave a dramatic eye roll, made even more pronounced by the lavender contacts she'd started wearing recently. "Hello, Bennet."

Lizzy had been bracing herself for an insult, but felt herself deflate when she realized Karoline's words had actually been...civil. "Hello?" It was more of a question than a statement, but nonetheless the polite thing required, and despite rumors to the contrary, Lizzy was no savage.

Karoline sighed, as though all of this were enormously taxing on her. "Let's just keep walking. I'm trying to be nice because you were, you know, victimized or whatever."

Not the most tactful exchange she'd had on the topic, but credit where credit was due, Karoline at least seemed to be trying to be kind. Lizzy blinked in surprise.

"I mean, it *was* kind of your fault for not listening to me about Wickham–" There it was. That was the Karoline Lizzy knew and loathed. "–but no one who saw the state of that bra could believe for even a second you did it on purpose, like some people are saying."

"On purpose?" Lizzy heard herself echoing, too blindsided by the verbal suckerpunch of it to stop herself.

"You know, for attention. But I mean, that bra was so tragic. Who patches up their underwear? Do you need bra money, Bennet? Seriously. I'm sure my parents can write it off as a charitable donation, or whatever."

Unbelievably, it turned out that Karoline trying to be nice was worse than Karoline trying to be mean. Lizzy took in a steadying breath, trying to recall some of the reassuring mantras Miss Bates had taught her but coming up blank. "Karoline," she managed, "stop helping. Just, stop talking, I beg you."

She escaped out the door before Karoline respond, stumbling through campus only half-aware of the usual mechanics it took to walk, turn, stop at traffic lights, and so forth.

It wasn't until Lizzy was almost home that the thought struck her: If Karoline knew about the article, knew about Lizzy's picture on that site, and had put together that Wickham had been a part of it (even though Lizzy had emphatically NOT suggested anything like this in the article to avoid being sued for libel), then that could only mean one thing.

Darcy almost certainly knew it all, too.

Lizzy didn't know why this bothered her so much, only it did. After everything that Darcy had written to her in that letter, Lizzy hated the idea of him thinking that she'd slept with Wickham, as the picture probably implied. Logically, she knew that it shouldn't matter because it would have happened before she knew the truth about Wickham and she was single and a legal adult and it would have been with another single, consenting adult.

And yet, the idea left an unpleasant sensation in the pit of her stomach. She told herself she'd done nothing wrong. That she didn't care.

And yet, weirdly, she did.

six

november - 4 days before darcy is expelled

"YELLOW FLAG!" Karoline shrieked.

Lizzy gritted her teeth. "I'm right, and you know I'm right. Now give me the Burberry!"

The agreed-upon stakeout of Darcy was not off to a great start, all things considered. Lizzy already felt morally dubious about following Darcy on one of his nighttime jaunts to see where he was going and what he was doing and if it had anything to do with what had happened to Wickham; all of that being said, if they were going to stalk Darcy ("Tail!" Karoline insisted, "Not stalk!"), they were going to do it the right way.

"The right way" to Lizzy Bennet meant wearing dark clothes so they, too, blended into their surroundings and could (ideally) follow Darcy without getting caught. Karoline, on the other hand, seemed to have actually bought into the delusion that they were private eyes and had decided to dress for the part, wearing a designer trench coat, suede heeled boots, and a fedora. It was a commendable Halloween costume, but not something designed to help her blend in. Between the absurd hat, the expensive coat, and the loudly clacking heels, they were guaranteed to announce their presence to anyone within a five-mile radius.

Lizzy had already tried explaining all of this to Karoline, twice, and yet here they were, physically tug-of-warring over the coat. "You really think Darcy won't notice you in that outfit?" she persisted, hoping that somehow this time it would manage to sink in.

Surprisingly, Karoline relented, letting go of the coat. "I guess you're right. I could never go unnoticed in something so chic." She motioned to Lizzy's own outfit. "I see now why you're dressed like that, Bennet. No one would ever look twice at you in that sweatshirt."

Lizzy bit back a retort. *She* was dressed for a stakeout, in clothing that was dark, nondescript, and easy to move in: dark jeans, a black hoodie, and sneakers. The clothing of a sensible human being. "Well then it must be your lucky day because I have another one just like it for you!"

The hoodie wasn't identical, of course; Lizzy wasn't the type of crazy person who went out and bought multiple versions of a clothing item if she loved it. The hoodie she gave Karoline was navy blue, not black, so...different.

Karoline begrudgingly threw it on over her black leggings, and put on a pair of Nora's sneakers that were the right size. With her airbrushed makeup and sleek hair, she still wasn't exactly neutral, but at least she wasn't a walking billboard anymore. "Here," Lizzy said, thrusting a baseball cap at her. "Maybe this will help."

To her surprise, Karoline didn't protest; then again, she was too busy examining herself in the full-length mirror. "This thing is so big. It's like I'm swimming in cheap cotton." She gave Lizzy a side-eye. "I guess yours fits a little big on you, too, but mine is *so* big on me."

This time Lizzy did not bother to suppress her eye roll. She and Karoline were obviously very different body types and weights, so Karoline didn't need to clarify that Lizzy's clothes fit loosely on her. "We get it, Karoline. You're thinner than me. Let's get going."

"That's not even what I was trying to say, Bennet. You're so sensitive..."

Thankfully, they fell into silence as they went to wait at the end of Greek Row. They'd decided to get ready at the Delta house, since Lizzy's and Karoline's dislike of one another was so well-documented that it would have been noticed if they were seen to be spending time together at the Kappa house. Unfortunately, this meant that they wouldn't be able to watch from the Kappa house to see when Darcy left the Theta house, but luckily Caty had volunteered to keep an eye out for him and text when he was on the move. (A little too readily, actually. They should probably find her some kind of hobby.)

They did not have long to wait. Ten minutes or so after Karoline and Lizzy had stationed themselves behind an accommodatingly large live oak tree, Lizzy received a buzz on her phone. *He's headed your way.*

"Darcy's coming," Lizzy told Karoline.

They waited in silence a moment, Karoline shifting every few seconds. At Lizzy's glare, she whisper-protested, "I'm sorry, but I'm not used to wearing such cheap fabric. It's itchy!"

"Shh." Lizzy fell silent at the sound of approaching footsteps.

Both Karoline and Lizzy watched as Darcy walked by. Just as Rushworth had described, he was dressed in all black, and he strode forward with confident purpose. To be fair, that didn't necessarily mean anything, since Darcy always seemed to walk with confident purpose, but in the all-black ensemble it landed differently. It looked like he was up to something–like he had a *mission*.

Karoline and Lizzy exchanged silent glances. Then, after waiting what felt like forever, they rose to their feet and followed after him.

δλε

Of all the places Lizzy had thought she might be following Darcy, late at night, dressed in all black, with Karoline Bingley in tow, this was not where she had expected to wind up. Lizzy had a pretty good imagination; her mother, for instance, loved to joke that Lizzy must be living in a dream world if she thought she could make a living (or, more importantly, snag a husband) with a journalism degree. Her father liked to counter that anyone in this day and age who thought they could make a living with a bachelor's degree (or survive off a single income) was living in a dream world.

So, yeah, her imagination was pretty impressive. (She was Gen Z; it had to be.) Thus, Lizzy had imagined Darcy might be leading them to an illegal gambling ring, or a secret speakeasy, or an illicit love affair, or maybe even a really intense game of nighttime hide and seek.

Instead, he went to campus.

Darcy reached the campus square–the same campus square where, notably, Wickham had been tied up, naked–and *waited*.

He just stood there, waiting. Eventually he pulled out his phone. Drug deal? Lizzy wondered. Coordinates for a secret CIA mission?

But after a moment, she recognized the muted sounds drifting across the empty square. He was playing Tetris.

Tetris. In an empty, darkened campus square, wearing all black. All alone. Lizzy wasn't entirely clear if this made him seem innocuous, or even more suspicious. What kind of weird energy was this, and why was Darcy putting it out into the world? It must be some kind of rich person thing.

The confused expression on Karoline's face, however, negated this idea. "What is he doing?" she whispered to Lizzy. "And how much longer do you think he'll be doing it? I need to pee. Do you think I have time to go pee?"

How on earth she expected her to know this, Lizzy had no idea. "You peed right before we left the house," she reminded Karoline in a whisper.

"I have an unusually small bladder." This said proudly, as if Karoline had managed it through sheer willpower, like cutting out sugar and gluten. "I think it's because I'm so small-boned and delicate–"

"Shh," Lizzy hissed–not only because she would rather puncture her eardrums than listen to another moment of Karoline bragging about her bladder, but also because someone else had just stepped into the campus square.

For a moment, just a moment, Lizzy wondered if Darcy was meeting someone here. As in, meeting *someone* here. And it surprised her, the little jolt her heart gave, almost painful in its intensity. Which was silly, really, because you couldn't lose something you'd never really had.

The moment dissipated quickly as the new person moved into the light and Lizzy saw it was Knightley. Not, of course, that Darcy couldn't be meeting for a tryst with another boy, especially if Tilney's personal fanfiction was anything to go by. But Knightley was very much dating

Emma Woodhouse, and Emma Woodhouse was very much not an open relationship type of girl.

Darcy put his phone into his pocket, and the two met in the middle of the square, conversing for just a moment (too quietly to overhear) before walking together toward the Student Union.

"Oh my gosh!" Karoline hissed, and for a moment, Lizzy thought she might know something that she didn't know, and all of the pieces had just come together. Then Karoline continued, "Caty was right! Knightley is a murderer, and Darcy is his accomplice." Gleefully, she added, "Emma is going to be so devastated."

"No one's been murdered, Karoline," Lizzy sighed. She did not remind her, though she could have, that Caty hadn't accused Knightley of murder since things had been sorted with Isabella's death the previous semester; and furthermore, that Karoline seemed to think it was impossible that Darcy could have assaulted Wickham but had jumped pretty quickly to the idea of accomplice to murder. But that might be a yellow-flag offense, to point out the obvious.

"Oh." Karoline sounded deflated. "Then what do we do?"

Lizzy wasn't entirely sure. "Follow them, I guess?"

So, they did. Wearing their dark clothing, Lizzy and Karoline followed Knightley and Darcy, also in dark clothing. Lizzy and Karoline didn't say anything to one another, and neither did Knightley or Darcy, aside from a few muttered words here and there. Their eyes were trained on the pathways in front of them, scanning the shadows of bushes, trees, dumpsters–but for what, it was impossible to say.

It was not the most exciting thing Lizzy had ever done, and apparently Karoline thought so, too. Without consulting Lizzy, or giving any warning, she suddenly shouted, "I can't take it anymore!" and marched forward to Knightley and Darcy, who had turned to look back at them in surprise.

So much for staying undercover. Lizzy begrudgingly followed Karoline, watching as she stalked up to Darcy and prodded him in the center of the chest with a taloned index finger. "You are the most boring person in the world to follow, Darcy. You're not saying anything, you're not *doing* anything, you're just walking and walking and walking and a girl always likes to get in her steps, but this is too much. It's too much!"

With a dramatic cry, she pulled off Lizzy's sweatshirt and threw it onto the ground, heaving for a moment before looking up again plaintively. "Does anyone have any Claritin? I think this cheap fabric made me break out in hives."

"Um," said Knightley, because really, what else was there to say?

Darcy took in the situation–Karoline, the sweatshirt–before finally landing on Lizzy. He stared. She stared. They stared, mutually and in plural.

Then at last, Darcy broke the silence. "You were following me?"

There was more to that sentence than just the surface level. It was both a general query–you were following me? And a pointed *you* were following me, to Lizzy, because he clearly didn't understand how she and Karoline could be in cahoots together, following him late at night through campus.

Lizzy didn't really understand it either, but here they were. "Rushworth told us you've been leaving the house, late at night, dressed in all black. So we decided to verify his information."

"And have you?" Darcy asked. "*Verified* it?"

There was nothing remotely sexual in that phrase on its own, but the *way* Darcy said it, Lizzy could not help but be affected. His tone was challenging, a little angry, like maybe he was daring her to prove him wrong. And his eyes never left hers the entire time, creating a potent charge between them.

Lizzy held his gaze, refusing to back down or break the current between them. "You appear to be dressed all in black. And out late at night. So, yeah. I guess we have, *verified* it."

Something flickered in Darcy's dark eyes. Smoldered, might have been the word Lizzy used, if she were suddenly in a bodice-ripper. Which she was not. (Right?) "Good."

"Good," Lizzy said back, because she had suddenly forgotten what else she wanted to say.

"Good," Karoline chimed in, apparently feeling left out. At the sound of her voice, the spell was broken and Lizzy blinked, looking away and trying to regather her thoughts as Karoline continued on: "So, what exactly are you doing here? With Knightley?"

Darcy looked irritated at the interruption, a muscle in his jaw churning. "Walking."

At that, Lizzy managed to regain her footing. "You and Knightley could go walking anywhere, at any time. Why do it late at night on campus, dressed in all black?" Before Darcy could trap her in his gaze again, she pushed on, determined to gain some ground. "And why were you dressed that way the night Wickham was assaulted?"

Darcy and Knightley exchanged a look. Neither man was very expressive, but their faces still plainly conveyed, *Say nothing.* "I was dressed that way the night Wickham was assaulted because I'm the one who assaulted him. I've already admitted as much. I didn't want him to see me coming, so I dressed all in black. Luckily, it worked."

It was the very thing Lizzy had feared when Rushworth first told them about the way Darcy had been dressed; but somehow, hearing Darcy say it out loud, Lizzy realized how little it made sense. "So, you assaulted Wickham on Friday and then continued wearing black every night after that because—you have other people to strip and hang up naked around campus?"

Darcy didn't say anything. Neither did Knightley.

Lizzy gestured to Knightley. "And since you're with him tonight, should I assume you were also with him the night that Wickham was assaulted? Maybe as an accomplice?" Darcy wouldn't speak up to save his own skin, but he might if he thought Knightley was going to get in trouble, too. "I think that's something de Bourgh might be interested in hearing. Mr. Collins has been itching to fill out all that paperwork for kicking a student out of university; just think of how happy he'll be to get to do it twice!"

She'd thought she might make Knightley nervous, maybe even a little angry. What she hadn't anticipated was the knowing look he gave her, as he looked back and forth between her and Darcy, biting back a smile. "Look, maybe the two of you should talk this out."

Feeling Darcy's eyes on her, Lizzy flushed; but luckily Karoline could be counted on to ruin a moment. "You mean the three of us. Lizzy and I are partners. And if anyone should be talking to Darcy alone, it should be me, frankly, because—"

Alas, her reasoning would never be given. Knightley interrupted with a plaintive look on his face. "Actually, Karoline, I was hoping you could help me. I wanted to do something for Emma and you're the only one who could give me the right advice."

Karoline looked torn; she wanted to be the de facto expert on all things Darcy; but to have the opportunity to wield some kind of power, however minute, over Emma Woodhouse, was entirely too tempting. "What kind of advice?"

Knightley clearly hadn't thought this far ahead. "Birthday?" he offered finally.

"Say no more." Karoline took him by the arm and guided him over to the light, where they would better be able to see their phone screens, compare Pinterest boards, and coordinate their calendars.

It didn't seem to occur to Karoline that Emma's birthday wasn't until April. (Lizzy only knew this because the entire town of Highbury celebrated it. Seriously. Apparently Emma had been named Little Miss Highbury for so many years in a row that they'd eventually retired the title and made her birthday a town holiday. School wasn't canceled, or anything, but they did hang up a banner every year outside city hall, and the Hartfield Bakery gave out half-price sugar-free strawberry cupcakes, Emma's favorite.)

Lizzy was almost amused by this entire charade, until she remembered that it left her alone with Darcy. She looked up to find him already looking down at her.

She swallowed.

"This way," Darcy motioned her closer to the administration building. This was, ostensibly, to give them some privacy away from Karoline; but as they rounded the corner and Lizzy turned suddenly to find herself in a dark alcove, alone with Darcy, her back pressed up against the wall, she realized that she was in danger.

Not actual danger, of course. Lizzy knew it hadn't been that long since she had suspected Darcy of being the one to post those disgusting photos on the Portraits of Pemberley; but she also knew that her opinion of him had changed drastically during that time. It was impossible to say if it was the letter that had begun it, or everything that had happened after, or if quite beyond her own knowledge and without her permission it had taken root before she even realized; but Lizzy now knew with certainty that Darcy would never take advantage, or push past any boundaries that were set. Not with her, not with anyone.

The danger came from Lizzy's own awareness of the darkness, the proximity of their bodies, this palpable pull between them. Her breath caught a little as Darcy stepped in closer–not close enough to be creepy and leering, but closer than was necessary. "Knightley didn't have anything to do with Wickham. I think you know that. There's no need to get him involved in this."

Lizzy was both relieved and disappointed to have this convenient distraction to discuss. "Fine," she agreed pleasantly. "Just tell me what the two of you are up to and I'll leave it alone."

He'd thought he had her for just a second; Lizzy saw it flash through his eyes, saw the flicker of irritation that had another, deeper undercurrent. "It isn't relevant to what happened to Wickham."

"I think I can make that call for myself. Once you tell me what you've been doing."

She said it in a tone that had been designed to be as annoying as possible to her three younger sisters–falsely agreeable, a little too cheerful. Darcy looked amused despite himself, and Lizzy felt the thrill of taking the upper hand–until Darcy suddenly switched tacks. He leaned toward her, and for a moment Lizzy truly thought he was going to kiss her.

Instead he leaned against the wall next to her. It was a calculated move, she saw, to gauge what her response might be. She was embarrassed to find that she was holding her breath. He was smoldering again, his eyes dropping down to her lips and then back to her eyes. "You and Karoline have teamed up to prove my innocence–is that it?"

If anyone were to come around the corner now, they'd think they were walking in on a couple seconds away from making out. (And were they???) "Stop trying to change the subject."

"You can't prove me innocent, Elizabeth. I did it. I attacked Wickham." There was something urgent in his voice. She almost would have thought it was *pleading*, except Darcy didn't ask or beg. He ordered, and was always obeyed.

Usually, anyway. "Liar." Lizzy straightened, aware that doing so brought her in even closer proximity to Darcy's face, but unwilling to give up the advantage. "I don't know what you're up to, Darcy, but I know it wasn't you. And I'm going to prove it."

Their gazes held again, combatted, volleyed. At last Darcy pushed away from the wall. He hesitated a moment, stopped himself from saying whatever he'd meant to, and walked off.

Lizzy watched him, realizing two things in that moment: That she had won the battle of wills against Darcy... and that it did not feel like a victory, not at all.

seven

november - 2 days before darcy is expelled

THE AUSTEN MURDER CLUB reconvened the next day at the Delta house. Surprisingly, Karoline was one of the first to arrive, and she handed over Lizzy's sweatshirt with a sniff of disdain before breezing past her into the room. "I would have washed it before returning it, but since it was retrieved from a pile on the floor, I'm guessing it would be a waste of time."

It had been a pile of FOLDED clothes on a *chair*, not the floor, but Lizzy refrained from making the distinction, as vital as it was. "Probably for the best. My pet rat's never smelled detergent before and I wouldn't want to put him off making his nest in here again."

Karoline glared at her for a beautiful three seconds of horrified silence. "You do not have a rat," she said finally. This seemed to be more command than question.

Of course Lizzy didn't have a pet rat; despite popular belief to the contrary, she was not a Weasley. But again, she refrained from saying anything, just smiled. Let that doubt percolate in Karoline's mind for a good long while.

The inseparable duo, Caty and Tilney, arrived next, followed not long after by Fania, then, Brandon and Anne (apparently, they had carpooled, which seemed very on-brand for the two ultra responsible GRAs). When everyone was there, Lizzy texted Nora to come out of her room; she had a lot of catching up to do on schoolwork, after everything that had happened with Marianne.

Tilney and Caty started things by catching everyone up on their findings. "Guanyin has an alibi, so it wouldn't have been her," Caty explained. "She was in South Carolina on some kind of sea turtle rescue–something to do with her marine biology degree?"

"Guanyin has such a good heart," Karoline cooed, almost condescendingly, as if she by extension was out rescuing sea turtles just by nature of being friends with the other girl. "I knew she couldn't have had anything to do with it."

"Good news, for Guanyin," Tilney reminded her. "Potentially bad for Darcy, since that means we're one suspect closer to it being him."

Lizzy didn't know quite how true that was. Even as little as she knew Darcy, she still knew enough to know that he'd prefer to be the guilty party over his sister.

"And not great news for Charlie either," Tilney continued. "He has no alibi for that night."

Karoline stared at him blankly. "What do you mean, he has no alibi?"

"I mean–he has no alibi. When we asked him where he was, he said he decided to stay at home that night and watch Netflix, by himself."

"But Charlie doesn't do anything *by himself*. He wouldn't even be able to choose something to watch without someone else's input. That doesn't make any sense..."

Something visibly shifted on Karoline's face before she managed to cover it up. Lizzy recognized that expression: Karoline was beginning to wonder if Charlie might actually be guilty. That couldn't be an easy thing to deal with–and the thought of this almost made Lizzy regret teasing her about the rat. (Almost. Karoline had started it with that laundry dig, after all.)

Seeming to realize that she'd been too obvious with her doubts, Karoline backpedaled quickly. "I'm exaggerating. Obviously. He probably just pulled up whatever was trending. That's so Charlie."

Lizzy couldn't help but dart a quick look over at Nora; but her quiet friend seemed to have gotten used to not reacting whenever Charlie's name was mentioned, and if Lizzy hadn't known about their almost-relationship, she would have never guessed that there had ever been any feelings there whatsoever.

"Be that as it may," Caty said tactfully, "without an alibi, Charlie remains a viable suspect."

Karoline clearly wasn't happy about this, but she seemed to have learned there was no point arguing with the two Bobbsey twins. She slunk back in her chair, folding her arms over her chest and pouting prettily.

"Darcy is also still a possibility," Lizzy informed them, taking a moment to catch everyone up to speed on what had happened during her stakeout with Karoline (minus a few of the more personal details).

Tilney and Caty seemed just as perplexed by the details as Lizzy had been. "He was wearing all black on the night Wickham was attacked—but he's also been doing it every night since then?" Tilney echoed the pertinent points, puzzling through them aloud. "And Knightley was with him?"

"Do you think Knightley could have something to do with it?" Fania spoke up. She'd been so quiet thus far that Lizzy had almost forgotten she was there.

It was nice that she'd finally come out of her shell a little—but unfortunate that it was for this purpose, since the response her question elicited was so resounding. "No," said a few people in unison—Anne, Brandon, and most surprising of all, Caty. The girl in question shook her head. "Knightley is not the kind of guy to get caught up in anything illegal."

Lizzy had to bite back a smile. This was a very far cry from the girl who had been all but convinced spring semester that Knightley was a murderer. But it spoke a great deal to Knightley's character that those who knew him best (which now included Caty) wouldn't even entertain the possibility that he might have done something to harm Wickham.

Tilney shook his head in agreement. "No offense, but Knightley is definitely not someone I'd choose for my team if I were breaking the law."

Nora gave him a wan smile. "I don't think that's something that would cause most people offense." She looked at Fania reassuringly.

"And it was a good question. We shouldn't count out anyone at this point."

That was Nora in a nutshell. Like Fania, she was so quiet one could almost forget she was in the room. But Lizzy was willing to bet she was also the most observant, with the ability to take in everyone's measure at a glance, knowing that Tilney needed to be put in his place on occasion and that Fania needed to feel included so she didn't retreat back into her shell. A gentle assassin, that Nora Dashwood.

"So, question mark on Darcy," Caty summed up, making a note in her little detective's notepad.

Yes, thankfully, the details didn't seem to add up to Darcy being guilty, at least not necessarily. But they also weren't any closer to finding answers.

Karoline groaned, breaking her self-imposed silence. "So this whole week was a waste of time?"

"Not wasted, just inconclusive," Caty corrected. "Maybe we should turn our focus in a new direction for a bit, see if that stirs anything that might be useful in putting the pieces together."

After a pause, Anne cleared her throat. "What about the girls from the Portraits of Pemberley site? Or if not them, someone close to them?"

Lizzy felt the unspoken tension in the room and decided to answer as tactfully as possible. "It's a good idea, but since most of them have remained anonymous, it would be hard to follow up on any leads with that. And if someone *were* guilty, they wouldn't have much incentive in coming forward."

"So if it's one of them, we may never find out," Brandon mused aloud.

It was a likely possibility, but one that wouldn't get Darcy off the hook unless they could find a way to prove it. "What about the whistle-blower?" Caty spoke up. "Whoever told Lizzy about the site in the first place. We don't know what their connection to the site was–they might be able to tell us more about who else was behind it?"

"Or they might have had something to do with assaulting Wick-ham," Tilney pointed out. "Whoever it was wanted justice–maybe it wasn't enough, when all was said and done."

No, it certainly hadn't been enough. Lizzy could imagine (maybe more than most) how the lack of retribution could frustrate someone, make them feel desperate. She looked questioningly at Fania. "Is that something you could figure out?"

Fania shrank a little under the collective focus of the group turning on her. "I–um, I'm not sure."

Sensing Fania's discomfort, Lizzy rushed in with reassurances. "We know it's not like the movies–it won't take just a few clicks of a button and you magically get all the information we need. Maybe it's not even possible?" She gave a self-deprecatory eyeroll. "I know literally nothing about tracking people down on the internet beyond what TV has taught me."

Tilney joined in with a mocking scowl of indignation. "I won't have you besmirch the good name of my beloved TV, Bennet. It practically raised me."

Normally Caty would be one to join in on the banter, especially as it regarded the supposed honor of television, but to Lizzy's surprise, she was watching Fania closely. "Is it possible, Fania?" she asked carefully.

Fania seemed visibly torn, her fingers gripping the armrest of her chair as her teeth worried her bottom lip. "It's possible," she said finally, in the tone of someone who would very much like to be able to lie, but couldn't quite manage it.

Seeing the war waging in Fania's expression, a new thought struck Lizzy. "Do you already know who it was?"

"I, um..." Fania stared down at the ground, then gave a resolute sigh. "It...was me."

δλε

The room fell into a long, protracted silence.

And then came the questions.

"How long did you know about the Portraits of Pemberley site?" asked Caty.

"*How* did you know about the Portraits of Pemberley site?" asked Tilney. "Did someone tip you off?"

"Do you know who was behind it?" asked Brandon. "Beyond just Wickham? He couldn't have acted alone..."

"Were you the one who attacked Wickham?" This from an eager Karoline. "No offense, but if it was you, you can't let Darcy or anyone close to him take the blame..."

Lizzy watched Fania's face as she was bombarded by each new query. The girl looked like she very much wished she could disappear back into her chair. She wished she could think of some way to rescue her, but Lizzy's forte was more in diffusing big personalities, like her mothers and her sisters. Nora, too, seemed to have sensed Fania's distress, but seemed likewise unclear how to best step in—Marianne was not the delicate, shrinking sort, so Nora, too, would have little experience in dealing with this kind of temperament.

Anne's quiet, reasoned voice cut through the din. "That was really brave of you to share that with us, Fania. I can tell that you were reluctant to share, but that you wanted to be honest. That took a lot of courage."

The calm authority in her voice effectively silenced everyone else. Fania's eyes were locked onto Anne, clinging as if she were a lifeline in a storm. "I didn't attack Wickham."

"No one here thinks you did," Anne reassured her.

No one here besides Karoline thinks you did, Lizzy refrained from adding—even though she really, *really* wanted to.

"I found out about the site, and I knew it was wrong. That's why I emailed Elizabeth." Fania took in a deep, steadying breath, glancing at Lizzy. "I was afraid to go to the police or the administration because I didn't think they would take me seriously, or maybe they would take me too seriously and track me down. But I'd read some of your articles in the paper and I didn't think you would let something like this continue to happen at our school."

Lizzy felt touched by this admission. It had always felt like she was writing into a void, but there had been someone out there who had read her work and trusted her to try to make things right. She also felt a renewed need to protect quiet, morally courageous Fania at all costs.

"What was your involvement with the site? How did you find out about it?" Seeing the panic flare once again in Fania's eyes, Lizzy hastened to reassure her, "We won't jump to conclusions." She leveled a quick, warning glare at Karoline. "We just want to find out the truth."

Fania seemed to be warring with herself once again. She shook her head. "He didn't have anything to do with this."

"He?" prompted Tilney eagerly, but Lizzy waved him off with a sharp jerk of her head. For whatever reason, Tilney's exuberance seemed a little too much for Fania, and they needed her to open up now, not close off completely.

"Did someone tell you about the site?" Lizzy asked gently. Seeing that Fania was still wary, she added, "Whoever it was, it was incredibly brave of him to expose this. This information won't leave this room."

At last, reluctantly, Fania sighed. "It was my brother, Wa'il. He's a member of Sigma Rho–he's in the NROTC."

Lizzy had no idea what this meant, but Brandon nodded in understanding. "The Naval Reserve," he clarified for the non-military folk in the room.

"He had nothing to do with attacking Wickham," Fania hastened to add. "When he found out about the site from some of the others in the fraternity, he was horrified. He only told me about it to see if I could figure out some way to take it down on my own."

Lizzy believed this part of the story. She hoped any decent human being would be horrified to learn about a site like that and do everything in his power to stop it. She'd meant it when she said it was admirable for Wa'il to enlist Fania's help in trying to expose it. That didn't, unfortunately, mean he was incapable of attacking Wickham, especially if he'd felt threatened, or thought that Fania might somehow be at risk if Wickham learned her part in the whistleblowing.

Caty seemed to be on the same train of thought as Lizzy. "Do you happen to know where Wa'il was the night that Wickham was attacked?"

Fania's face paled. "This is exactly what I was afraid of. That you would find a way to blame him, when he was the one trying to stop all of this."

Anne put an arm of comfort around her shoulders. "No one is trying to blame Wa'il. We're just trying to find answers."

Brandon spoke up quickly. "I know of Wa'il more by reputation than personally–I oversee more of the army recruits, and the naval group mostly keep to themselves. But I can vouch from everything I've heard about him that he's well-respected and liked."

Well-respected and liked people could still do stupid things, sometimes. But Lizzy also refrained from saying this out loud, less gleefully this time around.

Fania shook her head, visibly shaken by the entire encounter. "Wa'il was out with friends that night. They'd gone to New Orleans for a concert."

That would be easy enough to verify, if Wa'il and his friends would cooperate. Lizzy found herself strangely relieved. She wanted to find a way to absolve Darcy, but not at the expense of someone else. She believed in justice and fairness, but she also didn't know that Wickham hadn't gotten what he deserved. She would hate to see someone like Fania or Wa'il have their life ruined because of it. If only someone in a dark cape with a twirling mustache would appear and make themselves the obvious villain, that would make solving this crime a much more pleasant experience.

"We'll check in with him," Caty said, looking meaningfully at Tilney–as if there had been any doubt about who the 'we' in question could be. "And I guess that will be our primary focus until the next time we meet, unless anyone has any other ideas–?"

"What about Willoughby?"

The name startled the room into silence. Lizzy looked at Brandon in surprise. His face was set with resolve, and it was clear that he'd been itching to ask this question for a while, but holding himself back. Having spoken the words out loud now, he braced himself, clearly anticipating pushback. "It's possible, isn't it?"

He spoke to the room in general, but his eyes were on Nora. She gave her head a little shake. "Willoughby doesn't have anything to do with the site. And he isn't a Sigma Rho. What reason would he have for attacking Wickham?"

Nora was always careful, a little guarded, but she looked almost angry at the suggestion. Truthfully, that surprised Lizzy; she wouldn't have thought Nora would still be protective of Willoughby–not after what he'd done to Marianne.

"We've assumed there's no connection between Wickham and what happened with Marianne," Caty said slowly, as if piecing it together aloud. "But what if we were wrong?"

"I can look into it," Fania spoke up, uncharacteristically forceful. But then, Lizzy supposed, if she could somehow prove Willoughby's involvement, that would mean Wa'il was officially off the hook.

Silence fell over the room as they pondered through the possibilities. Before any more could be said on the matter, they were interrupted by a loud knocking on the front door.

Karoline rose to her feet. "That's probably Lucy. We have spa appointments in half an hour." At everyone's incredulous looks, she shrugged. "What? Like me getting a facial is really going to throw a wrench in us solving the case?"

Seemingly unfazed by the fact that this wasn't her home, Karoline disappeared to answer the door—only to reappear a moment later, looking positively stunned. "Um," she said, atypically at a loss for words.

Before Lizzy could mock her for her confused, fish-out-of-water look, a figure strode past Karoline into the room: Willoughby. The man himself. With his dark curls wind-tossed and his dark coat drenched, he looked like a Byronic hero stepped out of the pages of some Gothic romance. Maybe even Byron himself. Lizzy hadn't realized it was raining outside, and maybe it wasn't. Maybe that was just a testament to the power of Willoughby's Romantic intrigue.

"Where's Marianne?" he demanded, eyes half-wild with inner torment. "I need to speak with her, to explain everything..."

eight
october - 2 weeks before the event

THE PORTRAITS OF PEMBERLEY, and Lizzy's involvement with it, had been more than enough drama for the small Delta household. Alas, it was not to be the only scandal of the semester. Another strange development had taken place shortly after the Portraits of Pemberley site was finally uncovered: Willoughby had suddenly, and unaccountably, ghosted Marianne.

Marianne, like Lizzy and Nora, hadn't been too alarmed at first when Willoughby didn't respond right away to her texts about rewatching their favorite AOC documentary that night. As Marianne later, tearfully, told her sister and roommate, she and Willoughby liked to watch documentaries that broadened their social consciences on Thursday nights, so the plan was pretty much already set. She assumed that Willoughby was busy with coursework or grading or lost in a particularly tricky stanza, and that she would hear back from him as soon as he surfaced again.

Even when night came and still Willoughby hadn't responded, Marianne was more irritated than worried. She knew better than anyone, after all, how one could get caught up in a whirlwind of artistic passion, but would it really have been so disruptive to the creative process to send her one text?

By the time morning came and with it still no word from Willoughby, a frantic Marianne roused both Nora and Lizzy from their beds, demanding they help her form a search party. "I already called the police to report a missing person, but I can tell they don't take me seriously."

Nora looked at Lizzy, and Lizzy looked at Nora, both of them silently communicating the best way to deal with this. But Marianne was too wired on her several cups of coffee and adrenaline to be redirected, and despite all attempts at negotiation with sanity, Lizzy and Nora somehow found themselves roped into distributing the 'Missing' posters Marianne had apparently made and copied in bulk at the campus print shop at 3:00 that morning.

Finally, after passing out all the flyers, circling Willoughby's apartment several times, and driving a loop through Highbury to look for his car at his favorite vegan restaurant, coffee shop, and the animal shelter where he volunteered, Nora managed to persuade Marianne that they should return home and wait for Willoughby to get back in touch with her. "Maybe his phone died... Maybe there was a family emergency... Maybe he had to go to the ER..." Were the words used to lure a resisting Marianne back to the house.

While Marianne went to her room to call all the hospitals in a 50-mile radius, Lizzy and Nora conducted a whispered conference about how they should proceed. There was a slight likelihood, after all, that Marianne could be right and something terrible had happened to him, but in the age of cell phones and the multiple other ways to keep in touch, the far more likely scenario was that Willoughby was choosing for whatever reason to not get in contact.

"Did he seem distant to you the last time he was here?" Nora asked, fretting with the mug handle of her tea.

Lizzy shrugged her shoulders. "They were attached at the lip, like always. I had to clear my throat three times to get them to stop making out against the refrigerator." In short, business as usual.

"I'm sure there's some explanation," Nora said loyally, although her eyes said otherwise.

When a second night had passed and still no word, Marianne became more and more withdrawn, ignoring classes and all other social engagements as she scrolled, endlessly, through her phone, desperate for it to provide some answers.

And then, in the early hours of the next morning, a shriek.

Lizzy stumbled, only half awake, into the kitchen to find Nora rubbing Marianne's back, and Marianne deep into what seemed to already be a very long rant. "...so it could have been pre-scheduled, or we can't rule out the idea that someone else has his phone..."

Nora looked up, meeting Lizzy's gaze grimly. "Willoughby posted on Instagram this morning."

Lizzy took the phone from a trembling Marianne, looking at the seemingly innocuous image. It was a filtered sunrise over the Mississippi River, with a caption simply of a heart, along with a few lines written by an obscure Tibetan poet. She wouldn't say so out loud, but it seemed very much like the sort of thing Willoughby might post.

Something of this must have read on her face because Marianne slumped back into her chair. "I've texted him 32 times. I've left 13 voicemails. Why won't he answer me? Did I do something? Is this a test?"

In the silence that followed, Marianne rose to her feet, her cheeks flushed with indignation. "I don't care what it looks like. I won't believe the worst of him. He loves me, I know he does."

Lizzy didn't want to believe the worst in Willoughby either–for Marianne's sake, yes, but also because she too had genuinely believed in the weird connection the two of them shared.

But Lizzy's judgment wasn't exactly infallible, as she was increasingly learning.

By the time the end of the weekend rolled around, they had gotten used to this new normal: a silent, tense house, Marianne pacing or locked on her phone or both, Nora and Lizzy walking on eggshells.

Then, when Lizzy was out for one of her walks, she got the text from Nora:

Come home. Now.

And somehow, things only got worse from there.

ᎤᎴᎬ

It has been said that a picture is worth a thousand words, and while this adage may very well be true, at least in the Delta house that November morning, Lizzy had exactly zero words for the three pictures now on the screen before her.

Each picture was of Marianne, nude, and looking directly into the camera, her smile enticing, her gaze provocative. Someone had posted them to the English Department's Facebook page under what appeared to be a burner account–named, The Portraits of Pemberley.

The department secretary had been contacted and would hopefully soon be able to do an administrative override for the page and delete the photos. The English Department site wasn't often updated and presumably wasn't often viewed, so there was some little hope that perhaps not too many people had seen the pictures in question.

Then again, Austen University was a small little village, and word tended to travel quickly. It had been Anne who had contacted Nora with the news, and as Anne wasn't an English major or in any way affiliated with the department, one could only guess as to how she'd come across the information.

Behind Lizzy, Nora was on the phone, yet again trying to reach the English department secretary. It was a Saturday, and this was proving to be a more difficult task than it should have been. As Lizzy listened to Nora leave her fifth message of the morning, she quietly closed the laptop and prayed to whatever feminist goddesses existed to extend some mercy to Marianne. As one of their most devoted followers, they seem to have abandoned her most heartlessly (as immortal gods were wont to do).

With a sigh, Nora ended the call. For another long moment, neither one of them said anything. They hadn't yet said anything on the subject, not since Lizzy arrived home and Nora wordlessly showed her the page before telling her what steps she'd taken to correct it. Marianne had gone back to her room and hadn't made so much as a peep since then. There wasn't much, it seemed, that could be said, by any of them.

"Will you come with me to talk to her?" Nora asked at last, and Lizzy nodded.

They found Marianne, fully dressed, lying in her bed and staring up at the ceiling. There was evidence of recent tears on her face, though her eyes were currently dry. If she noticed her sister and Lizzy entering the room, she did nothing to acknowledge them.

Nora took a seat at the edge of the bed, and Lizzy sat on the opposite side, waiting for Nora to take the lead. She wanted to be there for both her friends, but there was nothing in the world that could match the bond between two sisters, even those as different as the Dashwoods.

"We're still waiting to hear back from the English secretary." Nora let this sit for a moment before adding, "Do you want to talk about it?"

Marianne still didn't acknowledge that either of them had entered the room with so much as a blink, so it surprised Lizzy when she suddenly spoke up. "What is there to say? You thought he'd betrayed me and you were right."

The accusation in her tone was unmistakable. Nora flinched, but pressed on gently, "You think it was Willoughby?"

"Who else would I have sent pictures like that to?" New tears sprung to Marianne's eyes, leaking down the sides of her face unchecked. "I trusted him with everything."

"But why?" Lizzy hadn't meant to speak, but the question blurted out, unchecked. "What would he gain from posting those pictures on the English Department Facebook page?"

Marianne lifted her head. "You think it might have been someone else?"

The naked hope in her voice was painful to listen to–she wanted so badly for it to be true. Nora shot Lizzy a warning glance, and too late she realized she might be encouraging Marianne to continue to cling to a dream of reconciliation that clearly wasn't going to happen.

"I don't know," Lizzy amended. "Like you said, he was the only one with those pictures."

The light that had briefly flared in Marianne's eyes snuffed out again, and she lowered her head back to the mattress. "I'm tired. I need to sleep."

Nora took her hand, squeezing it. "I can stay with you, if you want."

"I need to sleep," Marianne said again, rolling on her side so her back was to her sister.

Wordlessly, Nora and Lizzy left the room. When Lizzy glanced back at the doorway, Marianne was staring at the wall, unmoving and unblinking.

Back in the kitchen, Nora tried, and failed, yet again to reach the English secretary. She slammed her phone onto the countertop with more force than was necessary, uncharacteristically overcome with feeling. "If you have six missed calls from a number, even if it's one you don't recognize, you'd think you'd eventually pick up your phone."

Lizzy sympathized, but she was preoccupied with another idea. "Do Willoughby and Wickham know each other?"

"Does it matter?"

Lizzy knew her friend was under undue duress, so she forgave her snappishness. "I think it does. If Willoughby was the one who posted those pictures, why would he use the name 'The Portraits of Pemberley'?"

"Probably because that site is all over the news right now, so he hoped he wouldn't get caught if people thought it was all part of the same scandal."

"Fair enough." It did seem unlikely that Wickham had anything to do with Marianne's pictures. Not only did he have no affiliation with the English department and no access to their Facebook page, but the picture was also unlike any on the Portraits of Pemberley site: Marianne's face was fully in view, and her surroundings had been un-edited out of the photograph. It made sense that whoever had posted the pictures had wanted people to assume that it had been done by the same person to avoid drawing attention to themselves.

What *didn't* make sense was why Willoughby would have posted those pictures. She expressed as much to Nora. "He'd already ghosted her, and even though she was still trying to get in contact with him, eventually even Marianne would have had to let it go. So why publicly expose her like that?"

Nora looked unimpressed by Lizzy's questioning, her face bleak as she took a long sip of a cold cup of tea sitting out on the table. "Why do any of what he's done? I thought he really loved her."

So had Lizzy. Marianne and Willoughby had been a blazing forest fire, fast and searing and reckless, but he'd seemed to match Marianne's intensity. Then suddenly, without warning, he was gone.

It didn't make sense. None of it made any sense.

Lizzy was so caught up in trying to piece it together that it took her a moment to realize Nora's eyes were filled with tears. She blinked against them. "How is she supposed to get past this? This is going to follow her forever."

The words echoed the warning Palmer had given Lizzy about her own photograph—and at least she had been partially clothed, her face obscured from view. The thought infuriated her anew, the unfairness of it all—that she and Marianne and all those other girls had all been betrayed, and they were the ones who were going to keep paying for it for the rest of their lives.

Just as Lizzy reached for Nora to try to comfort her, the phone buzzed on the counter, and Nora jumped to her feet, wiping furiously at her eyes with the back of her hand as she answered. "Hello? Yes, this is Nora Dashwood. Thank you for getting back to me..."

nine

november - the day of the event

FRIDAY NIGHT PIZZA nights were not what they once had been. Aside from the obvious changes, like Lucy insisting on ordering a salad and loudly commenting on the amount of calories in each slice, were more subtle variations. Lizzy hadn't realized how much Marianne's vibrant, impassioned commentary about the crafting show made the night so much fun. But in the past few weeks since the breakup with Willoughby, nothing about Marianne had been 'vibrant' or 'impassioned'. She rarely if ever got out of bed, *never* went to classes, and she seemed to have been wearing the same pair of sweatpants and t-shirt ("Sorry, I Can't Hear You Over Your White Male Privilege") for days on end. Even her voluminous hair seemed flatter, more listless.

Without Marianne's outraged enthusiasm, Lizzy had no one to rile up, and Nora had no one to slyly tease, and so they were just a group of girls, silently watching TV and eating pizza.

Not that Lizzy begrudged Marianne her funk. She, herself, was feeling in a bit of a rut, and she had only experienced a small degree of what Marianne had been through. She'd been partially clothed in her picture, and it had remained anonymous until she'd decided to come forward and reclaim the story. The person who had betrayed her had been someone she barely knew, not the person she loved. And her confused feelings about Darcy and his maybe-feelings and then seeming

turnabout were nothing in comparison to what Marianne's disorienta-
tion must be after Willoughby's abrupt ghosting.

It wasn't a competition, she knew, but Lizzy's experience didn't
really compare. She was, all things considered, okay. Marianne was
clearly not.

A knock on the door interrupted their third episode, and Nora
paused it with a "Thank God" that seemed to surprise her as much as
everyone else. "Maybe it's someone dropping by?" she followed up, and
the hope in her voice was easy to translate: Maybe it was someone more
lively who could brighten up the evening.

That hope was very quickly dashed as Nora disappeared and
returned a moment later with Brandon in tow. Though he was an
extremely nice person, no one would ever have accused him of livening
up a get-together.

He cleared his throat, clearly uncomfortable with all the female
attention suddenly foisted upon him. "Hello. I remembered tonight was
pizza night but thought you might want some dessert." He held up a
box of macarons, which everyone knew were Marianne's favorite. Like
all of her other passions, this preference had been loudly advertised to
the world.

Brandon was trying hard not to look at Marianne, but he couldn't
quite keep his gaze from darting over to her to gauge her reaction. Her
face remained stony, unimpressed, and Lizzy had to resist the urge to tell
Brandon it wasn't anything personal, that she'd barely touched her pizza
and had been taking no comfort in food whatsoever over the past few
weeks, a concept that was personally foreign to Lizzy but seemed to be
true nonetheless.

"What a thoughtful gesture." Nora gave Brandon the smile that her
sister withheld, taking the box of macarons from him. "Will you join us?
We seem to have ordered too much pizza."

Brandon hardly seemed the type to be into competitive crafting
shows, but he gamely took a seat on the couch. Nora brightened her
smile, showing Marianne the bakery box. "Look, Marianne, macarons.
Wasn't that thoughtful?"

Marianne just stared at them blankly for a moment. "Willoughby
used to make those from scratch."

Everyone in the room tensed at the mention of that name, but Marianne said it without any visible emotion. Then she picked up a pale pink cookie and turned it around and around in her fingers, lost in some memory, though she made no move to eat it.

This was getting as bleak as a Brontë novel. Lizzy searched, desperately, for some way to salvage the evening. "So," she said. "Anyone hear about that mono outbreak in Denham Hall?"

Okay, so it wasn't her best conversational segue, but at least it had nothing to do with macarons.

Nora, Brandon, and Lizzy were able to carry on a polite conversation on the topic for a few blandly pleasant minutes as both Marianne and Lucy zoned out on their phones. After a short time, Marianne suddenly let out a shrill gasp, jumping to her feet.

For the first time in weeks, Marianne had color in her cheeks, and maybe it was only Lizzy's imagination, but her hair seemed to have somehow volumized on its own.

"Willoughby. Posted." Her voice was breathless, quivering with something that was an uncomfortable mix of rage and hope and anticipation and agony. "He's attending the Croft Gala tonight at the campus museum."

Lizzy, for one, had no idea what the Croft Gala was, though Marianne quickly informed them in that same breathless voice that the museum was hosting a traveling exhibition of maritime art. It somehow managed to sound even more boring than talking about a meningitis outbreak, but apparently it was where all the movers and shakers of Austen University would be that night.

After finishing her explanation, Marianne rushed off to her room. Exchanging a wordless look of worry, Nora and Lizzy followed after her.

"What are you doing, Marianne?" asked Nora as she watched Marianne tear through her closet.

Marianne's eyes were alight with a fierce, feverish glint. "I'm going to the Gala, of course."

"Oh, Marianne," said Nora, as Lizzy simultaneously spoke up, "I really don't think that's a good idea..."

"It's the perfect idea. The perfect place. The perfect time." Marianne settled on a dress she liked, ripping it out of the closet, hangar and all. "He won't be able to ignore me there. Not without causing a scene. He'll have to give me answers."

Another worried exchange of glances. Nora cleared her throat. "They aren't going to be answers you're going to like, Marianne. It's over between you two, truly. You know that, right?"

Marianne stiffened, as if the words physically pained her. Then she shook her head, vehemently. "At least they'll be answers."

She began rummaging for shoes. Nora looked to Lizzy pleadingly, as if she could somehow resolve this situation. Lizzy thought quickly. "I'm sure it will be a ticketed event, Marianne. And you don't have a ticket. How will you even get in?"

Marianne stilled, and for a moment, Lizzy thought she might have managed to talk some sense into her—until she abruptly barreled down the hall. Nora and Lizzy had to run to keep up with her.

The redhead stopped in front of Brandon, acknowledging him directly for the first time in–ever, maybe. "You're the GRA for Sigma Rho, right? Did they offer you any tickets for the Gala?"

Lizzy took a minute to catch up; Sigma Rho was the fraternity with ties to the armed forces, and since it was a maritime exhibit...

Brandon blinked at Marianne, as stunned to be in her direct glare as a deer caught in the headlights. Icarus approaching the sun. "Um... they made a couple available–"

"Great," Marianne didn't even wait for him to finish. "Then you'll take me as your date."

"Marianne." Nora sounded firm now. This was not her usual gentle coaxing with her volatile sister. "This is a truly terrible idea. It can't end in anything good. I'm begging you, don't go."

Lizzy expected fire, rage, tempest–but unexpectedly, Marianne's eyes flooded with tears. "I need to see him, Nora. I've been to his apartment, but he won't answer his door. He's stopped coming to class, and Professor Grey just looks at me like I'm pathetic every time I ask about him. He doesn't go to the same coffee shops, or breweries, or restaurants. It's like he's disappeared, and it's so unfair. He doesn't get to do that. He doesn't get to just run away like a coward. He needs to be held accountable. He needs to tell me *why*."

She cut such a pathetic figure, standing there in her sweatpants and t-shirts and wooly socks, clutching a dress to her chest, begging for resolution. Nora remained silent for a long moment. Then, she looked at Lizzy, sighing in resignation. "We're going to need to find more tickets..."

δλε

It took a little maneuvering, but at last they managed to procure tickets for all five of them (because, yes, Lucy had decided she needed to tag along once she looked through her social media and saw how many 'important' people would be going). Brandon had the brilliant idea of contacting Anne, who oversaw the Pi Kappa Sigma house. As a PhD candidate in neuroscience, Anne had been offered a ticket, and she also tracked down some extras that had been given to her father, and so an impromptu invitation was extended to Caty and Tilney–strength in numbers, and all.

They all got ready in record time and met Anne at the entrance to the museum. It was obvious this event hadn't been in her plans for the evening. She'd put on a dress, and even a little lipstick, but her hair was in its trademark ponytail, and she looked like she'd much rather be holed up having a pizza night of her own.

Nonetheless, she greeted them with warm smiles. "Thank you so much, Anne," Brandon said, kissing her cheek in greeting.

Lizzy took this in with some surprise. If she hadn't seen firsthand just how besotted Brandon was with Marianne, she might have wondered about him and Anne, but the current between them seemed to be purely friendly. She imagined they must have bonded over both being graduate RAs and having to deal with the tumultuous highs and lows of undergraduate students. (Like getting last-minute tickets to a gala so someone could confront the guy who'd ghosted her and most likely posted her naked pictures on a departmental Facebook page.)

Inside, Lizzy took in the glitz and glamour of the event with a little awe and also some healthy disdain. The museum was, admittedly, beautiful, with its high ceilings and stained-glass windows. But it was also such an incredible waste of money, when Lizzy knew firsthand how underpaid and overworked so many members of faculty and staff were, how overpriced the education was for students, how many undergraduates were drowning in student loans for a nebulous future that might never pay off.

At least, as she had suspected, the food spread was good. Lizzy had already eaten pizza for dinner that night, but there was always room for dessert; and she'd made sure to bring her big purse to smuggle away any portable food items, since she was certain her tuition was paying for tonight's events, anyway. Might as well get her fair share.

While the others were searching for Willoughby in the crowd, Lizzy happily beelined to the food table. She would be there for Marianne when the big showdown occurred, of course, but the event was well-populated and spread out over many rooms, so it might take a while to locate him. Lizzy was confident she'd be able to find the source of all the yelling and tears as soon as the confrontation began, as Marianne was not one to keep things quiet; and in the meantime, Lizzy would load up on snacks to share with the house in the days of grief (and hopefully, recovery) to come.

As she munched on some carrots and hummus, Lizzy's eyes were drawn to a photograph hanging over the table. It was of a middle-aged woman, beautiful, though it looked like she'd suffered a permanent injury to her jaw. Her eyes were defiant and bold as she gazed dead on at the camera, her chin held high as if daring the world to underestimate her.

Lizzy didn't know much about photography, but something about the image arrested her. It was a stirring sight, a testament to resilience and bravery. It deserved more than to be hung behind the snack table (and that was really saying something coming from Lizzy). Curious about the artist, she leaned forward to read the plaque.

Pemberley: A Portrait, by Fo-Hian Darcy.

"Lizzy Bennet. I should have known I'd find you here."

Lizzy stiffened at the sound of the unfortunately familiar voice, turning slowly to see Wickham standing behind her with a smug expression on his face. It was jarring to come face-to-face with him again; she'd seen him in Eliás's class, but had been careful to keep her distance. She wasn't 100% certain, of course, that he was the one behind the Portraits of Pemberley. But all the same, she knew. It was him. Hopefully it was only a matter of time before the police could prove it and charge him. All the same, she'd been advised by Professor Palmer to be careful about making allegations that could be considered libel. Wickham had never been named directly, though rumors spread quickly at a small school like Austen University.

She fell back half a step out of pure surprise, then instantly regretted it as she saw the look of smug satisfaction on his face at the thought that he'd cowed her. Locking her feet in place, Lizzy raised her chin to glare at him. "What are you doing here? Offense intended, but you don't exactly strike me as one of the Austen University elite."

Wickham smirked. "I actually have you to thank for that, Lizzy. It turns out, there are a number of men on the board who are sympathetic to a young man being unfairly targeted by a hysterical, attention-seeking female. I've been welcomed into quite a few new, powerful circles. So, cheers." He lifted his drink in salute and took a long sip.

Lizzy stared at him, not wanting to believe it was true, but suspecting from what she was beginning to understand about the world, that it was. She searched her mind, desperate for something clever or cutting to say. "It's so nice when perverts can find each other. Best of luck to you all. I certainly hope none of you choke on overpriced appetizers or spontaneously combust from an overabundance of evil. That would suck."

With that, she tried to make a hasty escape, but Wickham was not about to let her out of his clutches so easily. He was enjoying this too much. "You might want to go easy on the desserts." He motioned to her newly heavy bag. "I'm not saying I had anything to do with those pictures on the Portraits of Pemberley site–which, of course, I didn't– but I did notice that whoever cropped your photo had to cut out quite a bit more of you than some of the other girls. I think it was supposed to be a sexy site, you know, and cellulite is one of those things that once you start, it's a slippery slope."

He was trying to get a rise out of her, Lizzy knew that, but it still stung, even though she really didn't want it to. She swallowed. "Funny. I've heard the same thing about male-pattern baldness."

She had never actually noticed any bald patches on Wickham–if anything, he had infuriatingly nice hair–but she must have struck a chord because suddenly Wickham's eyes darkened and he took a threatening step toward her. "I heard something interesting from one of my new friends. Apparently if you tell a journalist something off-the-record, they're not allowed to print it. So if I were to tell you something off-the-record, you couldn't attribute it to me officially, and even if you were to repeat it elsewhere, it would just be your word against mine."

Lizzy didn't say anything, just stared at him, half-wary and half-compelled to see where this was going.

"Well, off-the-record, I made that site. Off-the-record, there were over one hundred girls on there before I took it down. Off-the-record, the site might be down, but we still have ways of sharing those pictures that you'll never be able to trace. Off-the-record, I only chose you because we had a few requests for big boobs, but personally, I was glad you turned out to be such a frigid prude so I didn't have to go through with anything." Wickham grinned at her cruelly, letting all of this sink in. "And because of the way Darcy was looking at you at that bar, of course."

As if his mention of the name had summoned him, Darcy–the man himself–suddenly appeared at Lizzy's side. He didn't spare Wickham a single glance, his eyes honed in on Lizzy–determined, it seemed, to get her as far away from Wickham as possible. "Elizabeth, would you like to–"

"Yes," Lizzy agreed before he could finish, desperate to get out of Wickham's orbit, away from his cruelty and maliciousness.

It was only as Darcy took her by the elbow, the other hand on the small of her back, guiding her forward, that Lizzy realized what she had just agreed to.

She and Darcy were going to dance.

chapter
ten

"I'M SORRY IF I OVERSTEPPED," Darcy murmured into her ear as they joined the other couples on the dance floor. "You looked uncomfortable, so I wanted to intervene, but we don't actually have to dance. If you don't want to."

His voice sounded detached, almost monotone, and the old Lizzy might have been irritated, looking to this as proof of his condescension, picking apart every phrase, every word. Post-letter Lizzy, however, heard something else in his stilted tone, felt his uncertainty in the slight flex of his hand. Like he wanted to hold her there but knew he shouldn't.

Or maybe that was only fanciful thinking. Darcy had never outright expressed any romantic interest in her before the letter, and nothing in his behavior since then suggested that lingering look at her lips had been anything but her imagination.

"It's all right." Lizzy tried her best for nonchalance. "Any excuse to leave a conversation with Wickham is a welcome one." Remembering his cruel, disgusting words, Lizzy shivered. She swallowed, meeting Darcy's gaze. "Thank you."

Darcy didn't say anything in return, but the indecisive hand on her back finally settled into place on her lower back.

They danced in silence for a few moments. Lizzy ran through a hundred different things to say in her mind, before finally settling on, "I've been meaning to reach out to you. Since I got your letter. I'm..."

She shook her head, still trying to find the right words, before ultimately landing on complete candor, "...such a judgmental bitch."

Darcy laughed silently at that, his face breaking into a broad smile. That sight–his smile–was so rare that Lizzy's breath caught in her throat. It completely transformed his face, that smile, made him look almost...approachable. "Well, I'm an egotistical dick. So I suppose we're in good company."

Feeling his eyes on her, Lizzy looked away, fighting her own smile. Remembering the full contents of the letter, she sobered. "I'm really sorry about what happened to Guanyin."

She hated to be the reason that Darcy's infrequent smile faded, but she felt it needed to be said. Not just because what had happened to Guanyin was truly terrible, but because it had meant so much that he trusted Lizzy enough to tell her that information.

"I'm sorry about what happened to *you*," Darcy said after a moment.

Their gazes connected again, and Lizzy felt herself blurting, "I didn't sleep with Wickham. For the record. Whatever it might have looked like in that picture."

Darcy cleared his throat. "It wouldn't matter if you–"

"I know. But I didn't."

They continued to stare at each other, something nebulous and unspoken passing between them. Feeling embarrassed, though she didn't know precisely by what, Lizzy searched her mind for some way to change the subject. "I saw your photograph. It was...moving."

Darcy blinked in surprise, then looked away with a wry smile. "Not a bad shot for an amateur photographer. It was my aunt's insistence that got it hung up in the gallery, not mine."

His gaze darted back to hers, and she could see that he, too, was embarrassed. It didn't speak much to her character, she realized with a sinking feeling in the pit of her stomach, that people felt like they had to explain themselves around her so she didn't jump to conclusions. It was a conclusion she very well might have jumped to about Darcy not so long ago. "She was right. It's an impressive portrait. It deserves its place here."

Silence between them, but this time it felt less uncomfortable. Lizzy hated to ruin the moment, but her curiosity won out. "I couldn't help but notice that it was called Pemberley...?"

The rest of the question didn't need to be voiced. Darcy understood right away. "It's the name of the women's shelter. For the safety of the women who live there, I thought it better to call it by the name of the place rather than the person."

Pemberley–the women's shelter that Darcy had been trying to get Lizzy to write a story about for the school paper. She knew from Caty's sleuthing that Pemberley was the name of his family's charitable companies, but she hadn't realized it was also the name of the shelter itself. "Why doesn't it come up in an online search?" she asked aloud, clarifying, "The shelter, not the photograph."

"Again, for the safety of the women, we don't like to advertise the name of the shelter or where it's located. Many of the people who stay there are trying to escape from dangerous situations."

And Wickham had co-opted the name to create his voyeuristic porn site. The site on its own had already been despicable, but knowing this history of the name made Lizzy truly loathe the boy behind it. What should be synonymous with providing a safe place for women was now connected to the idea of exploiting and monetizing them.

They once again fell into an uncomfortable silence, this one not out of embarrassment, but what was perhaps a mutual anger and helplessness. If Wickham were telling the truth about his new connections, it seemed unlikely that he would receive much of a punishment, either from the school or the legal system. He had ruined so many lives, and tried to ruin even more, and he would get away with it all.

The thought was interrupted by a shout of righteous anger that echoed across the room–turning heads, even causing the live band to briefly stop playing in confusion.

There was only one person Lizzy knew who would wear her heart so fully on her sleeve, make such a public spectacle of her pain without any regard to what others might think.

Marianne had found Willoughby.

chapter
eleven

AS EXPECTED, all Lizzy had to do to locate Marianne was to follow the raised voices and general discomfort. She pushed her way through a crowd who had gathered to watch the show as Marianne worked her feminist magic and put Willoughby in his place.

Only, Marianne wasn't towering over Willoughby in her stilettos, quoting Gloria Steinhem at him as she reduced him to a quivering puddle of patriarchal pissant. Lizzy drew up in surprise at the sight of Marianne on her knees, tears streaming down her face as she held out her hands in supplication to a visibly embarrassed Willoughby.

"I don't understand *why*. Please, just tell me. What did I do wrong? I'll change it, whatever it is. I'll be whatever you want me to be."

Nora stood at Marianne's side, back turned toward Willoughby and the crowd, almost as if she could physically shield Marianne from any shame if she didn't acknowledge them. "Get up, Mar," she pleaded. "Come with me."

Lizzy didn't think–just reacted, instinctively, to the pain on both the Dashwood sisters' faces–and moved in to Marianne's other side. "Come on, Marianne," she joined in, sparing Willoughby only one quick, scathing look. "He's not worth it."

Then Tilney and Caty appeared, seemingly out of thin air, by their sides. They didn't say anything, just helped Nora and Lizzy to form a human barricade between Marianne and Willoughby. "Come on, Marianne," they all urged, until Marianne numbly reached out and allowed them to help her to her feet, never breaking her gaze from Willoughby's back.

Even with their combined efforts, the quartet struggled to support a nearly comatose Marianne. Someone moved in next to Lizzy, and she looked up in surprise to see that Darcy had followed her. Their gazes met briefly before he offered his arm to Marianne. "Here. Lean on me. I'll get you out of here," he promised her quietly.

Marianne doubtless had little idea who it was who had come to her rescue; she had never had especially flattering things to say about Darcy, but whatever small part of her was still functioning seemed to recognize the kind authority in his voice, and she sagged gratefully against him.

Watching them, and the unexpectedly gentle way Darcy supported Marianne through the crowd, Lizzy wondered if Darcy was seeing Guanyin in all of this. Knowing a little bit more about him now, Lizzy didn't doubt Darcy would help Marianne just because it was the gentlemanly thing to do. But she also suspected that a part of him was glad to be here for Marianne in this moment, when he might not have been able to do the same for Guanyin during the fallout from her experience, and the thought made Lizzy's eyes sting with unexpected tears.

As she followed behind them, Lizzy cast a last glance over her shoulder at Willoughby. He still hadn't turned to face them, but an older woman had approached him, touching his shoulder. She was the sort of person who would have been very attractive, if her expression wasn't so unpleasant; and the way she touched Willoughby was almost gloating, as if she'd managed to nab the last designer bag at a fire sale.

"Undergrads," she said, loud enough to evoke a round of uncomfortable chuckles from everyone within earshot.

With the help of Darcy, they managed to get Marianne to the exit, where they encountered a concerned Brandon. Taking one look at Marianne's state, Brandon set his jaw, swallowing. "I'll get the car..."

As they waited, Karoline found them, her radar–as always–honed in on Darcy. "There you are! I've been looking everywhere!" Her eyes zeroed in on Lizzy, narrowing. "Bennet. I didn't realize they were giving out charity tickets."

Lizzy was distracted from her scathing comeback by the realization that Lucy Steele was at Karoline's side, the two of them literally arm in arm. Lucy beamed, far happier than she had ever been in the Delta house. "Karoline and I have been hanging out all night," she gushed. "We have *so* much in common."

"So much," Karoline echoed. "I was absolutely flabbergasted to hear she was a Delta."

"I've only been staying there," Lucy hastened to correct. "Temporarily. As a favor."

Funny, how that seemed to imply that Lucy had been the one doing *them* a favor by staying there.

"Well, we'll have to correct that, won't we?" Karoline shot a sly look in Lizzy's direction, and Lucy giggled.

If Karoline thought that taking Lucy Steele off their hands would irritate Lizzy, she certainly wasn't going to do anything to disabuse that notion. Frankly, as far as she was concerned, they deserved each other. "We're leaving," Lizzy informed Lucy, casting a pointed glance over her shoulder. "Marianne is unwell."

"Oh no!" Lucy sounded genuinely distressed, and for a moment Lizzy almost clowned herself into believing it was on Marianne's behalf–until Lucy turned to Karoline. "We were having such a good time together."

"Don't worry, babe. I'll help you get home." Karoline beamed smugly at Lizzy. "You go look after your little friend."

"Great." Lizzy barely refrained from adding that it wouldn't be the worst thing if Lucy never came back. She had a feeling Karoline's interest in Lucy might fade the moment she realized the Deltas couldn't stand her, and Lizzy wanted to give Lucy enough time to worm her way in until Karoline could no longer get rid of her.

By then, Brandon had returned with the car. After helping Marianne inside, Lizzy moved to squash in alongside Nora, Tilney, and Caty in the backseat–then hesitated, realizing she hadn't said goodbye to Darcy, or thanked him, even for his help.

He was standing up a few steps, watching her. Their gazes met wordlessly for a long moment, but Lizzy realized she didn't know what to say.

"Darcy!" Karoline called impatiently from inside, and he turned his head at the sound of his name.

Flustered, Lizzy climbed into the car. There was some commotion as they tried to figure out how to fit four of them in (Caty and Tilney had ridden with Anne on the way over), so by the time all of that was sorted and the car began pulling away, Lizzy assumed Darcy would be long gone.

But when she dared a glance back through the rear window, she saw him on the steps, watching after them.

chapter
twelve

MARIANNE REMAINED VIRTUALLY catatonic on the ride home, responding to no one and nothing, her face the picture of pain as she stared ahead in agonized silence. It was, understandably, not the most pleasant car ride for those squashed into Brandon's Lexus, and even Tilney had conceded to the somber mood by agreeing to keep the radio off the entire drive (a none-too-remarkable sacrifice for most, but for Tilney, the sign of true friendship).

Back at the Delta house, Marianne dropped into the nearest chair, continuing to stare forward at nothing at all, but Nora finally managed to persuade her to take a bath. They disappeared to the back of the house, Nora's hushed voice being muted by the closed door.

"Go home," Lizzy told Tilney, Caty, and Brandon, taking pity. There was no need for all of them to wallow in this fresh misery. "We'll be okay."

"Are you sure?" asked Caty, brow furrowed with worry. Almost simultaneously, Tilney added, "Let us know if you need anything—*anything*. I have absolutely no compunction about using my father's credit card."

Lizzy promised them that she would contact them if the need arose for kindly commiseration or vaguely illegal splurging, then ushered Caty and Tilney out the door. She was surprised, then not surprised at all, to see Brandon lingering in the living room, unwilling to leave. He raked a hand through his hair. "Give me something to do, or I'll lose my mind," he told her gravely.

Taking pity on him, Lizzy decided to manufacture some task. There was not a scenario in which she could imagine Marianne actually returning Brandon's feelings; Marianne had once scoffingly referred to him as the "trifecta of the patriarchy," whatever that meant. But Brandon clearly needed something to feel like he was helping, if even in some small way. "Ice cream," she told him. Lizzy doubted Marianne would be wanting dessert any time soon, but surely there would have to come a time when the three Delta roommates sat together and ate ice cream again—she hoped.

Brandon perked up at the order. "What kind?"

"Yes," Lizzy answered, and Brandon nodded his understanding, exiting quickly.

With the living room now empty, Lizzy battled with her own feelings of helplessness. She doubted Nora would need her help with Marianne in the bathroom, but she wanted to do something else to help both her roommates, even if only in some small way. So she tidied the living room, put away the dishes in the kitchen, even cleaned out the microwave just for something to do.

When all of that had been accomplished and there was still no sign of Nora or Marianne, Lizzy began to pace, worrying her fingernails with her teeth as she tried to think what, if anything, might help Marianne. Her experience paled in comparison to what her roommate had been through, so she didn't fully trust her own instincts on the matter.

There was only one other person Lizzy knew who might begin to understand what Marianne was going through. Or at least, knew *of*. Guanyin Darcy had been in a very similar position to Marianne, and might very well be able to give some advice or perspective on the process of overcoming that kind of trauma.

It was tricky, of course, because the story had been told to Lizzy in confidence, and she didn't actually know Guanyin. She didn't want to be presumptuous, or pressure Guanyin into doing anything she wasn't comfortable with, but if Guanyin was willing and could offer Marianne even one iota of comfort...

Lizzy pulled up Darcy's contact information on her phone, hesitating. This didn't really feel like a texting kind of conversation, but it felt presumptuous to call him out of the blue. Especially after the moment they'd had at the gala–there had been a moment, hadn't there? She didn't know entirely what it meant, but she also knew she didn't want Darcy thinking that she was calling him with any kind of romantic pretext...

For some reason, it felt less daunting to approach Darcy in person. That way there wouldn't be any strange subtext between them because she could see his expressions, his body language, and make sure her request wasn't making him uncomfortable. Yes, in-person would definitely be better. She could just run over to the Theta house and see if he was back from the gala. If not, no harm, no foul, and no phone trail.

Lizzy checked the time, debating for a moment whether 11:00 was too late to knock on the door at the Theta house–then remembered they were a fraternity, and that doubtless, most peoples' nights had only just begun. After changing quickly into some more comfortable clothes, Lizzy sent a quick text to Nora to let her know she was heading out: **I HAVE AN IDEA. BE BACK SOON. CALL IF YOU NEED ANYTHING.**

δλε

It took less than five minutes to walk to the Theta house, but by the time she got there, Lizzy was already second-guessing herself. This was a bad idea, or even if it wasn't, it could probably wait until morning...

She might have talked herself out of walking up the long Theta drive if she hadn't bumped into Rushworth, heading in the opposite direction. He did a double-take at the sight of her, squinting as he studied her face. "Wait, I know you, right?"

Lizzy had to suppress a sigh. She and Rushworth had interacted several times in the past couple years. Regardless, he didn't seem to be capable of retaining her in his memory, oversaturated with beer pong as it was. "It's Lizzy Bennet." Seeing a still-blank face, she added, "From the Isabella Thorpe dinner-party thing?"

"Oh, yeah!" Rushworth stopped in place, as though ready to have a long chat to catch up, even though moments before he'd had no idea who she was. "How's it hanging?"

Realizing it might be a long night if she didn't excuse herself from the conversation quickly, Lizzy motioned toward the Theta house. "I'm just here to see Darcy." Too late, she realized the implications of coming to a frat house late a night, and flushed as she added, "I have a question to ask him about an article we're working on."

Rushworth shook his head before she'd even finished speaking. "Nah, Darcy just left. I saw him leaving the house."

That wasn't a scenario Lizzy had anticipated. She'd thought he might still be at the gala, or if not then at home; but where would he be going so late at night? Not that it mattered, really. Rushworth was also leaving the house after 11:00, and Lizzy wasn't second-guessing that–although, somehow it seemed fitting with him. Darcy didn't really strike her as a booty-call-at-midnight kind of guy. Maybe he was heading back to the gala? "Was he dressed up?" she asked before she could stop herself, even though she knew this was truly none of her business. "Suit and tie?"

"Um, no. It looked like maybe he was going to the gym? He was in, like, a dark hoodie and track pants."

The gym? At this hour? Lizzy supposed it was possible, knowing Darcy, but it seemed like overkill to work out late at night and swim laps first thing in the morning, too. Or maybe he was breaking his normal routine?

Or maybe, Lizzy reminded herself firmly, this was none of her business. She was not Karoline Bingley. She did not have Darcy's schedule memorized. "Okay, well. Thanks."

She gave a little wave and started back the other direction, only making it a few steps before Rushworth called after her, "You feel like hot wings? My treat?"

Lizzy didn't really know how to respond to that, so she just pretended she hadn't fully heard him and waved again. Rushworth waved back, seemingly not at all put off by this rejection, and continued into the night.

δλε

Since Lizzy hadn't heard back from Nora, she decided to extend her walk around Greek Row, if only to expend some of her restless energy that was making her anxiety flare up. She was not really one to dwell on morbid thoughts, or give much credence to omens or "bad energy." She liked to think she was very much grounded in reality, and that there was nothing so dire that she couldn't find a way to laugh through it. But tonight, that heaviness pressed down on her–Marianne's pain and Willoughby's betrayal and Wickham's cruelty and Darcy's... well, just Darcy altogether, full stop.

Without overthinking it too much, she pulled out her phone and called the one person who always managed to put the world into perspective and twist the lens of the kaleidoscope so all the pieces rearranged themselves into something good.

"Hi!" Lizzy's older sister, Jane, sounded gratifyingly happy to hear from her. "It's late there. Is everything okay? I'm so happy to hear from you!"

All of this was said in one cheerful train of thought, and Lizzy felt herself relaxing at even the sound of her sister's voice. They'd always been the closest of all the Bennet sisters, not because they had so much in common, but because they were so little alike, but admired each other in their differences. Lizzy was Jane's snarky alter ego, and Jane was the persistent sun that outshone Lizzy's cynical raincloud. Talking to Jane made Lizzy feel like she was being pulled into a different world, a life entirely separate from her time at Austen University. Jane Bennet belonged in only the happiest of stories, after all.

"It's not so late," Lizzy returned, falling–gratefully–back into their usual cadence, Jane's optimism and Lizzy's wryness and the two of them balancing out to somewhere pleasantly in the middle. "For vampires, or musicians, probably."

"Why are you calling? Not that I'm not excited to hear from you, but it's not Tuesday."

Jane and Lizzy had a regular routine of catching up on Tuesday nights. Sunday night, all of the Bennets chimed in to fill Lizzy in on the latest gossip and complaints and headaches, but Tuesday was sacred time set aside for just the eldest two Bennet sisters. Why Tuesday, of all days, had been chosen, Lizzy couldn't remember, but she imagined it must have something to do with trying to have something to look forward to on an otherwise completely unexceptional day of the week.

At Lizzy's pause, Jane's tone dimmed around the edges a bit. "Is everything all right?" She'd been worrying about Lizzy since the Portraits of Pemberley incident, and in turn Lizzy had been concerned that she was worrying too much. They made a happy pair, both of them fretting that the other was fretting.

Lizzy thought about explaining the entire evening to her, but decided ultimately it would only put her burden on Jane's shoulders, not ease any of her own. All she wanted was the chance to talk to her sister and have a happy diversion. "I've been thinking a lot," she said, "about Tom Hardy and dogs."

Jane laughed, seeming pleasantly surprised by the turn the conversation had taken. "Tom Hardy and dogs? Is Tom Hardy in a dog movie?" A sudden alarm filled her voice. "Not one where the dog dies though, right...?"

"No. There's a whole thing about Tom Hardy loving dogs and bringing his dog with him on the red carpet at film premiers and looking like the happiest kid in the entire world whenever he's in a picture with a dog. Like pure abandonment gleefulness. And it's wonderful, but it's also given me a sort of existential crisis. Has anything ever made me as happy as dogs make Tom Hardy? Would dogs make *me* as happy as they make him? Or would I be the dog in this scenario, and it's just that I haven't found my Tom Hardy...?"

She continued to ramble on with similar bright, sparkly nonsense, with Jane obligingly going along with it, until Lizzy at last decided it was time to stop looping around Greek Row and head back to the Delta house. "Well, that's me," she said as she reached her driveway. "Thanks for helping me channel my inner surly but lovable British movie star."

"No problem. Talk to you Tuesday?"

"Talk to you Tuesday," Lizzy agreed.

She had just stepped into the front entryway when she bumped into Nora, who gave a start of fright. "Oh." She clutched at her chest, her face flushing a bit as if she'd just run up a hill. "God, you scared me. I was just coming to lock the front door—I didn't know you were still out."

"Sorry." Lizzy shut the door behind her, lowering her voice. "Is Marianne asleep?"

"I think so. I *hope* so. She's been quiet for a while."

Lizzy searched her friend's face. "Are *you* okay? What can I do for you?"

Nora managed a small smile. "Nothing. Really. I think I just want to go to sleep. I'll check on Marianne first, make sure she's all right."

Lizzy followed her back toward the bedrooms, intending to get ready for bed herself. She had only managed to put toothpaste to toothbrush when Nora called her name, frantic in a way that felt antithetical to Nora Dashwood. "Lizzy!"

Racing into Marianne's bedroom, Lizzy found Nora standing over the bed, which was conspicuously empty and Marianne-free.

"Where is she?" Nora's eyes were wild, filled with the same dread that had filled Lizzy at the all-too-ominous sight of that empty bed. With any other roommate, she might have assumed some innocuous explanation before jumping straight to dread. Maybe said roommate had decided to spend the night at a friend's, or was studying late at the library. Those were the reasonable explanations one usually assumed in such circumstances.

But Marianne and reason did not really go hand in hand. With everything that had gone down that night with Willoughby—and frankly, with all of Marianne's behavior since Willoughby had ghosted her—the fact that she'd snuck out of the house late at night without telling anyone where she was going did not bode well.

Lizzy couldn't afford to spiral, though; as the sister, Nora had that privilege. Lizzy would need to be the designated adult. "I'll text Tilney," she said. "He'll loan us his car."

chapter
thirteen

TILNEY, true friend and secret softie did one better than loaning them the car: He drove them all around Highbury, reasoning that three pairs of eyes were better than two. While this might have been true, Lizzy knew the real reason was that he wouldn't have been able to sleep knowing that Marianne was missing, and she loved him for it.

They drove around campus, along Greek Row, past the bar that sometimes hosted open mics that Marianne read her poetry at, and even past Willoughby's apartment, but there was no sign of her anywhere. Nora grew more and more still with each passing minute that Marianne remained missing, like she was afraid to move or even breathe. Like even the act of taking in air might break her open.

"Maybe the Crescent?" Tilney suggested. "Marianne likes their scones?"

The Crescent wouldn't be open for a few more hours, but no one had any better ideas, so they headed in that direction. Then Nora's phone rang, shattering the silence.

She jumped, then blinked at the name flashing across her screen. "It's Brandon," she said aloud, dumbly, before answering. She listened for a moment as her face somehow became even more pale and twisted with agony, before murmuring, "I understand," and hanging up.

To an anxious Tilney and Lizzy, she broke the news: "Marianne's in the hospital. She's been hit by a car."

δλε

Brandon was sitting in the hospital waiting room, his face in his hands, his posture a portrait of agony. He was wearing dark running pants and a white t-shirt—and, notably, the t-shirt was drenched in blood.

This was such a striking and horrifying sight that Lizzy somehow didn't realize—until long after Nora had gone in search of Marianne's doctor, insisting that she needed to go alone—that Anne Eliás was sitting next to Brandon, hand on his shoulder, offering him quiet comfort.

She was the one to explain to Lizzy and Tilney, since Brandon was too distraught to do so, what had happened. "Brandon was out jogging when he found Marianne on the side of the road. Whoever hit her hadn't stopped. He didn't know how long she'd been there, but she was semi-conscious and bleeding pretty heavily. Brandon used his sweatshirt to make a tourniquet and called 9-1-1. We've been here for about half an hour and we're still waiting to hear back on how she's doing."

A long moment of stunned silence followed this retelling, as Lizzy and Tilney processed the information. Lizzy swallowed back tears. The thought of vivacious, beautiful Marianne lying injured on the side of the road, no one stopping to help her... it made her sick to her stomach. The thought of poor Brandon, finding her like that... "But she's going to be okay, right? They said she's going to be okay?"

Anne swallowed. It was not in her nature to give false hope, Lizzy knew. So she said nothing.

Another long silence fell. At last, Tilney spoke up: "Brandon, you go jogging at midnight?" At everyone else's blank stare, Tilney shifted. "I know that isn't the point of the story, but it's...it's kind of weird. Impressive—"

Brandon stood up abruptly and left. Tilney looked after him, crestfallen. "I'm sorry. I always say the wrong thing at the wrong time." He shook his head, dragging a hand across his eyes. "How could someone just leave her there?"

Lizzy couldn't answer that. She couldn't fathom it. Another long silence fell.

"I'm gonna buy him a t-shirt in the gift shop." Tilney motioned after Brandon. "He probably wants to change, right? That would be helpful?"

Anne offered him a small smile. "I think that would be very thoughtful, Tilney. Thank you."

After he left, Anne exchanged a glance with Lizzy. "Some people just need something to do, when something like this happens."

Lizzy understood. She felt restless, crazy with not knowing what to say or do. She desperately wanted to find Nora and make sure she was all right. She wanted, even more desperately, to hear that Marianne was going to be okay.

Before she could form this into a reasonable plan of action, Brandon returned, his eyes bloodshot. Anne rose to her feet and enveloped him in a soundless hug, rubbing his back and offering him silent comfort. This lasted for a few long moments, before Brandon pulled back a little. "Has anything–"

"No change yet." Anne continued to smooth her hand along his back, trying to smile a little. "Tilney went to–"

She stopped suddenly, the smile on her face fading as her eyes locked on something across the room. Fearing that it was the doctor returning with obviously bad news, Lizzy turned–but was surprised when she saw that Anne was looking at a familiar-looking man in his early thirties. It took Lizzy a moment to place him, but then she remembered he was Wentworth, one of the detectives who'd been conducting investigations into Isabella's death the previous semester. He stared at Anne a moment before coming over, seeming reluctant to do so.

Good old Southern manners. One didn't simply ignore an acquaintance in a hospital waiting room. "Hi, Anne." Wentworth's voice was guarded, but his gaze was assessing as he looked her over. "Did something happen?"

"Our friend was hit by a car." The usually unflappable Anne sounded uncomfortable, and a little bit winded, like she'd just run up a flight of stairs. "You?"

"I'm here on a case." Wentworth's eyes darted to Anne's hand, still on Brandon's back.

She quickly dropped it back to her side. "Oh."

A long, uncomfortable moment passed. Wentworth cleared his throat. "Your friend, was it a hit and run?" Anne nodded, swallowing and blinking back tears. "You spoken to the police yet?"

Another nod from Anne. "I think his name is Harville?"

Wentworth nodded back at that. "Good. Good. He's a good guy. He'll get it sorted out."

More awkwardness ensued, before Wentworth jerked his thumb toward the door. "I better..." But the sentence remained ultimately unfinished as he turned and abruptly left the room.

That was...weird. In the grand scheme of the entire night, though, it wasn't the strangest thing that had happened, not by a long shot. Lizzy decided it was time to find Nora. "I'll be back," she said to the room at large before turning to wander down the direction that Nora had disappeared a few minutes ago.

She'd only been doing so for a few seconds before her phone buzzed. Hoping it would be Nora, Lizzy quickly checked her screen–and was surprised to see it was Caty.

A surge of unexpected panic, mixed with sadness, filled Lizzy at the sight of her friend's name. Caty didn't know yet what had happened to Marianne. Lizzy would have to be the one to tell her. The thought of it filled her with dread.

But when she opened the text, this thought was temporarily distracted by Caty's ambiguous message: **HAVE YOU SEEN WHAT HAPPENED TO WICKHAM?**

volume three

"I think I am justified—though where so many hours have been spent in convincing myself that I am right, is there not some reason to fear I may be wrong?"

- Jane Austen, *Sense and Sensibility*

one
november - 3 days until darcy is expelled

OF ALL THE divisive personalities that had populated the Austen Murder Club, however unwittingly, Willoughby might actually be the worst. While Lizzy might have once wished for a different personality to liven up the new meetings of the Austen Murder Club, she hadn't meant someone quite so divisive as Willoughby. He'd ghosted Marianne, most likely had something to do with posting her naked pictures online, caused her further public humiliation at the Croft Gala, and had led to her being hit by a car and left for dead in the early hours of the morning. Granted, this last part had not been entirely his doing, but even indirectly, he had most certainly been the cause.

Lizzy looked to Nora to gauge her friend's response, but was surprised to find Nora looking at Brandon. It was a brief, furtive exchange, but it struck Lizzy as being odd. She couldn't quite pinpoint what was strange in it; she could hardly have even named the emotion behind that look, it had come and gone so quickly. Perhaps what was notable was that it had happened at all. Why would Nora look at *Brandon* during a moment of emotional distress?

Unless...Lizzy reassessed everything she'd observed about the Sigma Rho GRA thus far. She'd always assumed that Brandon's regular visits to the Delta house, his courteousness in looking after Marianne, had been because he had feelings for *Marianne*. Was it possible that it was Nora who he was actually interested in? He had seemed to go out of his way to do things to please Marianne, like bringing over macarons when everyone knew they were her favorite. (Notably, he'd never brought over the ice cream Lizzy had sent him to get—maybe because she didn't have that Dashwood charm?). But Lizzy of all people should have known that when there were sisters involved, sometimes a suitor might go out of his way to impress the sister he *wasn't* interested in to curry favor with the sister he *was* interested in. How many times had Lizzy herself benefited from free pizza, lavish birthday gifts, and early morning rides to the airport from guys who were trying to impress Jane?

The revelation was hardly the most relevant matter at the moment, though, so Lizzy decided to revisit that possibility later. Nora had now turned her cool, collected attention back to Willoughby. "You don't get to come in here and demand *anything* about Marianne. You forfeited that right a long time ago."

To everyone's surprise, Willoughby deflated in front of them, sinking down to his knees and covering his face with his hands. "I know. I've made the worst mistake of my life. I fell in love with a beautiful Titania, and instead of cherishing her I tore off her wings and threw her to the wolves."

It was sort of jarring to see someone that emotionally bare, an open wound in human form. This quality elicited sympathy, certainly, but also a strong desire to cover it with a bandage before it spurted out all over everyone in the room.

Seeming to sense he might be gaining some leeway, Willoughby held out his hands to Nora, imploring. "Let me explain myself. Please. I'm a bad guy but I'm not *the* bad guy you think I am. Let me tell my side of the story and *you* can tell it to Marianne, if you think I deserve that kindness."

Nora looked at Lizzy, the uncertainty in her face a perfect mirror. They were both too practical to know what to do with this kind of unfettered emotional display. Marianne would have been much better at handling this... but then, that was why they had been drawn to each other, and most likely why things had gone so catastrophically wrong.

One person in the room, at least, was unmoved by this saccharine display. "I'll go make the popcorn," Tilney drawled as he rose to his feet. He cast an unimpressed side-eye at Willoughby. "This oughta be good."

δλε

John Willoughby had never intended to fall in love with Marianne. How could someone anticipate a force of nature that would completely upend one's entire life? She was like an unexpected hurricane in a day that had started out sunny and cloudless, and with no preparation whatsoever he'd been forced to hold onto whatever he could get hold of for dear life.

("Terrible metaphors," Tilney heckled him as he munched heartily on the bowl of popcorn that he had actually gone to make. "I thought you were supposed to be a writer?")

Willoughby had come to get his MFA at AU for one reason and one reason only: to work with Sofia Grey. In the world of spoken-word poetry, she was pretty much a rockstar. (The others in the room would have to take him at his word for this, since none of them had ever heard of her.) Unlike many of the others in his cohort, Willoughby didn't come from family money. He wasn't just getting this degree with mommy and daddy paying all his bills. He needed Sofia to like him, to mentor him, to recommend him and open some doors for him so he could actually make a career out of following his passion. He didn't have any other contacts, any other foot into the spoken poetry world. If he left graduate school without any prospects, he had no way of supporting himself.

Luckily for Willoughby, he had been born with the kind of natural charm that allowed him to ingratiate himself easily with most people. Luckier still, Sofia and Willoughby not only got along, but they also had a certain undeniable chemistry. It wasn't long before the two entered into...an unorthodox relationship for a mentor and mentee. Willoughby fetched her dry cleaning, helped her grade undergraduate writing assignments...and performed other services as needed by the attractive, older professor.

("We get it," Caty said, pulling a face. "Please don't elaborate.")

It seemed that everything was going according to Willoughby's plan...until he met Marianne. The possibility of a Marianne had never entered any of Willoughby's plans. His focus, his time, his energy were all so directed toward keeping Sofia happy that no other woman had even been on his radar, until Marianne showed up for the poetry seminar. She was beautiful, of course, a vivid Elizabeth Siddal reincarnated, but it was more than just that. She'd been so insistent upon being let into the class, even though she was only a sophomore and the spots were usually reserved for juniors and seniors, that Willoughby recognized in her a drive similar to his own.

Sofia noticed their electric connection right away, and initially she encouraged it. With Sofia's blessing, Willoughby explored an open relationship with his mentor and Marianne. (At this, Nora blinked, but remained otherwise visually unmoved by the telling of this tale.)

At first, Willoughby assumed his connection to Marianne would be similar to what he felt for Sofia: an electric bond, but he would reserve his sole focus and love for his work. The closer they became, however, the more Willoughby realized he was truly falling in love with Marianne, in a way that he was not with Sofia. He tried to deny this to himself, tried to downplay things to Sofia, but his insightful mentor began to sense the change in his attentions. Even though she had once been the one to sanction the relationship, Sofia now had a drastic change of heart, and with it, she issued an ultimatum: Willoughby would have to cut ties with Marianne, or he would be cut off from Sofia.

If love had been the only factor, Willoughby would have chosen Marianne, no questions asked. He had never met someone who had seen into him so very clearly. Willoughby had always found *Wuthering Heights* pedestrian, but now he understood Catherine Earnshaw as no other person perhaps ever could; whatever his soul was, his and Marianne's were the same.

But love was *not* the only factor. Willoughby had his poetry to consider, his career, and Sofia was his tie to almost-certain success. He could not afford to alienate her so completely. He told himself that there would be others like Marianne, all the while knowing that there would never be, not again. He broke her heart, but in doing so, he broke his own.

δλε

For a moment, they were all silent, processing this story. There could be no doubting Willoughby's sincerity; whether his account was *true*, was another matter, but it was clear that he entirely believed his version of events. And as such, it was hard not to be a little moved.

Hard, but not impossible, it seemed. "So is that why you posted the revenge porn? Because of your broken heart?"

The question, surprisingly, came from Anne. Of all the people in the room who might be susceptible to a good sob story, Lizzy would have thought that Anne would rank rather high on the list; but then, Lizzy supposed, Anne had listened to her fair share of sob stories as a GRA, and it was probably pretty hard to get past her BS-detector.

Willoughby responded to Nora, as if she had been the one to ask the question. "It wasn't me. I never would have done that to Marianne, *never*." He swallowed, throat bobbing, before he reluctantly continued, "But the pictures did come from my phone. Sofia told me to cut off all contact, but I thought I could keep some memories for myself...and she wasn't pleased when she found them."

Even Anne looked surprised at that. "Professor Grey posted those photos to the English Department Facebook page?"

He ran a hand through his dark, tousled hair. "There's no way to prove it. She would deny it if you asked her, and I'm sure she was smart enough to cover her tracks. But it couldn't have been anyone else."

"What about Wickham?" Lizzy surprised herself by asking the question.

Willoughby stared at her a long moment before seeming to process the name. "The guy who got tied up on campus? I've never met him before."

Willoughby's credibility wasn't something that Lizzy would rank especially high, but if he was acting, he was doing a pretty convincing job of it. All the theatrics of his confessional were gone; he just seemed genuinely confused. Still, she persisted. "The pictures were posted under the username 'The Portraits of Pemberley.' Just like the site Wickham was running."

"Sofia must have been trying to throw people off the scent. I guess it's possible she knows him? But I doubt it. She was outraged by his site. Thought it was disgusting."

Only women *not* involved with her boyfriend could warrant Sofia Grey's empathy, it seemed. Still, Lizzy thought it was unlikely Sofia would have been collaborating with Wickham, all things considered. The scenario of a bitter love triangle seemed ultimately more plausible in Marianne's case.

"So to sum up, none of this was your fault. You loved Marianne, but you loved your career more, and who could blame you for pursuing your dreams? You kept those photos on your phone as—what, creepy tokens of your relationship?—and how could you have possibly known that your crazy, possessive girlfriend would have a problem with that? You're really the true victim in all of this, aren't you?" Leave it to Tilney to cut through all the bullshit. He glared at Willoughby, unimpressed. "Did I get it right, or is there another part of the story you want to throw in? Did you have a rough childhood, or maybe your mom never really loved you?"

Willoughby drew himself up to his full height, but he didn't spare a glance to Tilney, or anyone else in the peanut gallery; his eyes once again focused on Nora. "I'm not perfect. I know that. I made mistakes. But whatever they were, my intention was never to hurt Marianne. Never. Will you let her know that?"

Nora didn't respond. Her face was blank of any emotion, but Lizzy thought she knew her friend well enough by now to detect that the wheels were turning in her mind. She was really processing what Willoughby was saying, taking it all in.

Instinctively, Lizzy looked to Brandon to find him also watching Nora closely. His face was easier to read. He looked worried, though *why* was only Lizzy's guess. Because he was worried about the emotional strain this might cause? Because he was afraid that Nora might be persuaded by Willoughby's eloquence and passion?

Or some other reason, that Lizzy had not yet guessed?

two

november - 2 days until darcy is expelled

LIZZY WAS AT A LOSS. While Tilney and Caty checked Wa'il's alibi, and Fania used her computer magic to verify Willoughby hadn't been the one to post Marianne's photos, she currently had no leads to follow. No loose threads. With just one more day until she would have to report to President de Bourgh, Lizzy felt like she should be doing *something* to help resolve the case one way or another. But short of kidnapping Darcy, forcing him into a clown costume and makeup, and taking blackmailing photographs to coerce him into revealing the truth (a tempting idea, but one that seemed difficult to carry out), she had nothing.

It came as a relief, then, when her phone pinged, even when she saw the text was from Karoline Bingley—that was how frazzled she was in her current state.

GET TILNEY TO LOAN YOU HIS CAR. PICK ME UP IN 15.

That was Karoline in a nutshell. Give an order when it would have been just as easy to pose it as a question. Luckily Lizzy was too intrigued to take (much) offense. She quickly secured use of Tilney's car and pulled up outside of the Kappa house, right on schedule.

"What's with the vagueness?" she asked as Karoline slid into the car, wearing Old Hollywood sunglasses and a scarf tied around her head. "Don't tell me you just missed me and wanted to see me. Aww. I wish the feeling was mutual."

"As if. Though I would need to wear a disguise to be seen in public with you, so I understand the confusion."

Lizzy had to turn her face away so Karoline wouldn't see her begrudging smile. Another solid burn from Bingley. Maybe she was rubbing off on her crime-solving partner, just a little.

"I have a lead." Karoline was practically beaming, she was so pleased with herself. Lizzy couldn't remember ever seeing her happier, except for maybe that one time she bullied the cafeteria vendors into stocking her favorite flavored water. "A good one."

"Do tell."

"Well, I had posted a few selfies I took the night of the Croft Gala, but I received notice from the school that they had to be taken down because they were shot on private property without permission." Karoline waved her hand, like this sort of thing happened all the time. And it probably did, Lizzy realized, considering how often Karoline was photographing or filming herself. "Not so uncommon in the life of an influencer, but I was, of course, irritated because the lighting in one was *so* good. Like, *I got comparisons in the comments to Beyonce* good."

Was there a point to all of this, or was this just a weird humblebrag? With Karoline it was genuinely hard to tell. "The lead?" Lizzy prompted.

"Right. I got to thinking how stupid it is that these old dinosaurs are still enforcing these kinds of laws about photography and whatnot. I mean, EVERYTHING is online these days. Everything is being monitored, recorded, photographed. It's the wave of the future. Get onboard or go extinct."

"The lead," Lizzy reminded her again.

"You're not paying attention, Bennet. *Everything* is being recorded these days. It's so much a part of society that we don't even notice it anymore." She looked at Lizzy expectantly, clearly waiting for her magical aha moment.

Lizzy did not get it. "Are you recording me now?"

"No, but that camera on the traffic signal is. If you run a red light, you get an automatic ticket. There were security cameras filming everything happening at the Croft Gala that night. And...?"

It was such a good realization that Lizzy wasn't even annoyed she was being fed lines like a toddler. "There are security cameras around campus."

"Bingo. Gold star to Isles."

Lizzy was (still) *so* not the Isles in this dynamic, but she decided to let Karoline have this one. "And? Do you have some way to access the footage?"

"Already taken care of."

Karoline directed Lizzy to a small building behind the administration building that she'd never noticed before–likely because it was little more than a glorified shed, located so close to a row of dumpsters that it couldn't be pleasant to work in there during the summer heat. "The security building," Karoline explained as she undid her seatbelt. "My ex, Elton, put me in touch with the guys who put in the CCTV cameras at the Crown Inn, the bar he manages. Turns out it's the same company that did the ones for the school."

A university seemed like a much more complex project than a lone piano bar, but maybe the security operations were more impressive than they appeared to be from the outside.

After being ushered into the building by a guy named Carter (first name? Last name? This remained unclear), Lizzy realized that the security operations were NOT more impressive on the inside. If anything, the lone, dated desktop computer and swamp cooler made the entire thing seem much more depressing.

"Hurry inside," Carter snapped. "You're letting out all the air."

Once he'd secured the door behind them again, he rounded on Karoline, correctly sussing her out as the wealthier between the two of them. "You Karoline? Did you bring what we agreed on?"

Karoline, who had not removed her sunglasses or scarf after coming inside, reached into her coat and pulled out an envelope. At first, Lizzy thought it might be packed full of cash, until she realized it appeared to be online printouts of some kind of ticket. "The gun expo," Karoline explained to Lizzy.

Weird choice. But then, Carter seemed to be a pretty weird guy. He hadn't made eye contact with either one of them since they entered the room, and seemed nervous to be having actual human contact. Or maybe it was *female* human contact?

Either way, the sooner they could get this over with, the better. Lizzy once again didn't mind when Karoline skipped all social niceties and skipped straight to the point. "Do you have the footage or not?"

Carter slipped into his desk chair, much more comfortable now that he could focus his attention on the computer screen. "There are no cameras directly overlooking campus square, but I checked the feeds from some of the footpaths nearby. I got a hit."

The guy sounded like he probably watched too many episodes of *Criminal Minds*, but Lizzy was too excited by this news to care much. "Can we see it?"

A moment later, all three of them were hunched over the computer screen, watching the shadowy footage of a footpath on campus that night. Just when Lizzy had begun to worry she might have missed whatever Carter seemed to have thought he'd found, a figure all in black appeared on screen.

"Pause it!" Karoline demanded, and Carter complied. Lizzy and Karoline leaned in even closer. "I can't tell who it is."

Neither could Lizzy. It was too dark, and the person was in a baggy hoody and a baseball cap. Their face was turned away from the camera. "Zoom in," Karoline demanded.

"This doesn't do that. It just records it."

"Do they ever face the camera in the shot?" Lizzy asked. "Do you get a clear glimpse of their face?"

"Nope," said Carter, sounding pleased with himself. "But there is something else you should see..."

He pressed play again, and as the figure continued hurrying on the path, another figure all in black followed them into the frame, following them again out of the shot.

δλε

Lizzy and Karoline were silent in the car, still in the security building parking lot, processing what they'd just seen. "It could be someone else," Karoline said finally.

Possibly. It could be Wa'il and one of his navy buddies, or Willoughby and one of his poet friends, or someone else they hadn't yet considered.

Or it could be Darcy and Knightley, who by their own admission had been out on campus that night, dressed all in black.

"Maybe it was Darcy and Knightley in the video, but they were just out patrolling and had nothing to do with what happened to Wickham."

This time, Lizzy couldn't agree. "Carter said the camera was positioned on the footpath between the square and the student union. If Darcy and Knightley were coming from that direction at that time of night, they would have seen Wickham tied up in the square."

"It's someone else." Karoline folded her arms. "We just haven't figured it out yet."

A sudden idea struck Lizzy. Probably, it was pointless. Probably it really had been Darcy. But she had to know. She couldn't leave any stone unturned. "There is someone we could talk to. Someone who might have a reason to attack Wickham."

Karoline eagerly buckled herself in. "Well then, what are you waiting for?"

"They have an alibi, but it isn't very convincing."

"Of course not, because they're probably lying." Karoline sounded pleased at the prospect, until the words finally caught up with her. "You don't mean–"

"No stone left unturned," Lizzy vowed, and turned on Tilney's car.

δλε

It took the entire drive over to calm Karoline down and convince her that interviewing Charlie again was a necessity. They were running out of time, and an unconvincing alibi just wasn't going to cut it anymore. If Karoline hadn't been wearing Veronica Beard, Lizzy wasn't entirely certain she wouldn't have thrown herself out of the moving vehicle. As it was, Lizzy had the six-minute drive across Highbury to Charlie's place to make her case.

"I'm not saying that Charlie did it," Lizzy said, though she wasn't *not* saying that, either. "But if anyone would have some insight into what's going on, it's him. Either Darcy confessed to him that he *did* do it, or Charlie knows why Darcy is keeping it quiet. It's bro code. You don't string a naked guy up in campus square, or cover up for someone else who did it, without telling your best friend. You just don't."

There could be little arguing with logic such as that. Still, Karoline glared at Lizzy as they pulled into a free space outside of the apartment building. "Fine. But just know if I get any whiff of coercion or entrapment, I have my father's lawyers on speed dial."

"I wouldn't expect anything less."

Karoline let them inside Charlie's apartment, because of course she had her own key. "It's just a temporary place while Charlie figures out what he's doing next," she explained. "That's why it's so basic."

One man's basic was another's #goals, Lizzy thought wistfully as she took in the open-concept layout, the crown molding, the big bay window overlooking campus. She guessed it was probably the lack of decor that made Karoline so defensive about it, but it was an objectively nice apartment, even without all the trimmings. Charlie was set up with his own giant flat screen TV, a gaming console that looked too complicated for Lizzy to even attempt to identify, and a bean bag where he currently sat. He was in his pajamas, a half-empty bag of potato chips open next to him, his eyes glued to the screen.

Charlie made what looked like a reflexively polite attempt to rise to his feet, though the bean bag made this unnecessarily difficult, and after a moment he gave up and plopped back down. "Hey. What are you doing here, Karoline?"

This was said a little louder than necessary, probably because the video game was blaring at such a high volume. Karoline seemed to have the same thought, and switched off the TV. Charlie groaned. "Come on. I was in the middle of that..."

"Were you?" Karoline challenged. "'Cuz from here it looked like you were wasting your life away." She snatched the bag of potato chips, thrusting it toward him accusingly. "Barbecue? Seriously?"

Lizzy had no idea why barbecue potato chips should inspire such specific rage, but that was the thing with siblings. There were layers upon layers of shared history, memories, betrayals, inside jokes, and trigger points. She decided to side-step the chips, since she didn't see that conversation leading anywhere productive. "We wanted to ask you a few questions. If you aren't busy."

"Well, Karoline just lost my place in the game, so no. I guess I'm not busy."

Lizzy tried not to let her surprise show on her face. Siblings always had their own rhythm with each other, but it was very out of character for Charlie Bingley to be so petulant and rude, especially in mixed company. Lizzy had only ever seen him cheerful, upbeat, and unfailingly polite. Everyone had their hidden sides, she supposed; she herself could not be held accountable for anything she said before she had her first coffee of the day. But this seemed notably out of place for Charlie.

Even Karoline seemed taken aback. "Don't be rude, Charles."

The irony of Karoline Bingley telling her brother not to be rude to Elizabeth Bennet was not lost on Lizzy in the moment, but again, she was determined not to be derailed. Today was too important.

"Sorry," Charlie grumbled. He ran a hand over his face. "Do you want anything? I don't have much. Coffee? Water?"

"I'm fine." Lizzy motioned to an overturned crate near the beanbag, waiting for Charlie's nod of assent before she sat on it. "It seems like you aren't feeling like your normal self these days."

Something flickered through Charlie's gaze that looked very much like panic. "I've had a lot on my plate."

Lizzy pretended not to have noticed his flash of anxiousness, not wanting to push him too far, too quickly. "We just wanted to follow up on the other day, when Caty and Tilney asked where you were the night that Wickham was assaulted. Have you thought of anyone who could vouch for where you were?"

Charlie visibly relaxed, sagging back a little in the beanbag. "Oh, that again?" He shook his head, gesturing toward his gaming console.

"Uh, no one, I guess. Unless you want me to track down some of the guys I play Call of Duty with online."

"You were here all night, playing video games?"

"Yep."

He'd previously told Caty and Tilney he'd been watching Netflix. He could have done both, she supposed, but the discrepancy was still notable. Lizzy decided not to push it right away. "Did you hear from anyone else that night?"

Another nervous flicker in Charlie's gaze. "Like who?"

"Like Darcy?" Lizzy prompted, waiting. Was that why Charlie was so nervous–because maybe Darcy had texted him something that indicated what he was up to?

But again, Charlie instantly looked relieved by this line of questioning. "Uh, no. Darcy's not much of a texter. Like I said, I just played Call of Duty until about two in the morning, then went to sleep."

Disappointed, Lizzy struggled to figure out what she was missing here. There was some piece she didn't have, something that Bingley was holding back. "And Darcy never said anything to you about that night? Anything that might indicate why he'd done it?"

Charlie shrugged. "We haven't talked a lot lately. Like I said, a lot on my plate." Another weird, shifty look that was hard to read. "He's not really the type to attack people, you know. Not usually. But it's pretty obvious why he did it."

"Why's that?"

"Because of what Wickham did to Guanyin. The pictures."

Lizzy cast a quick look at Karoline. She'd had her doubts before that Karoline knew anything about what had happened with Guanyin, but those were confirmed now as she saw the look of confusion, then alarm, flash across Karoline's face. "What pictures?"

Charlie seemed to realize he'd unintentionally put his foot in his mouth. "Uhh..."

"What pictures?" Karoline demanded.

There was little to be done when Karoline had that look in her eye. Charlie recounted the whole terrible story in awkward, halting sentences, finishing with an eloquent, "That guy sucks."

During the whole story, Lizzy watched Karoline's reaction. It was crystal clear now that Karoline had had absolutely no idea what had happened to her young friend. There was no gloating, no lording her own superior life choices or "bless her soul"-ing. Just a quiet processing of this terrible new information. Karoline really loved Guanyin, Lizzy saw with no little surprise; and she was hurting deeply for this pain she'd never realized her friend was going through.

Lizzy didn't think it was her place to offer comfort, and she doubted it would have been accepted. Tactfully, she refocused the conversation to allow Karoline some more time to process. "So you think Darcy did it?"

Charlie sighed, shrugging again. "I really don't know. But if he did, who can blame him?"

No rational human; but unfortunately, there were many on the Board of Trustees who likely did not fall under that category. And if Darcy had done it, as it seemed increasingly likely, then he would be officially expelled in two days' time.

In the silence that followed, something clattered in another room. Karoline's head shot to the side, her eyebrows narrowing. "What was that?"

Charlie struggled to his feet, managing to make it this time. "It must have been the apartment next door. Thin walls." But that nervous, jittery look was back. "I actually have somewhere I have to be, so if you guys wouldn't mind..."

They would never know if Charlie could have successfully herded his sister out the door, since a figure appeared in the hallway, chin held high in defiance as she stepped into the room.

"No, Charles. It's time they know," said Lucy Steele, coming up beside him to take his hand.

chapter
three

FOR A MOMENT, there was only a terrible, awkward silence. Then all at once, Karoline rounded on her brother, eyes glowing with murderous rage. "What the absolute hell is going on here?"

Charlie swiftly withdrew his hand from Lucy's, holding both palms up in the air in an attempt at a placating gesture. "Hold on, Karoline. Just listen for a minute–"

"Has this bitch been living here with you?"

If Karoline had been thinking logically, she likely would have remembered that Lucy had just moved into the Kappa house. But 'logic' did not seem to be the prevailing sentiment of the moment. Charlie shook his head. "No. Of course not." He darted a quick, urgent glance at Lizzy–likely, she realized, because he assumed news of this would be getting back to Nora. "She stopped by right before you two showed up. When I saw y'all park on the street, I panicked and made her go into the back room."

So that was why Charlie had been announcing them so loudly, and why he had been so dismissive. That much made sense. But it still didn't explain why Lucy Steele was hiding in Charlie's apartment.

"Kar," Lucy spoke up, her big blue eyes wide and pleading. "We've been wanting to tell you forever. I just didn't know how. I knew you would be on our side if you knew the whole story, but I didn't want you to get the wrong idea."

Karoline rounded on her, advancing as Lucy retreated until the smaller girl's back was literally up against the wall. "What wrong idea might that be? That you've been pretending to be my friend so you could seduce my brother? Been doing a little digging on the Mattress King, I see. Figured out how much his net worth is and decided you wanted a piece of the pie?"

It had been a tactical error for Lucy to try to use their so-called friendship to diffuse the moment, that much seemed clear to even Lucy. Her big blue eyes welled with tears. "We never meant to hurt you, Karoline. I love him. I really do."

"Barf." Karoline spared a withering glance at her brother. "We always knew you weren't the brightest Bingley sibling, but this bitch? Seriously?"

Lizzy could have reminded Karoline that not a day before she'd been gushing about how wonderful Lucy was and that they were basically bffs a week after meeting. But that seemed unnecessarily petty in the moment.

Charlie shook his head. "We aren't in love." Again, to Lucy. "We aren't in love. We hooked up, one time, over a year ago." Another quick glance at Lizzy. "Before the start of the school year."

AKA, before he'd met Nora. Lizzy kept her face expressionless, but it was good information to have.

"I told Lucy I wasn't looking for anything serious with her, and I meant it." Charlie sighed, running another hand over his face. He looked like he'd aged about twenty years during that one conversation. "I still mean it. I'm sorry you wanted more, Lucy, but I just don't feel that way about you."

Once again, Lucy's eyes flooded. "How can you say that? After what happened with our baby?"

A shocked silence once again descended upon the room as everyone processed this new piece of information. Then Karoline rounded on her brother yet again. If her eyes had looked murderous before, they now looked positively genocidal. "Your *what*?"

Charlie shook his head quickly, eyes comically wide. "There was no baby. Honest, Karoline, I think she's actually crazy." He winced, glancing at Lucy. "Sorry, but it's true. You need help, Lucy."

Tears gushed down Lucy's face. "How can you say that to me? Do you have any idea the emotional duress I've been under?"

Charlie looked like he wanted to crawl out of his own skin, he was so uncomfortable. "I'm sorry," he said again. "But, I mean, we didn't even have sex. Just fooled around. How could you have gotten pregnant?"

"I sent you that TikTok explaining how it could happen," Lucy accused him. "It's not my fault you don't want to believe it."

"And why did you wait to tell me that you'd lost it until a year and a half later, when there was no way to prove anymore if it had or hadn't happened?"

"I was traumatized, okay? I needed time to heal."

Lizzy silently put together the timeline in her head. If Lucy and Charlie had been together the summer before he and Nora met, and Lucy hadn't told him about it until over a year later, would that coincide with when Charlie had abruptly left university last spring to go to Paris?

Karoline seemed to be putting it together, too. She turned back to Lucy, making her full six-feet-in-heels presence known. "Wait, *you* were the one who was trying to blackmail Charlie with a fake pregnancy last spring?"

The *you* all-but confirmed it, at least in Lizzy's mind. She could see how it would have happened. Sweet Charlie, confused and wanting to believe the best in Lucy, had refused to divulge the name of the girl who was trying to extort money out of him for a pregnancy that had never happened. Knowing how much Charlie liked Nora, Karoline had assumed *she* was the girl in question, and had convinced Darcy and her parents that it would be in Charlie's best interest to leave campus (and the country). That would explain more of Karoline's passive-aggressive hostility toward Nora all this time. Not *excuse* it, maybe, but it certainly made more sense now why she was always rubbing in Nora's face that Charlie had moved on.

It seemed to Lizzy that Karoline had some serious apologizing to do. But that would be later. For now, Karoline had some other catfish to fry. "So let me get this straight. You thought you could trick my dumb brother into thinking he'd gotten you pregnant even though you never actually had sex, then—what? Force him into a relationship so you could mooch off him? Maybe try to get some kind of settlement from my dad?"

Lucy's tears refreshed. She really was alarmingly good at that. "I'm in a very emotionally fragile state. I would appreciate it if you wouldn't take that tone with me."

"And you thought you'd try to be my best friend so I'd be on your side when it all came out?" Karoline shook her head. "You must really think we're a bunch of dumb hicks, don't you? Well guess what? You gave a good effort, but no one out-bitches Karoline Bingley. This is done here. If you ever contact my brother again—and I mean so much as a like on one of his social media posts—I'll sue you so hard that your kids will be paying it off. The real ones, not the made-up ones."

As quickly as they'd sprouted, Lucy's tears miraculously dried up. She glared back at Karoline, the set of her jaw indicating that she realized she'd lost. "Fine. Who would want to be tied down to your dumbass brother anyway?" She made a face at Charlie. "*Offense.*"

Charlie looked too relieved to be free of her to care much that she'd insulted his intelligence. "Okay?"

Seeming to realize that the dagger hadn't landed quite as deeply as she'd hoped, Lucy threw out one last parting shot. "Y'all can judge me all you want, but I came here because I needed *help*. And I'm obviously not the only one." She looked pointedly at Karoline. "Maybe if you didn't throw up after every meal, your breath wouldn't be as toxic as the way you treat your friends."

Lizzy assumed this was just run-of-the-mill cattiness, until she saw the look on Karoline's face. She looked like she'd been sucker-punched. Oh. *Oh.* Lizzy thought back through every time she'd rolled her eyes at Karoline's careful calorie-counting, her obsession with her size, her pickiness about ingredients and designer clothes, and realized that she'd made an awful lot of assumptions about Karoline because of the way she looked. And okay, yes, because she was difficult, but so was Marianne, and Lydia, and frankly even Lizzy herself at times. Instead of seeing Karoline as a person, Lizzy had dismissed her as a caricature, and probably ignored the very real warning signs that she would have called out in anyone else she knew.

She had been very, very blind, Lizzy realized, and not for the first time. She had always believed herself to be a good judge of character, but she'd allowed her own personal biases to keep her from seeing some very obvious truths about people. Darcy. Karoline. And who knew who else?

δλε

After Lucy left, Karoline surprised Lizzy by walking her down to Tilney's car. They faced each other in an awkward standoff on the sidewalk, Karoline hugging herself tightly and not quite meeting Lizzy's gaze. "I think I better stay and help Charlie sort some things out. I don't think I'll be able to help you with the rest of your investigation." Glaring against the sun, Karoline blinked a few times and looked down at her shoes. "Sorry."

"It's okay." Lizzy didn't really know where to go from here, anyway. She'd been so sure that Charlie's suspicious behavior meant he was hiding something. And he was, but it had absolutely nothing to do with Wickham. And all the other leads seemed to be going nowhere. No, it seemed more and more likely that either Darcy had done it, or she would never know what had really happened. Maybe that was just something she'd need to accept. "You should be with your family now, anyway. What Charlie's been through..."

To her surprise, Karoline glared at her—not her usual *Why are you breathing in my vicinity, Bennet* sneer but a full-on mama-bear death stare like she'd been giving Lucy upstairs a few minutes before. "Let me guess. Can't wait to publish an article about it. Baby mama drama for the Mattress Prince. Don't forget to throw in my eating disorder, too. I bet that'll get more clicks."

Lizzy stared at her blankly. "What?"

"The Mattress King's wild offspring. You can take the trash out of Mississippi, but you can't take the Mississippi out of the trash." Karoline shook her head. "Believe me, I've read it all. But at least this time you'll have a new scoop."

Lizzy shook her head. "Karoline, I'm not going to write about any of this."

Karoline rolled her eyes. "Sure. For a price, right? How much do you want? Let me give you an insider's tip–go too big and Daddy's lawyers will start digging up dirt on you. Even if you think it doesn't exist, they'll find it."

It was clear that Karoline had been down this road one too many times to take Lizzy's protestations at face value. She folded her arms, mimicking Karoline's stance. "All right. There is something I want."

Karoline scoffed, waiting.

"If anything that Lucy was saying about you was at all, in any way, true and not just something she made up to get revenge, I want you to promise me that you'll make an appointment with Miss Bates tomorrow so that she can recommend a good counselor for you."

At the unexpected turn, Karoline's eyes prickled with tears–real tears that contorted her face with the effort of fighting them back, not Lucy Steele-tears. She turned her face away for a moment, composing herself. "Why would you want that? You don't care about me. We aren't friends."

Lizzy caught herself from saying something nice but ultimately insincere. "Sworn enemies don't have to like each other. But I need you at your fighting best. Who else is going to make fun of my outfits?"

Karoline laughed a little at this, catching a stray tear with the heel of her palm. "Literally anyone with eyes." She sniffed, and abruptly changed the topic, still not looking at Lizzy. "My dad got rich over a long period of time, but he got famous really fast. Like, crazy fast, with those stupid viral commercials. He didn't even care that people were watching them to laugh at him. He still got treated like a celebrity in the South. People would stop him on the street and take pictures. Sometimes they wanted me in the pictures, too. I liked it at first. I thought it made me, I don't know. Special or popular or something. Then I saw what people were writing about me in the comments. Chubby. Whale. Moon pie. That kind of stuff."

Without being prompted, she pulled up a picture on her phone and held it out. It took Lizzy a moment to recognize Karoline. She was much younger, her face rounder and less made-up. Her clothes looked like they came from the department store, and her smile was big and genuine. She certainly wasn't the fashion plate that Karoline was now, but she was just a girl. Just a normal girl. "You look fine," Lizzy told her honestly. "They shouldn't have been saying that stuff about you. Even if it were true, which it wasn't, they had no right to talk about you like that. You were just a kid."

Karoline winced away, like it physically pained her to think about that time. She quickly minimized the photo and tucked her phone away again. "I was a heifer. Whatever. It's fixed now." Before Lizzy could protest this, she rushed on, "I think that honestly wasn't the worst part. It was when my own friends started joining in–tagging unflattering pictures or popping up in the comments with 'insider stories' of things I'd said or done so people could laugh at us. Or the distant relatives who came out of the woodwork to 'borrow' money from my dad, like he owed them something. You learn pretty quickly that the only people you can trust are your family, and other people like you."

The Darcys, Lizzy guessed. Emma Woodhouse. Knightley and Rushworth. Other people who'd grown up rich and knew what it was like to have people only interested in their friendship because they wanted something. As much as Lizzy wanted to protest it wasn't true, what were Wickham and Lucy if not proof that those kinds of vultures existed? She knew, of course, that she wasn't that way. That Nora hadn't had any ulterior motives with Charlie, that others like Caty and Tilney and Anne and Brandon cared more about who people *were* than what their money could buy them. But she could maybe begin to understand, after seeing some of the underbelly firsthand, how hard it must be for people like Karoline and Darcy to trust people outside of their circle.

"People suck," Lizzy agreed, for lack of a more eloquent way to express it. "I won't pretend that's not true. But they can also surprise you. And, God help me, I can't believe I'm saying this, you've surprised me, Karoline. You aren't who I thought you were." At the look on Karoline's face, she rushed to add, "I know, way too sappy. Believe me, I don't think you're a saint. We don't need to hang out, or anything."

Karoline made a face. "That wasn't even on offer, Bennet."

Lizzy rolled her eyes, but affectionately this time. "I guess what I'm saying is, as an acquaintance who doesn't hate you and doesn't want anything from you, I hope you'll get some help. I hope that Charlie will see someone, too, because I bet these last few months have really messed with him. And I just don't know how you get better unless you learn to trust someone. That's all I'm saying. And Miss Bates would be a really good place to start."

Karoline looked skeptical. "The whole university will know about it by the end of the day. She never stops talking."

"Yeah, but that's kind of the great thing about Miss Bates. Have you ever noticed that, even though she can go on forever, she's never really talking about anything that matters? She could talk for an hour about the best way to cook rice, but I've never ever heard her give away a confidence. And she must know a *lot*, having worked at that school for such a long time."

Karoline considered this, seeming maybe not fully convinced, but on the path to being so. At last, she shrugged. "Whatever. I'll think about it, okay?"

As a sworn enemy/vague acquaintance, Lizzy supposed that was all she could really ask.

four
november - the day before darcy is expelled

WITH KAROLINE OUT OF COMMISSION, Lizzy realized she was basically on her own. She knew the Austen Murder Club, and especially Tilney and Caty, would always be game to lend a hand; but with Karoline, this investigation had been as personal as it was for Lizzy. No one else cared as much about proving Darcy innocent...or understanding why he'd done it, if he wasn't.

Lizzy could own that part to herself now. The stakes had never been particularly high in finding out who'd attacked Wickham, because Lizzy frankly felt like he'd gotten what he deserved, and was lucky that his comeuppance hadn't been much worse. But if Darcy had attacked him, Lizzy wanted to know why. Was it revenge for Guanyin? That would be more than understandable. But why now? What had been the instigation? It was becoming increasingly difficult not to get a little self-important about the entire thing, because try as she might, no matter how Lizzy looked at it, the cause had something to do with her. If Darcy was lying about committing the crime, then he must be doing it to keep her from getting expelled, right? If he had done it, then the reason for doing it *now* would have to be about her just as much as Guanyin, wouldn't it?

But then, that was also the part that didn't make sense to Lizzy. Darcy was known for being protective over his younger sister, and after Wickham had blackmailed her, Darcy hadn't retaliated, at least not physically. So why would Wickham posting a picture of Lizzy in a bra send him over the edge? She knew—she *suspected*—he cared about her, but more than his own sister? Or maybe it was just that realizing Wickham was up to his old tricks had pushed Darcy over the edge?

It was all a tangled mess in Lizzy's mind. Each possible answer seemed to only open up more questions. And there was only one person, she realized, who could answer them.

Luckily, Lizzy knew where to find Darcy early on a Sunday morning.

δλε

Sure enough, there he was—the lone swimmer today, slicing through the far lane, his rhythm sturdy and steady and strong. Lizzy watched him a moment before grabbing a kickboard. She moved to the end of the lane, waiting until Darcy was a few yards away before plunging the board into his line of sight underwater to signal someone was there.

Darcy stopped short, treading water as he looked up to see who was intruding. It was impossible to read much emotion with goggles obscuring his eyes, but Lizzy could read the tension in his neck and shoulders at being interrupted.

For a moment, he said nothing, taking her in. Then abruptly, he disappeared underwater, re-emerging a moment later sans cap and goggles and running a hand through his dark hair. Despite this gesture, he made no effort to move closer. "What are you doing here?"

They both knew, of course, but Lizzy had to say it. "This is my hail Mary." She wrinkled her nose, realizing suddenly she might be a little out of her depth. "That's a sports term, isn't it? Did I use it right?"

A long pause. Then a reluctant, "Yes," from Darcy.

"Tomorrow's the deadline, you know. De Bourgh will have to expel you. For something we both know you didn't do."

"I thought you had something new to say, but since you clearly don't—" He gestured broadly toward the exit. "The pool area is for lap swimmers only."

Lizzy didn't think, just reacted to the instinctive part of her that bristled at anyone—but especially *him*—giving her orders. She took off her shoes, pulling down her jeans next. Pausing only briefly to worry about her mismatched bra and underwear, Lizzy pushed through her self-consciousness and pulled her t-shirt over her head.

She dove into the lane adjacent to Darcy's, surfacing a moment later with what she knew must be an infuriatingly smug grin. "Look at that. I'm a lap swimmer."

For a long, charged moment, Lizzy stared down Darcy as he stared right back. Their eyes tug-of-warred, danced, parried. Then Lizzy's victorious smile faltered, as Darcy's eyes slid downward. Somehow she had not entirely thought this through—that in taking off her clothes so she could jump into the water, she would be *taking off her clothes and jumping into the water*. Flushed and flustered, Lizzy resisted the urge to cover herself, which felt like a surrender, and tried to remind herself that Darcy was technically in even less clothing than she was, although in truth, that acknowledgment did not make her feel any less unsettled.

Darcy's eyes snapped back to hers. He swallowed. "What are you doing here, Elizabeth?" Despite himself, it seemed, his voice softened when he said her name.

"Who are you covering for? There has to be somebody you're protecting, but it isn't Guanyin and it isn't Charlie. So, who?"

Lizzy swam a little closer, right to the edge of the lane. "Or maybe you're just fed up with being here. You have the money anyway, right? Who cares about getting kicked out if you can just buy your way into another school."

That, at least, had gotten under his skin, though Darcy looked more irritated than ready to confess. "Nice try."

Lizzy didn't have to feign her anger now. She was trying to help him and he was being so stupidly stubborn. "Or maybe you just want to take credit. You know that someone should have given Wickham his comeuppance, and it should have been you."

He no longer looked even remotely amused, just angry. "We're done here."

Desperate to keep him in the pool, Lizzy called after him. "Don't you want justice? Whoever did this is just going to get away with it, and let you take the punishment."

That didn't stop him, either, so Lizzy surged forward, trying to get ahead of him so she could get between him and the edge of the pool. Physically prevent him from climbing out, if that's what it took.

If they'd been racing, there was no way she could have beaten him—captain of the swim team, and all. But he'd clearly underestimated her, so she managed to slide between him and the wall right as he reached it.

It should have been a moment of triumph, only Darcy wouldn't look at her, and he just started to swim the other way, and Lizzy realized she couldn't chase him all over the whole pool. She wasn't up for it physically, certainly, but not emotionally either. It felt so deflating, realizing he was really and truly giving up without a fight.

"I've thought you were a lot of things, Fo-Hian Darcy," she called. "But not a coward."

That stopped him short. Realizing this was her very last shot, Lizzy swallowed. "Isn't there anything about this place you don't want to leave behind?"

A beat, and then quite suddenly, Darcy was right in front of her, forcing her back into the wall. He leaned forward, one hand pressed against the edge of the pool, right next to her head. "You haven't found whoever did this?"

Swallowing, Lizzy shook her head.

"If I say it isn't me, de Bourgh will turn it back on you without another suspect." Anticipating Lizzy's argument, he spoke over her. "You know she will. If that happens, you'll be expelled. Either way, I lose you." The ghost of a smile crossed his face. "At least *I* can afford to bribe my way into another school, right?"

Lizzy stared at him, wordless, uncomprehending. "You're..." But even having suspected the possibility, it sounded too absurd to say out loud, that Darcy would allow himself to be expelled—and more, to have his name legally and publicly connected with Wickham's forever after—for *her*.

Darcy laughed ruefully. "I know. Look at me throwing money at a problem to fix it. What a hero—"

He clearly didn't expect the kiss, and truthfully, Lizzy didn't either.

No logical decision was made. There was no clear train of thought. It was some heady combination of realizing how much he liked her, how much *she* liked *him*, now that she finally understood who he was. And realizing, too, that this had all come too late. He would be expelled, for something he didn't do, for her. She would lose him just as she'd finally found him.

So, Lizzy kissed him. It seemed the only real thing to do, given the circumstances. Darcy seemed surprised at first, but he quickly conceded to the superiority of her decision-making. After the initial awkward shifting and fumbling of two peoples' mouths coming into contact for the first time, they quickly found their eager rhythm, and then not much conscious thought followed for some time, beyond Lizzy acknowledging to herself that Darcy was actually a fantastic kisser, and she hoped he would find that spot again, and...*oh*...

It is uncertain how far this encounter might have progressed if the sound of the far gym doors opening hadn't caused Lizzy to jerk away from Darcy and put some sizable distance between them. He swore, uttering a truly imaginative combination of words that might have made Lizzy laugh under other circumstances. She pulled herself out of the pool, without much of a clear plan of where she was going or what she intended to do next, only a sharp, sobering reminder that she was in a very public pool in her underwear.

Fortunately, Darcy seemed to be a bit better in a crisis. "Take my towel." Lizzy did as he instructed, for maybe the first time in her life, and wrapped herself up in the generously sized terry cloth.

Only once she was covered up did Lizzy stop to meet Darcy's gaze. He was still in the water, watching her. She stared back at him a long moment, not knowing what she would have said, even if an oblivious underclassman hadn't been readying himself to jump into the water two lanes down from them. This might very well be a goodbye, Lizzy realized with a pang.

There was so much to be said in that moment, and none of it that could be. So Lizzy simply held his gaze for a moment longer before leaning down to gather her clothes and hurrying to the locker room.

chapter
five

AS SHE HURRIED AWAY from the pool, Lizzy found herself in the very unfortunate position of being what no woman wants to be: confused about a boy. She realized that despite the confrontation, she was no closer to discovering the truth about Darcy's role in Wickham's attack (though she had, for the record, set to rest another pressing concern she'd long held about Darcy, which was wondering if he was a good kisser. Also, for the record, he was).

The prospect of spending the next few hours dithering over Darcy, how he looked in a speedo, and whether he would actually be expelled the following day was so bleak that Lizzy decided to pursue the best antidote she knew to worrying about a boy: paying a visit to Marianne Dashwood.

Much to Lizzy's relief, Marianne was not only looking remarkably well despite having been hit by a car two weeks before, but she was also reading Mary Wollstonecraft's *A Vindication on the Rights of Women*. That had to be a good sign. At Lizzy's entrance, Marianne looked up with a slightly painful-looking smile, thanks to the generous bruising around her jawline. "Lizzy. It's so good to see you."

There was nothing wrong with what Marianne said–in fact, it was very nice, and said in a completely sincere and friendly tone–but still, something about it gave Lizzy pause. She realized that it was because Marianne very rarely offered any kind of pleasantries. She seemed to find it beneath herself to have to conform to the societal norms that mere mortals deigned to follow. But there was nothing forced or condescending in her tone now; she seemed genuinely happy to see her roommate.

The best thing, Lizzy decided, would be to play along, and not draw attention to the nicety in case it caused an immediate regression. "It's good to see you, too. I come bearing gifts." She held out a milkshake; she'd thought about bringing macarons, but had decided with Marianne's injured jaw that something more liquid-y might be easier to manage. "I'm sorry I haven't been here in a few days. Things have been a little...crazy."

"Nora told me about the investigation." Another wincing smile. "Caty must be so happy there's another case to solve."

"She's been walking on sunshine all week," Lizzy confirmed.

The two of them laughed. Lizzy watched as Marianne took a halting sip from the milkshake, then had to look away, it seemed so painful. She motioned to the Wollstonecraft book. "A little light reading to pass the time?"

Marianne ran her fingers over the spine of the book. "You know, I've never actually read it? I haven't read a lot of feminist theory, if I'm being honest. I picked up a lot of it from the Internet and latched onto it because I knew it was the 'right thing' to support." A rueful laugh. "It made up so much of my identity, but I don't know if I ever really understood it. I certainly didn't act like I did."

Lizzy blinked, taken aback by the confession. She shook her head, not liking the self-recrimination she heard in Marianne's voice. "You trusted the wrong person. It happens to all of us. You don't deserve to punish yourself for that."

"I don't," Marianne said firmly. "I don't blame myself for trusting Willoughby. That's what we do when we love–we trust. And if we can't, then it isn't love." She shook her head. "I blame myself for how I behaved afterward. I let him take over my life. I lost sight of who I was. I *begged* him to come back to me–someone who had shown me in every way possible that he wasn't worthy of the love I had to give him." She shook her head. "But *blame* is the wrong word. I don't judge that girl. I pity her. And I don't want to be her, ever again."

Not knowing what to say, Lizzy reached out and squeezed her arm. She thought back to her own self-discovery over the past week, all that she'd learned about herself and about how she viewed the world around her, and she shook her head. "We are all fools in love, I think."

Marianne smiled, wryly. "That's very wise of you."

Lizzy laughed. "I think I got it from a book...?" She motioned to the Wollstonecraft. "Maybe even that book?"

Marianne shook her head. "Mary doesn't have much to say about love, thank goodness."

Mary, was it? Lizzy hadn't realized they were on a first-name basis; she smiled a little to herself, glad to see that some things never changed. Oblivious, Marianne continued: "And neither do I, for the foreseeable future. I'm not planning on dating for the rest of the semester. Maybe the rest of my life. We'll see."

Poor Brandon, Lizzy thought reflexively, then corrected herself, remembering what she'd seen at the Austen Murder Club meeting. The shared glances between Brandon and Nora. For some reason, she had a hard time wrapping her mind around the idea of it; she'd been so certain he was into Marianne.

Marianne must have thought so, too, because of the segue that followed this announcement. "By the way, could you return something to Brandon for me?"

She motioned to the counter, where Lizzy saw a folded-up, black hoodie, with a card on top. Lizzy recognized Marianne's handwriting on the envelope. "Brandon's sweatshirt?"

"He used it as a tourniquet, when he found me." Marianne glanced down at her leg, concealed under her blanket. "I was bleeding pretty badly, I guess." She blinked, coming back to herself. "One of the nurses washed it for me, and I'd like to make sure he gets it back. Along with a note I wrote to him. Thanking him for what he did."

"Of course." Lizzy could have pointed out that Brandon would likely have been happy to come visit her in the hospital. Whether he was into her, or Nora, or no one, he'd doubtless want to check in and make sure she was doing okay.

But Marianne seemed pretty set on this decision. "I just don't feel like seeing too many people, for a bit," she said by way of explanation, before offering another pained smile. "I'm happy to see you, though."

Lizzy stayed for a while longer, catching her up on some of the latest developments in reality TV, intentionally keeping the conversation light. She sensed Marianne was recovering from more than just physical injuries, and needed some time and space to heal.

As soon as she saw Marianne was starting to tire, Lizzy made her excuses, careful to pack the sweatshirt and note into her bag. "Is there anything else I can do for you before I go? Anything you need?"

Marianne was starting to get a little fuzzy; Lizzy suspected some of her pain meds were starting to kick in. She smiled woozily at Lizzy, then reached out abruptly to grab her hand. "I want you to know I still believe in the goodness of people. I really do."

Lizzy had to fight a smile. She was glad to see that, even amidst all of her personal growth, the core of Marianne remained unchanged; she was still the same passionate, intense girl Lizzy had always known, even if some of her energy had been refocused. "Good," Lizzy said, for lack of anything better to say.

"Someone left me for dead on the side of the road," Marianne said, sounding bewildered by the idea of it.

Smile fading, Lizzy squeezed her hand back. "I'm sorry, Marianne." She had a hard time comprehending it, too. How someone could just drive off after doing that to another person. How they could possibly live with themselves, knowing what they'd done.

Marianne sighed. "But someone paid my hospital bill. Did you know that? Anonymously. I would have been paying those bills off for the rest of my life, you know? And someone just..." She snapped her fingers, then leaned her head back, eyes closed. "Like it was nothing."

Huh. Lizzy *hadn't* known that. It seemed significant somehow, even though she couldn't quite piece together how. "That's wonderful, Marianne. I didn't–"

But it seemed that Marianne had drifted off, or was otherwise very close to it. Lizzy gently extricated herself, quietly slipping out the door.

δλε

Part of Lizzy's visit to Marianne had genuinely been inspired by wanting to see how her friend was doing. In truth, though, part of it had to do with wanting to delay going home as long as possible. How did one break the news to one's best friend that the boy she'd been pining for since last fall had randomly left school in the middle of the semester because a random hookup had tried to convince him he'd gotten her pregnant? And that the reason the sister and best friend of this boy had been so cold to her ever since was because they thought *she* was the girl who'd been doing the blackmailing, when in actuality they had never so much as even kissed? And that the girl who'd been doing the black-mailing was the same obnoxious girl who had been living with them the past few months, making their lives absolutely miserable with her sneaky, two-faced presence?

They did not write Hallmark cards for this kind of scenario, it turned out. Lizzy had no idea how she was supposed to explain all of this to Nora, when she could barely wrap her mind around it herself. It felt like some kind of dessert was in order for a revelation of this magnitude, though she couldn't quite decide if it were more of a cupcake or a brownie vibe.

Why not both? Lizzy ultimately decided. If there was a situation that warranted multiple dessert offerings more than this, Lizzy did not think she cared to experience it.

Bearing her gifts in a deceptively cheerful pink box, Lizzy cautiously approached Nora. She was engrossed in her laptop, her textbook open on the couch next to her, a variety of well-used index cards spread out across the coffee table. It was such a familiar *Nora* sight that Lizzy felt another pang of regret, at the chaos that she was about to impose on this orderly life.

Nora looked up, then did a double-take at the sight of the familiar pink. "You went to Denham's?" Her brow furrowed. "Uh-oh. What happened?"

Lizzy took the seat opposite her, setting down the bakery box as an offering. "I have something to tell you, and it isn't going to be easy for you to hear."

A flash of panic passed through Nora's eyes, covered quickly by her usual wry, calm expression. "Did you find out something about the assault?"

Lizzy blinked in surprise. For the first time in several days, her thoughts had actually not been on who had assaulted Wickham. "No. Nothing like that." She took in a bracing breath. "It's about Charlie and..." There was really no easy way to say it. "And Lucy Steele." She rose to her feet, finding it suddenly impossible to sit still. "I honestly don't even know where to start. I know it won't make much sense, but–"

Nora held up a hand, cutting her off. "It's okay, Lizzy. I already know."

Of all the reactions Lizzy had anticipated to this news, it was not that one. Her jaw did not actually drop because she was not a cartoon character, but it probably came as close to that as a normal response could. "You–know? How can you know?"

"Lucy told me." Nora spoke matter-of-factly, but with the air of someone who was saying something they had rehearsed in their head many times, and was trying very hard not to let any nerves or emotion show through. "Not long after she came to stay with us."

Now Lizzy's jaw did drop. "She told you?"

"I think she must have suspected that we were...that Charlie and I were connected somehow. She pretended that she was confiding their relationship to me because she knew how much Charlie trusted my opinion, but it was obvious she was trying to stake her claim and make sure I backed off. It was a waste of time, of course. I've barely seen Charlie since he left last spring, and even if there ever *was* anything between us, well... that was all over a long time ago."

Nora was softening it, but Lizzy could easily imagine how it had all played out. Passive-aggressive Lucy cornering Nora and forcing her to listen to all the sordid details of her fling with Charlie, likely trying to play it up as more than it was. All the while pretending to be her friend as she twisted the knife deeper and deeper with every word.

"I'm sorry, Nora." Lizzy meant it. She added, gently, without accusation, "Why didn't you tell me?"

"She made me promise not to say anything." Nora shrugged, but in that little gesture, Lizzy could have wept. If she hadn't known it already, this would have been all the evidence she needed no one in the entire world had more integrity than Nora Dashwood, and no one was more concerned with putting the comfort and ease of others first. Even now, Nora was putting on a show, trying to convince Lizzy that the experience hadn't been pure hell–not for her own pride, but so *Lizzy* wouldn't have to feel bad. "And anyway, what was there to tell? Things were over with Charlie a long time ago. They never even began, really." A rueful laugh. "It might be hard to find out the guy you like has a secret girlfriend, but it's better in the long run to know who you're dealing with."

Lizzy was so busy nodding along in solidarity that it took her a moment to process what Nora had actually said. "Lucy isn't his girl-friend, though," she corrected.

Nora rolled her eyes–a very un-Nora-like gesture that let Lizzy know just how much this whole ordeal had rattled her. "I don't know if they've made it official, or whatever, but in my book if you're sleeping together for over a year and playing house, you're girlfriend and boyfriend. Call me old-fashioned."

Lizzy shook her head. "I don't know what Lucy told you, but she was never Charlie's girlfriend. They hooked up one time before he met you, and she's been trying to convince him he got her pregnant ever since, even though they didn't have sex." She'd been planning how to rip the Band-Aid off more gently, but the misconception–or, more likely, Lucy's misleading retelling–had to be corrected, immediately and completely.

Nora stared at her, unblinking. Then she shook her head. "You're wrong. Lucy sent me a picture yesterday, from Charlie's bed."

Wincing for her friend and the sheer hell that Lucy must have put her through, if this was even a small glimpse into that, Lizzy reached forward and took her head. "I was there yesterday. She dropped in unan-nounced and Charlie made her hide in the bedroom when he heard us coming. She definitely wasn't sleeping with him, though probably not for lack of trying on her part. When Karoline found out, she freaked out and kicked Lucy to the curb." Lizzy laughed, a little. "It was kind of awesome."

Nora did not smile, just continued to stare at Lizzy, searching her face. "Charlie and Lucy aren't together?"

"No."

"They were never together?" Nora repeated, as if she couldn't quite trust the words. "They haven't been dating for almost two years?"

"She was the reason Charlie left in the spring. She was still black-mailing him with this baby that had never existed, and Charlie must have told some of it but not all of it to Karoline. I think she thought it was you. That's why Karoline's been such a bitch—well, to you, anyway. They never even went on a date or anything like that. It was just a random hookup."

Another moment of blank-faced silence. And then Nora burst into tears.

Not dainty, feminine tears, either, but huge, guttural sobs that seemed to be coming from somewhere primal deep inside of her. She turned half-away from Lizzy, curling up into the fetal position on the couch, where she continued to rock and sob with something that was both release and sorrow, joy and agony.

Lizzy let her cry for a moment, rubbing her back reassuringly, but otherwise not knowing what she could possibly say to fix this. Finally, the perfect words came to her: "Brownie or cupcake?" she asked.

chapter
six

A LADY WILL NEVER DIVULGE how much of a full pastry box two other ladies have consumed in a relatively short amount of time, but suffice it to say that the brownies and cupcakes provided at least a little comfort in a moment of dire need. Nora's textbook, laptop, and note cards had been put away for the foreseeable future, and other necessary comforts of pajamas, streaming services, and tea had been acquired.

When a comfortable lull had finally been reached, Lizzy paused the next loading episode. "You ready to talk? Or do we need to see another house flip?" Anyone who said laughter was the best medicine had clearly never watched HGTV.

Nora sighed from her supine position on the other end of the couch. "I don't know what there is to say." But she sat up a little and sighed again, indicating that there was, perhaps, something to be said on the subject.

Lizzy sat up, too, brushing some crumbs off her pajama top. "Does this change anything for you and Charlie? Or are things still over?"

Nora gave an exasperated shrug. "Who knows? I've barely heard from him since he came back. For all I know, he stopped thinking about me a long time ago."

Not likely, Lizzy thought, but didn't press the point, since she knew Nora would only dig in and deny it more. "More to the point, do *you* still think about *him*?"

Nora tossed a pillow at her head. "That's a very uncharitable thing to ask your friend when she's down." She raised a challenging eyebrow. "And as long as we're calling each other out on our bullshit, how long have you been thinking about Darcy?"

"What are you talking about?" Lizzy hedged, all the while knowing it was futile. Nora was the secret assassin, after all. She noticed everything, about everyone, all while keeping her cards close to the chest.

Accordingly, Nora gave her a skeptical look. "There's been a *thing* between you two for a while now, but I noticed a definite shift when we ran into him at the Crescent. Probably, that you've actually started to notice he's been pining for you since the moment you met."

Lizzy felt her traitorous face heat up. Dammit all. She had never been a blusher before Darcy, she was fairly certain. What was it about him that made everything feel so furtive and private? She wanted to guard her heart and everything in it, keep it safe from the cruel world outside–but she supposed, if she was going to encourage Nora to confide in her, then she should be willing to offer the same in return. "We made out in the pool this morning."

Nora gaped at her, clearly not expecting *that*. "What?"

Lizzy still had a surprise or two up her sleeve, it seemed. Unable to help herself, she barreled on. "I was in my underwear."

"*What?*"

"It was really, really hot." Lizzy took the pillow Nora had thrown at her and pressed it over her face. "I think I want to do it again."

Nora laughed until she was near-weeping once again, this time with hilarity. "I don't think this conversation is going to pass the Bechdel test."

"Don't tell Marianne," Lizzy agreed.

After a moment of shared laughter, Nora regained her composure, wiping at her eyes. "Well, you should." At Lizzy's questioning look, she clarified. "Make out with him again. If you want to. For what it's worth, I never saw any reason to hate him." Reading even the merest flicker in Lizzy's eyes, she continued, "And yes, that includes the fact that he likely had something to do with Charlie leaving in the spring." She sighed. "There are far worse people out there, who do far worse things, with not nearly so much good intention."

Lizzy realized that they were in danger of focusing entirely on her own love life, and not at all on Nora's, which had been the intention for the entire conversation. Sneaky Nora. She decided to subtly segue, turn her friend's own tactics against her. "Luckily Brandon isn't like that," she said with a knowing look.

Nora frowned at her. "No, I guess you're right." Her tone said, *I have no idea why you're saying that, but okay, weirdo,* and there didn't seem to be any telltale giveaways that she was hiding anything. But knowing that Nora was extremely good at hiding her emotions, Lizzy decided to press it further.

"I thought that maybe there was a little something there. Between you two."

Another perplexed look from Nora. "Between me and Brandon? I thought it was obvious that he was into Marianne." She sighed, shaking her head. "Those macarons..."

"I thought so, too. Until the other day, at the Austen Murder Club meeting, when you two were, you know." Lizzy moved her eyebrows meaningfully. "Exchanging *looks.*"

Nora's face did shift then, but not in the way Lizzy had expected. There was no blush, no averted gaze, nothing that would indicate a potentially lovestruck individual who had been caught out in their crush. Nora paled, and blinked, and chewed her lip, as if she had been called out, but not about anything that would be pleasant to share.

And all of a sudden, a few things clicked into place for Lizzy. She thought of those secret, charged looks between Brandon and Nora, and realized that they weren't the looks of two people pining for one another. They were looks of two people who were *complicit* with each other in some way. It was strange, really, how similar those two things could appear.

And once Lizzy realized this, different pieces began to slot together in rapid succession. The two figures in the CCTV footage. Both in all black. The black sweatshirt that Marianne had sent home with her from the hospital, that Brandon had used as a tourniquet when he found Marianne when he had supposedly been out for an extremely late-night run. She remembered, too, that she had tried to call Nora that night, but received no answer, so she had called Jane instead. Then, when she had come back to the Delta house that night, she'd seen Nora at the door. She'd assumed Nora was coming to lock the door, but what if she had come in only a moment before her? That would put her out and about at roughly the same time...roughly the same time that Wickham had been assaulted on the campus square.

These details had been there all along, but they'd seemed unimportant to Lizzy, because Nora and Brandon were not the type of people to assault anyone. And even if they were, what reason would they have to attack *Wickham*?

As usual, Nora seemed to have read her train of thought perfectly. Her own face was set in pale resignation as she met Lizzy's gaze.

Lizzy skipped the details, and asked the only question that was really important. "Why Wickham? I didn't think you knew him all that well."

"We didn't," Nora sighed, and for a brief moment, Lizzy thought she'd misunderstood, that Nora was telling her they hadn't done the thing she'd thought they'd done–until Nora continued on, and it all fell into place: "We thought it was Willoughby."

chapter
seven

NORA DASHWOOD WAS NOT the type of person one would expect to commit an assault. One could easily imagine her graduating with honors, earning a Fulbright, becoming a promising up-and-coming green architect, or maybe less ambitiously (or *more* ambitiously, depending on one's perspective) color-coordinating her bookshelf on a weekend night, for fun. Even Nora would not have imagined it possible of herself to commit such a crime even a few months ago at the start of the fall semester.

But then, at the start of the fall semester, she had not yet met Willoughby.

For anyone who does not have a sister, it would be difficult to explain the complex relationship between Nora and Marianne. They were each other's best friends and harshest critics; their shared history ensured that no one else could make them laugh harder, nor could anyone else name and exploit the other's weaknesses quite so easily. They drove each other crazier than any other person could ever possibly manage, and their fights were the deepest and most cutting, bringing out sides to them that no one else in the entire world would ever see; and Nora would absolutely kill for Marianne if she had to, and vice-versa. That, in a nutshell, was sisterhood.

It wasn't so much that Willoughby had broken Marianne's heart. Nora was not some kind of avenging angel, hellbent on destroying anyone who wounded her poor dear fragile Marianne. Marianne was not fragile, for starters, nor was she anyone's poor dear; Nora knew first-hand, more than anyone, that she could be difficult, and impulsive, and prone to hysterics. (As a rule, she didn't like that term or its root word, hysteria, that had been weaponized against women's emotions, but Nora had to own that it captured Marianne's volatility rather well.)

No, Willoughby would have been pardoned for simply breaking things off with Marianne. Not forgiven, necessarily, because the enemy of one beloved sister is the enemy to both, but no retribution would have been required. Hearts get broken. People move on. Such is life.

He might have even been pardoned for ghosting Marianne. It was a cowardly way to behave, and Nora would have given him the cold shoulder if ever they happened to meet in public again, but such was the reality of modern dating. It happened.

What could not be forgiven was when Willoughby posted Marianne's pictures on the English Department's Facebook page (or so she believed at the time). He had already ended things with Marianne. She might have been pestering him, but even Marianne would have eventually had to give up. Posting those pictures–that revenge porn, to call it by its real name–was needlessly cruel. It was a betrayal that was unnecessary, that was done purely out of spite.

Even this, though, might not have resulted in a physical response from Nora, even if it might have warranted it. (This author will not sit in judgment of *that*.) The tipping point was that night at that gala. Willoughby, *appearing* at least unmoved (though his later words seemed to contradict that) while Marianne wept on the floor in front of him. After everything he'd done to her, he couldn't offer even the smallest kindness, the tiniest sliver of pity. He was exposing her to everybody yet again, but somehow it was worse this time. As Marianne herself would have argued, what was the body? Nothing but a physical, material, ultimately mortal thing. He had put her *soul* on display for everyone that night, and scoffed at it, and laughed at it.

And that? That was unforgivable.

The plan was made in haste. It was not a usual Nora Dashwood plan, with intricate layers and fallbacks and safeties to suss out every foreseeable loophole, which is perhaps why there were so many mistakes.

For one of the few, rare times in her life, Nora was acting on her heart, not her head. She knew Willoughby would be leaving the gala. She hoped he would be on his own.

As soon as Marianne seemed to have gone down for the night (another error in foresight that Nora would never forgive herself for), and Lizzy had left the house, Nora called Brandon. He was the one person whom she knew would be able to physically manage what she had in mind, and whom she suspected would be willing (if not eager) to help her.

They had to move quickly. Dressed in black, they waited outside the gala for Willoughby to leave. It would be entirely a matter of chance if he left on his own, and if they managed to seclude him in an area without witnesses. If they managed both, then perhaps it would be fate. (Another very un-Nora like notion, but she seemed to be embracing those this evening.)

As to how they made such an egregious error. Nora had a few ideas. It was a dark night. Nerves were running high. And there was that uncanny resemblance between the two men, at least from a distance. By the time they realized their mistake, the deed had been done, and it seemed unwise to risk someone coming across them in the square, or Wickham waking up and recognizing them.

Either way, Nora consoled herself, the punishment fit the crime. It may not have been intended for Wickham, but there were few who would argue he didn't deserve it.

δλε

What Nora hadn't intended was for Lizzy to get caught up in the entire thing. "I was going to tell you before you got expelled," Nora told Lizzy. "There was no way I would let you take the punishment for my crime. I guess I somehow hoped some other resolution would present itself."

And some other resolution had, in the form of Darcy. Nora wasn't entirely sure why Darcy had spoken up and taken the blame. She suspected, after bumping into him with Lizzy at the Crescent, that Darcy had done so to keep Lizzy from being expelled. It was obvious that day, according to Nora, that Darcy would not sit idly by while Lizzy's future was jeopardized. "You'll have to ask him," Nora finished.

Lizzy intended to, when she had the chance. But first, there was something she needed to know. "So you were going to let Darcy take the fall?" She wouldn't blame Nora for it, necessarily; she knew her friend was practical, first and foremost, but she couldn't quite see her justifying letting someone else get kicked out of school.

Nora shook her head. "I know I should have come forward sooner. I think I kept hoping that some other solution would present itself. That maybe de Bourgh would back off since it was her nephew. I think Darcy was maybe hoping she was bluffing, too." She sighed ruefully. "But I wouldn't have let him go through with it. I was planning on telling you this afternoon, and going to de Bourgh myself in the morning, until today's conversation got a little...derailed."

Lizzy looked at what remained of the Denham's pastry box on the table. Ah, yes, there was that. There had been a lot going on with Nora this semester—more than Lizzy would have ever guessed. People and those damned layers of theirs.

"You shouldn't blame Brandon, either," Nora continued. "He wanted to come forward, but I asked him to let me handle it. He would never let Darcy be punished for him."

Somehow, Lizzy hadn't fully put it together. It wasn't just Nora's future at stake, but Brandon's as well. All of these people who were going to suffer—because of their own choices, yes, but also because of the choices of others. People like Willoughby and Wickham, who had wreaked so much havoc, and who would be getting away with so much, comparatively speaking.

It wasn't fair. But life rarely was, as Lizzy was beginning to discover.

chapter
eight

THERE WAS ONLY one thing about Nora's story that Lizzy hadn't entirely believed. Nora thought that Darcy had taken the blame because he didn't want Lizzy to be punished for the crime. But knowing that Darcy and Knightley had been out doing their mysterious prowl on the campus at night, Lizzy had to wonder if there was something more at play. Was it possible that Darcy and Knightley had seen Nora and/or Brandon leaving the area, and connected later that they must have somehow been involved with what happened to Wickham?

There was really only one person who could answer that question.

Once again, Lizzy found herself marching over to the Theta house, determined not to let anything deter her from learning the truth, the *whole* truth, this time. She would not let Darcy get away with evasive answers. She would not get distracted by lips, even if they were remarkably full and soft and kissable. She would definitely not let him anywhere near that spot on her neck, at least not until she received a full confession. (Maybe that was something she could use as leverage. Lizzy was not above bribery in the form of making out with a very attractive millionaire in exchange for answers.)

She was let into the house by a sophomore she didn't recognize, who disappeared upstairs to tell Darcy she'd arrived. He did not make her wait long, appearing soon at the top of the stairs. His expression was difficult to read, but so, she imagined, must be hers. He stared at her.

She stared back at him. The energy between them was maybe even more charged than it had been before, because before the weird, unspoken chemistry between them had only been in the hypothetical, and now Lizzy could remember (with eloquent intensity) how it felt to be pressed up against his bare chest.

She imagined, judging by that look in his eye, that he could do the same.

Darcy cleared his throat. "Do you—want to come upstairs?"

"Yes," said Lizzy, and she did.

Inside his room, Lizzy did a quick, surreptitious sweep with her eyes to see if she could catch him out with anything embarrassing before he had time to hide it. She'd hoped for something endearingly nerdy, like a Harry Potter lego set or some Star Wars figurines; but the room was meticulously clean and devoid of any personality, almost like a hotel room. She did smirk a little, though, when she saw that one dirty sock had fallen out of the hamper onto the floor—more because she knew it would embarrass Darcy for her to see it, than that it was in and of itself embarrassing. So he was human after all.

Darcy followed her into the room and shut the door behind him. Then, seeming to feel this was presumptuous, he opened it again. Turning back to face her, he swallowed, running a hand through his hair. "How are you? Are you—uh. Good?"

Lizzy might have laughed at him, had she not also been feeling enormously self-conscious and unsure of herself. She hadn't really thought this through, she realized, marching over here. Her primary thought had been on getting answers; she hadn't fully realized just how much remained unspoken and unsettled between them. "I am. Good. You?"

"Good," Darcy confirmed.

Another charged moment of staring ensued, this time intensified because they were alone, in Darcy's bedroom. Lizzy looked away, gathering herself, before meeting his gaze with purpose. That was *not* what she had come here for tonight. (Mostly.) "So when did you see Nora that night? It must have been after she attacked Wickham, right?" A ghost of a smile. "I'm trying to put together a timeline."

Darcy was silent for a long moment. "What makes you say that?" he hedged finally.

"Well, you had time to come back to the Theta house and change before you did your rounds with Knightley. Rushworth saw you leaving in all black."

Darcy sighed and glanced at the wall. "Rushworth," he said, shaking his head.

Lizzy continued, "I guess it's possible you could have gotten back in time to run into Nora before she attacked Wickham, but it would have been tight, with how late we left the gala. And that probably would have spooked her off, if she'd seen you, too. More likely you saw her afterward, when she was leaving the scene of the crime."

Darcy said nothing this time, just watched her.

"How long did it take you to put it together?" Lizzy prompted. Guessing the partial cause of his reticence, she informed him: "Nora's already made a full confession, by the way. You aren't outing her."

Another sigh. Darcy ran a hand over his face. "I didn't suspect her right away. The direction I saw her coming from that night, I assumed she was leaving the library."

That *did* seem like more of a Nora thing to do–a late-night study session was more on-brand than a cloak and daggers attack. But people could surprise you. "I had my suspicions after I found out what happened to Wickham. But I told myself she couldn't have managed it on her own–not with him tied up the way he was. It wasn't until later that I realized she must have had an accomplice." It was his turn to level Lizzy with a probing gaze. "Did she?"

"She did." Lizzy didn't know yet if she felt comfortable naming Brandon. Not until she figured out what all of this meant, and what it would mean for Darcy's future. "So, why did you cover for Nora?"

"I knew she was here on scholarship, which likely means her family wouldn't have the funds to buy her way into another school." *Not like mine*, went the unspoken part of that. "Wickham deserved what happened to him. I don't know that I would have done the same in Nora's shoes–but I don't know that I wouldn't have, given the opportunity. She was only doing what I *should* have done, and I can afford the repercussions–she can't." He shrugged. "It seemed like the right thing to do."

Lizzy really didn't know what to think. This whole situation was a moral gray area, at best. Attacking someone, forcing them into a public spectacle of nudity–it was wrong. But hadn't Wickham done essentially the same thing, to so many other undeserving people? Nora had committed the crime, so she should accept the consequences. But truthfully, she couldn't afford to lose her scholarship and get kicked out of AU. With that black mark on her record, she likely wouldn't get accepted into any accredited green architecture program. That would be her whole future, gone. For Darcy, the financial hit would be a drop in the pond, and his family connections would probably cover the scandal and ensure he got into any other school of his choice. His future would be fine...but it would be completely removed from Lizzy. As a wise sage once said, one makeout session in a pool was not enough to sustain a long-distance relationship. Whatever weird thing had started between them would just be over.

But Lizzy could not look at what she felt about this too closely in the face; she focused, instead, on something else that Darcy had mentioned to her. "If you didn't suspect Nora for certain right away, why did you tell President de Bourgh it was you?"

Darcy was silent again for a long moment, holding her gaze. He didn't need to say the words for Lizzy to understand. He had risked expulsion, blackened his good name, and forever tied himself to Wickham, to prevent her from having to do the same.

Still, it was nice when he confirmed for her out loud, simply, "You. I believe I thought only of you."

Lizzy's intentions for going to the Theta house that night had *not* been to kiss him again. On that point, she was adamant. But after such a confession, dear reader, is there any among us who could blame her for doing so?

δλε

After some time had passed (this author will not disclose the exact amount), Lizzy and Darcy sat side by side against the headboard of his bed, limbs playfully intertwined, and discussed only the most important of details.

"You need some personality in this room, stat," Lizzy told him, looking around with a critical eye. "Literally anybody could live here, except for maybe a fraternity bro in college. I'm going to have to buy you a poster or something to hang up. What do 20-something-year-old guys like?" She snapped her fingers, an aha moment. "Musicals! I'll get you a *CATS* poster to hang on your wall."

Darcy smiled tolerantly at this. "Fine."

"Fine?" Lizzy challenged skeptically. "If I bought you a poster of the musical *CATS*, you would hang it on that wall, right there?"

"If you bought it for me, I would."

Lizzy felt another pleasant surge at the realization of the power she had over this man. Her feminine wiles had never been employed to such good use. It was entirely reciprocal, of course. If Darcy came to her room (a likely scenario) and asked her to put up a neon beer sign, or something, she might consider it. That was how smitten she currently felt.

The pleasure subsided as Lizzy remembered that Darcy might only be so agreeable in the moment because he knew that, likely, this room would not be his for much longer.

Sobering from her giddy, fizzy Champagne-happiness, Lizzy realized there were still a few loose threads that needed to be tied up. "Since you're in such a generous mood, maybe you'll finally tell me what you and Knightley have been doing patrolling around campus at night?"

Darcy *was* in a very good mood, but maybe not THAT good. "Maybe, if you want to tell me who was Nora's accomplice?"

"A journalist never reveals her sources," Lizzy reminded him.

"A fraternity president makes some sacred oaths of secrecy," he returned.

"So it has something to do with the fraternity?"

Darcy sighed and shifted away from her–though not far enough that they were no longer touching, Lizzy noted with no little gratification. (He *liiiiked* her.) "Is this how our pillow talk is always going to be? You prodding me for information?"

Lizzy liked very much that he was anticipating future pillow-talk sessions. "It's your own fault. There are plenty of floozies out there who would want you for your money and your bod. You had to go and fall for the plucky ace reporter who wants you for your mind."

She was in full playful banter mode, so it took Lizzy a moment to realize what she'd just inadvertently implied. She flushed. "Not that you've *fallen* fallen, I'm not saying–I just mean, there's obviously an interest. Right?"

Darcy responded by pulling her into a straddle over his lap. Lizzy let out a surprised little *oh,* and he smirked. "You never get flustered, Lizzy Bennet. It's kind of cute."

"You've never seen me trying on bathing suits," Lizzy quipped, trying to lighten the mood.

"I'd like to."

It took a moment for Lizzy to process that. Her mouth popped open a little, she was so surprised. Darcy's smirk deepened, and he smoothed his hands over her shoulders, down her back, causing her to shiver. "For the record, there's nothing you could assume about my feelings that would be overstepping or presumptuous. It is cute when you're flustered, but you don't have to be. And I would really *love* to see you in a bikini."

Eloquent and witty as she could be, there was not much Lizzy could think of to say to that.

chapter
nine

AFTER SOME MORE TIME HAD PAST, Lizzy found that she was suddenly in a much more amenable mood to share confidential information. "It was Brandon. Nora's accomplice? They thought they were attacking Willoughby." At Darcy's surprised look, Lizzy shrugged. "Pillow talk is confidential, right? Officially off-the-record. And anyway, you're getting expelled tomorrow anyway, so who are you gonna tell?" This last part said with a lightness she did not really feel.

Darcy took a moment to process this, nodding as the pieces slotted into place for him. "That makes sense." He sighed. "Does that mean I have to share my secrets now?"

"I told you mine. You tell me yours. Quid pro quo, baby."

Another sigh from Darcy. He buried his face in his hands. "Knightley is going to kill me. He hasn't even told Emma."

Lizzy did not want to look too directly at the thrill she felt at the knowledge that she would be learning something that Emma Woodhouse did not know. "I'll make sure to plan a really nice funeral," she promised him.

Shaking his head at her, Darcy relented. "Have you heard of the Skull and Bones society?"

"That super-secret society at Yale, where all the rich dudes pat each other on the back for having money?" To be fair, what Lizzy mostly knew about the society was because of the Paul Walker film (from when

Jane was going through her Paul Walker phase), but it still wasn't great. "I'm not going to like where this is going, am I?"

"Austen University has its own secret society. The Knights of White's. Think less gentleman's club, more community minded. We try to secretly and quietly correct the wrongs of society, or at least society in Highbury. You've probably already guessed that Knightley and I are members. I can't divulge who else is involved. One of the things we do is patrol the campus at night and try to make sure that it's a safe space for anyone out walking alone."

That hadn't really worked out too well for Wickham, but Lizzy refrained from saying so. "So, you guys are like a secret Batman-vigilante society? Trying to use your resources and power to fight the evils of Highbury?"

"Something like that."

Lizzy could recognize the nobility in the intention. But she also couldn't help but shake her head. "That is...such patriarchal bullshit. Because you guys are rich and have penises, you get to decide what's best for campus?"

Darcy had clearly never thought about it in that light before. "We're trying to help people. To make Austen University a safer place."

"I don't doubt that. I get it, the idea is nice. But why keep it a secret society? Why exclude people based on gender and income?"

"Income isn't a factor," Darcy protested quickly.

Lizzy suppressed an eyeroll. Sure, Jan. She believed that *he* believed that, but she'd be willing to bet that no one in the special club came from a working-class background. Darcy was a good guy overall, but there were some definite blinders they'd need to work on.

"As for gender, well..." Darcy shook his head, seeming to realize how bad his answer was before he even said it. "The general feeling of the group seemed to be that people wanted it to be *chivalrous–*"

"Patriarchal. Nonsense," Lizzy reiterated.

"Maybe," Darcy agreed. "But can you imagine if, say, Emma got wind of this society? It would completely change the nature of what we're trying to do."

Lizzy realized the sense of his point, even if she didn't entirely agree with it. "Poverty would be ended in a week. All student loans would be paid off. Free low-carb lunches for everyone."

"It would be too efficient. We would become obsolete in a month."

Lizzy pondered. She wasn't thrilled about the secret society nonsense, but it at least accounted for why Darcy had been out the night Wickham was attacked, dressed all in black, and why he'd been so cagey about the whole thing. Maybe it also answered a few other questions as well. "The night patrol isn't the only thing the Knights do, right?" At Darcy's nod of confirmation, she continued, "Were you the ones to pay off Marianne's GoFundMe?"

"I'm not sure what you're talking about."

He sounded genuinely perplexed. Darcy was many things, but Lizzy suspected that a great actor wasn't one of them. Which was why she believed that he'd had nothing to do with Marianne's hospital bills. Lizzy explained to him what Marianne had told her about some anonymous benefactor covering the enormous costs accrued by someone with only the very basic student insurance offered by the school.

"It seems like the kind of thing the Knights might do," Darcy agreed, "but so far as I know, it has nothing to do with us."

Something passed over his face, which made Lizzy think he'd had some sort of realization. He really was not very good at hiding his emotions. Why had she always found him so cold and aloof? She must not have been looking very carefully. "What?" she prodded him. "You can't hide anything from me, Darcy–I can read you like a book."

He gave her a grudging smile. "I was wondering if maybe Charlie had something to do with it. He has access to that kind of money. And I know he still really cares about Nora."

There was a half-question in that statement, but Lizzy kept her face a careful blank. She might be able to read Darcy's every expression, but at least in this instance she hoped he couldn't do the same. There were sacred bonds of trust in friendship that couldn't be broken, not even for extremely cute boys. If Nora wanted Charlie to know how she felt about him, that was up to her.

Luckily, she was saved from having to come up with a distracting response when the door opened and Karoline strolled in. She looked unusually dressed down–for Karoline, anyway. Her hair was in a simple ponytail, and she was wearing an oversized t-shirt and pajama shorts. The t-shirt had a Theta symbol on it and looked as though it likely belonged to a boy, unless Karoline was really changing up her usual form-fitting aesthetic; and the shorts, though a simple cut, had the Gucci insignia on them. Still, casual overall.

"Actually," Karoline announced, "it was me."

chapter
ten

IF KAROLINE FOUND it strange to be barging into Darcy's room and to find him in bed with Elizabeth Bennet, none of this showed on her face. Luckily everyone in question was fully dressed, but Lizzy nonetheless pulled up the bedsheets a little higher, looking incredulously at Darcy.

His jaw was set in a firm line. "Karoline. We've talked about this. You can't just walk in any time you feel like it."

They'd *talked* about this? Lizzy did not love the sound of that. She was so distracted by this idea that it took her another moment to realize the significance of what Karoline had said. "Wait—you're the one who paid off Marianne's hospital bill? Why?"

Karoline had not looked at all ashamed at being called out for barging into Darcy's room without invitation; but she did look a little chagrined now. "I figured I owed the Dashwoods one." She shrugged. "It's basically the same as a spending spree during New York fashion week—Daddy will never notice."

That answered one question, but raised another, more disturbing. "How did you know that we were even talking about that?"

"The walls are incredibly thin, Bennet. Something you might want to keep in mind for the future. Thank God for noise-canceling headphones."

As if to prove this horrifying point, Rushworth's disembodied voice called out from the other side of the wall: "Proud of you, babe! I always knew you had a heart of gold underneath all that...gold."

Karoline smiled–a genuine, giddy, happy little thing that Lizzy had never seen on her face before, nor expected to. "Thanks, hon. Why don't you and Darcy run downstairs and make us something to eat? I need to talk to Lizzy for a minute."

She looked pointedly at Darcy, who in turn looked at Lizzy, his face the picture of unhappiness. "I hate everything that's happening right now."

"It's fine," Lizzy reassured him. "Maybe just invest in some sound-proofing. And a deadbolt."

She only remembered, as he paused in the doorway to look back at her, that he would be expelled soon. So the need for all of that would likely be very low.

Karoline waited until he was gone, then shut the door. She turned back to Lizzy, folding her arms. "So. I leave you on your own for one minute and look what you do."

Despite herself, Lizzy blushed; and even Karoline looked a little mortified. "I meant about the case, Bennet. Geez. Get your mind out of the gutter." She raised an eyebrow. "Although, you finally nabbed Darcy. Good for you."

"There's no *finally* about it. This is a very new development."

Karoline shrugged. "Maybe for you. I saw it coming a long time ago."

There was no sadness in her voice, or bitterness, only resignation. Lizzy motioned toward the general direction of the wall where she'd just heard Rushworth's voice. "Is that officially a thing now?"

It was Karoline's turn to look discomposed. She rolled her eyes, but Lizzy could see she was pleased. "He's an idiot. Still. But, I don't know. He actually likes *me*. Not my money." Her expression sharpened all at once, and she leveled a finger at Lizzy. "But don't think you can distract me, Bennet. I came in here to warn you about Darcy. Not because I'm still hung up on him, or whatever, but because he's a good one, okay? Be nice to him. We might not be enemies anymore, but we aren't friends, and I will still kill you if you hurt him."

It was the sweetest way anyone had ever threatened to kill her–even knowing that, coming from Karoline Bingley, this was likely no idle threat. Lizzy did her best to smile. "I don't plan on hurting anyone. But it's probably a moot point anyway, since he's going to be leaving AU."

"Why? He's not the one who attacked Wickham. We know that for sure now."

The slow-dawning realization that Karoline must have heard Lizzy's *entire* explanation of who had attacked Wickham sent her stomach falling. "You heard all of that?"

"I mean, I didn't catch *every* single detail–you really need to learn how to enunciate, Bennet–but I got the overall gist of it. Nora and Brandon? I never would have guessed."

Lizzy watched her carefully. "So I guess you're going to go tell de Bourgh."

Karoline shrugged. "Well we can't just let Darcy take the blame."

"But we should let Brandon and Nora get expelled?"

Another shrug. "It's not like I want that to happen, but they are the ones who did it. That's not my fault. And that's not me being petty. That's just the truth."

Lizzy wanted to be angry at Karoline for throwing Nora under the bus again so quickly after realizing she'd made a mistake in doing so the previous semester; the problem was, she agreed, at least in terms of not wanting Darcy to be expelled. It felt like a terrible, impossible choice.

Unless...unless there was another option, one that Lizzy hadn't yet considered. She met Karoline's gaze, and the other girl sighed and shook her head. "Oh, boy. What fresh nonsense is this?"

"Hear me out..."

chapter
eleven

FOR THE SECOND time that semester, the university was abuzz with an entirely new scandal–or rather, the conclusion of the first. Just when it had seemed likely that President de Bourgh would have to follow through on her threat to expel her own nephew, an impassioned poem to the editor appeared on the university newspaper website.

The poem, penned by the person responsible for attacking Wickham, outlined their reasons for doing so. This author could merely summarize the contents of the verses, but as it was written by a *true artist*, it would be best to let them speak for themselves:

To the Austen University Community,

Justice is not blind, unless we are afraid to witness.
    It is not an eye for an eye–
    It *sees*, if we will open OUR eyes.
    It is not toothless–it has teeth
    That tear and grind and speak
    If we will open our mouths and bear our truths.
    All men are created equal
    But not all live equal;

Some give but others take and take
More than the fair share they've been given
And something, someone, must balance the scales–
That is justice. That is witness.
That is truth.
What are eyes and teeth? Useless tokens
Unless we act when we see injustice
Unless we witness and demand justice
When our community is attacked–
We must be the justice we wish to see.

While it is doubtless true that, to the poet, these verses perfectly illustrated why Wickham had been attacked, the editor of the piece, Lizzy Bennet, found it necessary to add an addendum to the bottom, wherein the poet outlined their intentions in prose for those uncultured swine before whom their pearls had been cast:

When I learned of the incomprehensible injustice that had been enacted against the women on campus on the Portraits of Pemberley website, I was moved to take action. Attacking Wickham was not about punishing the individual, but demonstrating to the world the larger issue that those who identify as cisgender men must stand up against those of our sex when their behaviors are toxic, abusive, and unacceptable. We must not leave all the work of feminism to women and non-binary individuals; we must be active participants in the change we want to see. I realize that I may have overstepped my bounds–not for the alleged crime I have committed, but for presuming to speak for those involved. As a firm ally, I pledge my continued support, but now I will step back, listen, and follow their lead.

- J.A. Willoughby

chapter
twelve

WILLOUGHBY MIGHT HAVE BEEN EXPELLED from Austen University, but his dramatic ally-ship transformed him into a folk hero for the feminist cause. It was fortunate that, alongside his impassioned diatribe about equal rights, he linked to his social media accounts, where viewers could follow his spoken-word journey and lend him financial support through his Patreon. Now coupled publicly with renowned poet Sophie Grey, another fierce advocate for women's rights, Willoughby was primed and positioned to have the career he'd always wanted.

His only real regret was that he had been forced to cut ties with Marianne. Willoughby still thought of her often. His feelings for her had been genuine, or at least as genuine as those belonging to someone like Willoughby can be. He tried reaching out once or twice to her, but either she had his number blocked, or she was choosing not to respond. Either way, Willoughby did not blame her. He recognized that he had treated her badly, even while failing to admit to the role he had played in abandoning her. What little self-reflection he possessed was directed toward longing for something that had once made him happy, without fully acknowledging that choosing Marianne over Sophie would have hampered his professional career, if not derailed it completely. His advocacy for love was as impassioned, if as baseless, as his advocacy for women's rights; he believed in both, so long as it was convenient for him to do so, and so long as it would not cost him anything of real significance.

Wickham did not fare so well as his double, I am sorry to say. As he had reported to Lizzy at the Croft Gala, Wickham seemed primed at first to benefit from his public attack, as many powerful men had sympathized with his position and taken him on as a mascot for their cause. For a while, Wickham thrived under this attention; his charm, as always, earned him many friends, but his selfishness and greed ensured he never maintained them for long. Initially buoyed by his new connections, Wickham began to slack off in his duties as a TA, ensuring the irritation of Professor Elías. Without Wickham there to grade, Elías's own faults became all the more glaring, and that, coupled with some other personal issues, ensured he did not earn the promotion he sought to gain that semester. Wickham was not hired on again for the spring; and by that point, he had gotten into some trouble with one of his new patron's underaged daughters, as well as getting caught up in ill-advised scheme with some of the valets at the club he'd been brought to as an honored guest.

Having burned all of his new bridges, Wickham returned to one of his old ones: attempting to prove his paternal connection to Mr. Darcy, Sr. It is unknown how Wickham managed to obtain the necessary DNA sample, and probably best left that way; when the results came back conclusively that Wickham bore no genetic relation to Fo-Hian and Guanyin Darcy, he quietly destroyed the evidence. Darcy and Guanyin were never the wiser that this had taken place, though Wickham continued to insinuate the family relation whenever it was in his best interest.

Nora and Brandon were never publicly linked to the assault on Wickham, and it was privately agreed by those few who knew the truth that it should remain this way. Willoughby might not have committed the crime directly, but he was part of a larger system corrupted by patriarchal privilege and could act as its scapegoat—or so Marianne might have once said. Now, when Nora and Lizzy sat down with her to tell her the truth, Marianne just looked out the window, and nodded to herself. "It's fitting," was all she said on the matter.

The Austen Murder Club continued to meet regularly, though no unsolved crime had been committed on campus for several weeks following Willoughby's letter, to the consternation of at least two of its members. Friday night pizza nights had become a regular occurrence, though tonight the guest list was more exclusive than it had been in weeks previous. After a long recovery, paid in full by her anonymous benefactor, Marianne was finally cleared to come home to the Delta house. There would still be months of physical therapy ahead, but Marianne was well enough to be released, and eager to get out of the hospital. She, Lizzy, and Nora would celebrate with their own pizza night tonight, followed by a low-key celebration with the rest of their friends the following day. Baby steps, for Marianne, which would be appropriate, since she was learning to walk again (her joke, which both Nora and Lizzy tried to laugh at).

Let the reader be assured that the first part of the evening passed the Bechdel test, with talk focusing mostly on Marianne's recovery and plans for completing her incomplete courses from that semester; Nora's internship she would be applying for shortly; and Lizzy's ongoing battle with Palmer to publish her diatribe on university fees, during the short window remaining when people might actually be paying attention to the student newspaper.

Talk soon devolved, however, as talk so often will, to relationships. "Your date with Charlie seemed to go well the other night," Lizzy hedged, exchanging a quick, furtive glance with Marianne. (They had, of course, talked about this already in detail together, and waited as long as they possibly could before broaching the subject with Nora.)

"It wasn't a date." Two eyerolls at this. "It wasn't," Nora insisted. "It was more of a catchup. There's a lot that's been unsaid, that has to still be said."

Lizzy supposed that was true, since this was the third "catchup" they'd had since Nora had found out Charlie wasn't actually secretly seeing Lucy Steele and had never fathered her baby. Then again, maybe they *did* have quite a bit to sort through, with all of those factors in play.

"Will he be coming to the get-together tomorrow?" Marianne asked. It was a surprisingly tactful way for Marianne to ask if there would be more "catchups" between Nora and Charlie in the foreseeable future–

but then again, if there had been one noticeable change about Marianne after the hit-and-run accident (aside from the more obvious casts, cuts, and bruises), it was her newfound caution. She was *careful* in a way she never had been before; and even though Lizzy had one or two times in the past thought that Marianne could benefit from a little more thoughtfulness, she found herself hoping this wouldn't be too permanent a change. Loving wholeheartedly, feeling things passionately, was not a crime that needed to be punished. Tempered, perhaps, with a little age and wisdom, but not erased altogether.

Nora, despite her best efforts, flushed. "If that's all right with you? I don't want to overwhelm you–"

Marianne cut this off with a shake of her head. "The more the merrier–just as long as you don't invite his awful sister."

Lizzy winced at this. With all of the big revelations of the past few weeks, she had not yet told the Dashwood sisters about Karoline's role in paying off Marianne's hospital bills. She wasn't entirely sure that Karoline wanted her good deed to be made known–although, knowing Karoline, she was surprised it hadn't yet been posted on social media. She'd half-expected Karoline to meet them at the hospital on the day of Marianne's release with one of those giant checks, just for the photo opp.

But people could surprise you, as Lizzy was learning in more than one way.

"Will Brandon be at the party?" Nora asked.

It was a clear ruse to distract from her own romantic will-they-won't-they entanglement, since she had likely been the one to invite Brandon, herself; but it did the trick, handily distracting Marianne. Color rose up her neck–more out of irritation than embarrassment, it seemed–and Marianne lifted her chin. "I imagine he will. We are friends now. And I hope we're all mature enough adults to agree that two single individuals can be friends, and only friends, without any annoying insinuations."

Maybe there was still a bit of the old Marianne there, after all. Biting back a smile, Lizzy nodded her enthusiastic agreement. "Hear, hear! I, for one, am tired of all the rumors circulating about me and President de Bourgh. It's complicated, but it's not *that* complicated."

Actually, Lizzy had heard nothing from President de Bourgh since their discussion in her town car. The only communication between them had been the espresso machine that had arrived, complete with a handyman to do the installation in the kitchen. Lizzy's life had never been so good, with both of these factors (the coffee, and the absence of de Bourgh) likely contributing.

"Well, you aren't a *single* individual," Nora pointed out.

It was Lizzy's turn to blush. Rather than respond, she picked up the remote and started the next episode of the newest show that had become their obsession: *Rodeo Rehab*, a makeover show about...well, the title likely made it obvious. "One more episode?" she asked, already pressing play.

"Only one more? It's only nine o'clock."

Lizzy said nothing, though she knew she would be cutting herself off after this next episode. She had to be up early the next morning, after all. It was the best time of day, she'd discovered, for swimming laps.

acknowledgments

First and foremost, thank you to Mike, who believes in these books sometimes more than I do. Thanks for making me be brave.

Thank you to Johnny for being my heart.

Thank you to Jennifer Rands for proofreading drafts and offering feedback.

Thank you to Alicia and Sarah and my parents for being my cheerleaders. You are amazing! Thanks also to Alicia for gifting me with my awesome author photos.

Thank you for readers of previous books who have come back for more—truly, thank you! I'm so happy to have found my own Austen Murder Club.

Thank you especially for those who leave reviews. So much of writing is done on your own, it is so encouraging as an author to read and know that people are out there enjoying your book and that these characters are coming to life for others, too.

about the author

Elizabeth Gilliland is a writer, Dr., wife, mom, and lifelong Jane Austen fan. She is a playwright (whose plays have appeared off-off Broadway), a screenwriter (with a master's in screenwriting and production), an academic (with a PhD and a dissertation on Jane Austen adaptations), and now a published author! When she isn't writing or grading papers, she is most likely reading a good book, binge watching the latest hit, working on a puzzle, or hanging with her cute kid.

also by elizabeth gilliland

Austen University Mysteries Series

What Happened on Box Hill (book one)

Sly Jane Fairfax (prequel novella)

Dear Prudent Elinor (prequel novella)

As E. Gilliland

Come One, Come All (standalone novel)

Round and Round We Go (prequel novella)

bayou wolf press

Bayou Wolf Press is an independent publisher of quality fiction. If you enjoyed this book and would like to support us, the best thing you can do is leave a review on Amazon, Goodreads, or wherever you review books. If you'd like to learn more about our press, sign up for our newsletter, and stay informed on upcoming books, please visit www.bayouwolf.com .

Made in the USA
Las Vegas, NV
24 July 2023

75176039R00157